Beneath the Cedar Tree

Advance Praise for *Beneath the Cedar Tree*

'A beautifully written story about loss and grief and what lies beyond it. Funny and heartbreaking in equal measure. One of those books where you don't want it to end. I absolutely loved it.' – Paul Howard (Ross O'Carroll-Kelly creator)

'This twisty story ... is as unexpected as it is revelatory. With pathos and wry flair, Shouldice transports us to embattled territories of . . . the human heart. A remarkable multinational journey that is life-changing . . .' – Ethel Rohan, author of *Sing, I*

'A wonderful book with a brilliant comic voice and a poignant exploration of grief that is ultimately consoling, *Beneath the Cedar Tree* celebrates the redemptive power of human connection, and takes the reader on a journey that in itself feels like a pilgrimage.' – Andrew Hughes, author of *The Coroner's Daughter*

'I read it in one sitting; flew through it, in fact . . . an original story . . . a poignant and ultimately life-affirming read.' – Martina Devlin, author of *Charlotte: A Novel*

'A feast of dark sardonic humour, tragedy and joy, juxtaposed perfectly to give us a compelling journey of a mother's emotional struggle against injustice and bereavement, and the confederacy of dunces and villains she encounters along the way. Highly recommended.' – Sam Millar, author of *On the Brinks*

'Written in unsentimental gripping prose, this is a powerful story.' – Michael Harding, author of *I Loved Him from the Day He Died*

Beneath the Cedar Tree

A Novel

Frank Shouldice

The Liffey Press

the liffey press

Published by
The Liffey Press
'Clareville', 307 Clontarf Road
Dublin D03 PO46, Ireland
www.theliffeypress.com

© 2025 Frank Shouldice

A catalogue record of this book is
available from the British Library.

ISBN 978-1-0686645-3-3

Printed in Northern Ireland by W&G Baird

For Mam

Part One

Nobber, County Meath

Visits being both rare and unexpected, she is surprised to hear the doorbell. Lukewarm coffee in hand, she pauses at the security monitor and catches a navy coat sleeve withdraw from view. Assuming it to be the postman she buzzes him in only to be taken aback at finding Sergeant John Flanagan edge hesitantly into the hall.

He's a bit redder in the face, she thinks, her mind performing cartwheels for reason and context. Slightly heavier, maybe a bit thinner on top but no big change otherwise. Hands like shovels, fish fingers attached.

'Hello Irene,' he says.

She already knows there is more.

The sergeant removes his badged hat and offers her one of the shovels. Her hand disappears into his. She can guess what's coming. An excuse of some sort. The little shit probably used a bedsheet to hoist himself from a cell window. His way of giving the world two fingers.

She pictures a prison officer finding a scrawled note: *Hasta la vista pricks!* Or, the more remote possibility that guilt finally made acquaintance with conscience and he couldn't bear it any longer.

Maybe that's no harm. The Gogartys can move on.

Or maybe they can't.

I hope he burns slowly, she wishes privately.

'Sorry to be bothering you now. Is himself about?'

'He's at work,' Irene replies, pulling a loose thread on the cuff of her dressing-gown.

'Right. This won't take long.'

In that moment she recalls spring showers in Portobello five years previous. Competing with the high-pitched squeal of a taped-up Nilfisk she was unsure whether the bell had rung or not. Switching the hoover off with her foot she unintentionally carried it downstairs, opening the front door to find the broad-shouldered sergeant face out into rain, almost apologetic at having to introduce himself.

'Irene Gogarty, is it? Garda Sergeant John Flanagan.'

Little was she to know that Portobello visit would detonate a dull pounding in the base of her skull that would never quite go away. Sleepless nights dragged into days, a path worn from the city morgue to solicitors' offices, shuffling in and out of courtrooms, one statement after another committed to foolscap in leaky blobs by garda biros, traipsing from weeks to months between sunless chambers inhaling the stale air of the legal system.

So today, 5 AC, she finds herself many miles from Portobello. In a different hallway in a different house, opening a different front door to the same deferential policeman. She and Brendan spent long enough in the good sergeant's company for Irene to remember him mentioning he was originally from the Tipperary/Kilkenny border, although she can't remember which side. A decent man in a harmless sort of way. He said he had a daughter doing her Leaving Cert that summer and a son three years younger who 'wasn't one for the books'. Otherwise, he didn't talk much about his kids, which was quite considerate given the circumstances.

She recalls only too well the good sergeant accompanying the Gogartys through the murk. At times he would feel obliged to fill silences – and there'd be plenty of them – so he would rabbit on about life in 'the big smoke' and hurling. Pushed to breaking point Irene would raise a hand to demand quiet but most of the screeching came from within.

Much to her annoyance Brendan always addressed him as 'Sergeant'. Along the lines of, 'Sergeant, seven of the jury were in tears – what's wrong with the other five?'

Irene didn't address Sergeant Flanagan as anything. 'Your job,' she liked to remind him, 'is to make sure they throw away the key.'

It took seventeen days for Judge Rita Barrett to sentence Patrick James McGeedy to nine years. That's what he got. Irene and Brendan took up saying – before they tried to stop reminding themselves – that everything was either BC or AC.

Before Cathal. After Cathal.

Hard to believe so much time has passed.

Clearly, the good sergeant has built up on-the-job experience as a sounding board for bad news. She can see he knows how to hold a silence, when to nod, how to avert eye contact, how to fold his hands. Which brought to mind the revelation that her newly acquired stepfather, Myles, ran a thriving funeral parlour in Salisbury with two hearses, three black Mercedes and a vintage Wolseley limousine. Even the tyres are painted black, her mother remarked in unconcealed wonder.

It occurs to Irene that if Sergeant Flanagan is close to retirement he could easily double up as an undertaker – and aren't ex-garda sergeants always on the lookout for a sideline? She makes a mental note to ask her mother if Myles is in the market for a new body – unfortunate turn of phrase, that. Bound to be a nice little earner for the good sergeant except he'd have to up sticks and, for all Irene knows, there's no hurling in Wiltshire.

She motions him to follow. Sergeant Flanagan closes the door quietly, telling her what a grand place they have. He marvels at the amount of light spilling into the kitchen.

Irene has never been one for small talk, certainly not AC.

'After the city and all, you must find great peace in the countryside.'

She doesn't know whether that's a question or a statement but feels no obligation to confirm or deny. If this was 5 BC she'd probably joke about it being a counter-offensive to culchies taking over the capital but seeing as it's 5 AC she is more inclined to respond rhetorically: *Even if we went to the ends of the earth what makes you think we would ever find peace?*

Instead, she asks if he would like a cup of tea.

'I wouldn't say no. Thanks.'

'Or coffee if you prefer – filtered.'

'No, I'm a tea man.'

She half-fills the kettle and flicks the switch. His unexpected arrival has really thrown her. She pouts at the metaphorical aptness of him appearing out of the blue but starts to wonder what has him here. Gardaí, being gardaí, don't usually stray beyond their own patch. And if he's still based in Rathmines why has he come all this way to Co Meath?

'I'm out of biscuits.'

'That's no bother, Irene. Have to mind the oul weight.'

The kettle hisses into action but before the water starts bubbling the good sergeant clearly wants to unburden himself. He says this is a very difficult part of the job but it is his duty to inform the Gogartys that Patrick James McGeedy is about to be released.

The word drops to the floor like a grenade.

She swallows bitterly and wants to inhale and gasp at the same time. But there's more. Mr McGeedy has been a model prisoner. And although he chose not to attend psychotherapy or rehabilitation – *as was his right* – he did apply himself fully to reading and writing classes. His literacy teacher even felt sufficiently encouraged to loan the inmate her personal copy of *Moby Dick*.

Furthermore – *don't say there's more* – the prisoner demonstrated a natural flair for gardening and was awarded a photocopied certificate in horticulture. Given that there were indications he *might* feel some degree of remorse, the prison governor, together with the probation service *and* the psychological support unit, were satisfied that Mr McGeedy, now aged thirty-seven *and a father*, was no longer a threat to society.

'All things considered,' says the sergeant, 'it has been decided that the accused deserves a second chance.'

Calling him *the accused* slaps her in the face, another bum note at a really bad concert. The good sergeant is waffling now. She struggles to grasp what is coming out his gob, interrupting sharply to correct him by pointing out that Patrick James McGeedy is not 'accused'; he's *guilty as sin*.

The kettle clicks off automatically, steam rising. She drops a teabag into a mug but forgets to add hot water. It's all out of kilter, everything garbled like the discordant sounds now competing for her inner ear. To stay calm she speaks in a level but insistent tone.

'Five years ago he got nine years.'

'I know he did. But his legal team put in an appeal and Arbour Hill reviewed his case.'

'He got nine years – and it should have been longer!'

'I'm sorry, Irene. I have nothing to do with sentencing.'

'Five is less than nine the last time I looked – barely more than half! Why do they say nine when they have no intention . . .'

She trails off, bare feet padding the floor. Her soles hug heat through skin and bone but this is not a time to extol the virtues of underfloor heating. They stand yards apart. She fingers the cotton belt of her dressing-gown and tightens it sharply. The good sergeant can say no more about bright south-facing windows. He's not really undertaker material after all, his repertoire for condolence a lot more limited than she gave credit for.

Not that it matters for she is no longer listening.

He too stops talking and stares out the back garden. He sees four ceramic angels herald a water fountain where a sparrow pauses to bathe. Beside the fountain a wooden bench sorely in need of varnish squats under a flowerless cherry blossom. It's a barren scene of faded tranquillity that looks somehow unfinished. He notices sunlight catch a brass plate across the top of the bench. It is inscribed but the good sergeant's eyes are not what they once were.

'That's Cathal's seat,' she says, following his gaze.

He fingers his hat like he's threading a needle.

'Lookit, we did our best,' he says a little lamely.

'Did you?'

He's given up on tea and prepares to leave.

'I'm sorry Irene. Give Brendan my regards.'

Maybe it's because she stands rooted to the spot he doesn't actually move. The good sergeant finds himself wriggling through a vortex of grief, the force field of her desolation.

'Half way through his sentence,' she repeats.

Sergeant Flanagan shakes his head slowly and exhales. He does not wish to argue.

'I just thought you should know instead of reading it in the paper. Or you might be shopping up beyond in Dublin one day and spot him in the street. I'm not saying that'll happen now – it probably won't,' he pauses. 'I know you're upset, but that's how it works.'

'Works'? she splutters, like food going down the wrong way. 'If you ask me it doesn't *work* at all! They just tell you he's been a good boy who eats his vegetables – sure he even grows them now!'

'It's not . . . '

'Isn't that good enough to set him loose! After everything.'

Seconds pass, maybe longer.

'I'll let myself out.'

The good sergeant starts down the hall.

'That's probably what McGeedy told them.'

'I don't get you.'

'I'll let myself out.'

– 2 –

Cruising smoothly, soundlessly through this morning's downpour the motorway feels strangely subdued. He's already had a good meeting with the bank manager in Navan but it will take another 45 minutes to get to Gogarty's Marina Ltd. July should be busier but ever since icebergs started melting in the Arctic, summer has morphed into warm and heavy showers in the midlands. Who, but advance-booking Germans, would want to go boating in a deluge?

His ringtone blasts *Eye of the Tiger* and he knows without looking it's Irene. He presumes she's dialling from the bed seeing as she's taken to staying horizontal until lunchtime. On good days he's a quick and enthusiastic answerer of calls, tapping a rhythm against the steering wheel. Today the muscular rock anthem prickles him. He lets it ring three times so it goes automatically to message minder. Whenever she leaves a voicemail it's usually followed up ten minutes later, reminder of an urgent to-do list. Like, pick up a carton of milk on the way home.

Sometimes he does what he's told to keep the peace only to find three cartons unopened in the fridge. 'Didn't see them,' she'd say, waving him away like he's a fly in her soup. There's the message pips, sure enough. A crisis that can wait till he gets to the marina.

'One thing sure,' he sighs after the last note, 'we'll never run out of milk.'

The phone jumps again and Irene's name lights the screen. He isn't conscious of his foot pushing the accelerator and doesn't notice the Range Rover pick up speed. He also knows there's nearly a full litre at home because he actually checked before leaving. He considers switching it to silent so he can think clearly but how are you supposed to run a business if you can't hear your phone?

More pips. *Eye of the Tiger* rumbles again. He bangs the steering wheel with both palms. She's ringing like a mad thing. He's not going to answer – let her think he's in a meeting. Doesn't she know. Ah here . . .

'Irene, I'm in a meeting!'

'He's getting out.'

That's all she says. He stays in the fast lane and adjusts the wiper speed for no particular reason. The windscreen clears and blurs before the next wipe.

'How do you know?'

'Flanagan came over.'

'The sergeant?'

'Good behaviour.'

'Jesus.'

'That's what he said, Bren. Good behaviour.'

'I have to go.'

His mouth feels sour. The controls are electric so he presses a button to lower the window. He leans out and spits like a centre forward who has just missed a sitter. Saliva blows back in his face. He curses and closes it, wiping his cheek with the back of his hand.

The phone pulses again and he's fit to scream. Except it's Gary, calling from the marina.

'Yeah?'

'Good morning to you too.'

A wordless moment passes which tells Gary that the boss is in no mood for chat.

'Problem with the sensor. Can't switch it off.'

'Is the alarm actually ringing? Out loud, like?'

'No, but it won't turn off. I opened the shutter and nothing happened.'

'So it won't turn off but it's not working anyway.'

'That's it.'

'Fuck! Second time this month.'

'Will I ring the security crowd?'

'Yeah, do. I'll be there in half an hour.'

'Boss, can you pick up coffees? The kettle is banjaxed too.'

'Go on.'

Brendan fixes his eye on the median. Irene's call has floored him. He tries to clear his head of burglar alarms and coffee orders. Cathal is never far from his mind but five years of painful dissatisfaction return all at once. The sentence was nowhere near long enough in the first place. Way too lenient. And now it's the prison, or whoever-the-fuck is supposed to be in charge, bottling it at the half-way mark. If they were climbing Everest it's like someone has decided to ditch the tent at K2 and slide home.

Life for life. What's wrong with that?

During the trial Judge Rita Barrett twice cautioned Brendan to a vexed silence. Aching with rage he dipped a toe into DIY voodoo and directed all hostility towards McGeedy. To burn, choke, scald from within – whatever. Target the fucker. It didn't work. On numerous occasions he tried to catch McGeedy's eye. The prisoner denied him any satisfaction, training his gaze sheepishly on the floor each time he was led to a holding cell downstairs. Brendan's iciest stare was wasted, melting into a fluid brim that glazed and puddled his eyes.

A woman with a baby sat at the back of the court through this entire ordeal. Brendan and Irene noticed her taking the same seat every day, as far away as possible from the dock, her invisibility betrayed by a runny nose and a periodically uncooperative infant. Brendan took her for McGeedy's wife or 'partner'.

He knew the sniffling woman was not to blame for what happened to Cathal. She probably could not believe what she heard about her lover, her partner, her man. His conniving, his deception, his skill at luring the innocent with a very unoriginal promise of puppies needing a home.

Having to endure the detailed jigsaw of their son's final hour was off the scale for the Gogartys. If you were talking somewhere between one and ten Brendan would put it at eleven.

They discovered McGeedy had tried it earlier that day in Stepaside without success. Undeterred, he came down from the mountains to circle the city like a predator, armed with reliable pretext and an open car window until he spotted Cathal arriving home from school. He stopped and presumably made an identical appeal.

'Hey, am I near the dog pound? I have a few puppies in the boot and if I can't find someone soon they might have to be put down . . .'

It was enough to lure a kind-hearted boy. Cunningly identified as a 12-year-old who loved puppies too much to doubt a stranger.

Counsel for the defence – *and game for a laugh,* snorted Brendan – made every pathetic excuse that McGeedy grappled with an illness he could not control. That he was struggling with demons, the aftershock of a vaguely abusive childhood. A kiddie-fiddling uncle or some such convenience. 'His mother's brother, long deceased,' added counsel in a masterclass of extraneous detail. The jury looked to each other, increasingly confused as to who exactly was the victim in this pitiful episode.

'This frightful tragedy,' concluded counsel.

'Tragedy my bollox!' muttered Brendan. 'He knew what he was doing.'

The wailing baby roared in support from the gallery. For all Brendan knew the woman continued her snotting out of shame. Maybe it just sank in prior to sentencing that she could never really get away. She had well and truly tangled herself up with one sick excuse of a cunt.

Between one and ten he guessed it a seven for the sniffling woman.

In the hubbub after summation the baby started howling and made quite a racket until a court usher went over and suggested the woman take the child outside. When she stood to leave he impatiently pointed to clumps of damp tissue left behind.

'That's what ushers do,' whispered Irene, already in a daze. 'They usher.'

Granted, Brendan had nothing against the woman *per se* except wasn't she with him? And he presumed that the baby – a little girl by the sound of it – was McGeedy's spawn. Brought in to wring a little sympathy from the jury, no doubt. If we

13

punish the offender, pleaded the defence, what hope for his newborn daughter? Jury members shifted in their seats, part discomfort and part irritation. Maybe that's why he got nine years instead of fifteen.

Credit where it's due; the spawn did its job.

Brendan didn't believe in casting the sins of the father on the child but he could not tolerate the notion of McGeedy leaving legacy. His own issue rubbed together in spunk and slime, a perverse act of creation begat by someone who shouldn't be let near children. All things considered, why not – for the spawn's own sake – whisk her over to the nearest church, let the water run at the font and hold her little bonnet, face-down. All over in minutes, simultaneously baptised and drowned. Would the world stop turning? Not at all. Nothing against the colicky child, in fairness, but if the world gene pool of sick cuntery is down a carrier aren't we all winning?

Nine years! The Gogartys wanted the DPP to appeal. They wanted the sentence topped up. The prosecutor saw otherwise, insisting this was a fantastic result. That although the accused – *say his name for fuck sake!* – had taken the boy – *Our Cathal!!* – into his car under false pretences, defence counsel maintained there was no hard evidence that anything untoward *actually occurred* during their short onward journey.

In fact, counsel contended, tragedy could conceivably have been averted that afternoon had the boy not made a hasty but ill-advised decision to exit the accused's car at a red traffic light. Observed by seven eyewitnesses to blindly swing open the passenger door and race headlong in diagonal fashion across a busy intersection. Needless to say – *but say it anyway why don't you!* – the unfortunate driver of the oncoming Bedford coal truck was in no way blameworthy.

To the Gogartys the judge's summary made it sound like this was all Cathal's fault. A casual observer might well surmise that the boy was expected to stay put like prey and helplessly await his fate. That, if there was any sympathy going, the distraught coal man was probably most deserving.

Somewhere deep down Brendan felt a flicker of pride that his son, in the most fearful moments of his 12-year-old life, had indeed resisted. The boy ran to fight back. No such consolation for Irene who chose to berate herself for not warning the child enough not to talk to strangers, even ones with homeless puppies.

Nine years.

Upon sentencing, the prosecutor's bespectacled assistants were all smiles, backslapping their man like he had just got elected. Brendan and Irene, reduced to idle spectators, sat stranded through this laughless comedy in bad humour and failing grace. Only when the prosecutor took a moment to glance over did part of his clean-shaven neck redden beneath a fancy silk mustard tie.

'Mr and Mrs Gogarty, I feel I should emphasise that this is a splendid outcome,' he insisted.

'You think so?' replied Brendan, freshly irritated by elocution.

'Nine years? I most certainly do.'

'Well we *most certainly* don't!'

He wanted to declare loudly that the law had failed them. More than that, the Gogartys, punch-drunk after sentencing, were denied justice. From start to finish none of this went the way they wanted. Not a single thing. And for something so deeply personal to go so horribly wrong . . . he found himself unable to look away, unable to let go. Every unfixable aspect, replaying over and over in granular detail.

God, he remembers that day. He remembers that day every day.

It hung over him like a shroud, even shadowing his dream time. Whatever their boy was put through in his last moments Brendan wanted McGeedy to endure much, much more. None of this magicking nine-into-five mullarkey. No efficiently accurate firing squad or razor-sharp guillotine. No quick-action cyanide injection. No, no, no. Too good for him when you could instead go the scenic route by drawing it out, nice and slow. In recurring nightscapes he would frighten Patrick James McGeedy so badly that the little fucker would literally shit himself to death.

Following the trial you could say Brendan had a bit of a rethink about what he saw as crime *without* punishment. Bitter experience convinced him to dispense with any notion of fairness. He could see good reason to take a leaf out of Pakistan or Afghanistan or one of them -stan countries where they're not so hellbent on rehabilitation. That's not to say he'd go as far as turning Croke Park into Beheading Central, but even at his most reasonable he wanted to put an end to all this watering down of penalties. Everybody a soft touch, nobody held to account and victims' families battered into mute submission as collateral.

It left him with only one recourse. Retribution.

– 3 –

Irene is privy to a raft of boating enquiries daily, any possibility of a 5.00 pm curfew broadsided by Brendan's ever-intrusive Nokia and international time zones. When she once suggested he could switch the phone off he looked at her like she had two heads.

'Why would I do that?' he asked, incredulously.

'So we could have some *quality time*!' she hissed.

It's not that she'd want him around 24/7 – God forbid – but it's just he's never here. As in *never*. Sometimes the only sound she hears in this four-bed mansion is the tick of expanding metal as radiators heat up. Or the tuneless accordion of her own breathing. Otherwise, silence. Whenever that stillness feels either pronounced or prolonged she pinches herself until she draws blood. Then she doesn't feel so alone.

True, Brendan provides her with a *geansaí* load of home comforts in exchange for abandonment. Top dollar white goods, a Mazda RX-7 she calls Sylvia, a gold credit card subventing clothes and a Marcosian collection of shoes. And, as far as she is concerned, why not – if he's married to the job doesn't that make his stresses her in-laws?

Granted, he puts in the hours, but if you love working so much can you really call it work? It's a vocation without halos. Gogarty's Marina Ltd itself is a statement. Like any other megalomaniac who names a company after his or her self. I mean, *puleeaase* . . .

It's his escape for God's sake.

Escaping from me, more like.

He did buy her a red Ericcson once. 'To stay in touch,' he said. She found the idea of carrying a phone everywhere you go plain weird but he said it's something you get used to. The mobile barely fits into her handbag so she usually leaves it on the kitchen counter, uncharged.

Maybe it's too early to say, but if it turns out sticking a mobile phone to the side of your head can give you cancer, Brendan's days are definitely numbered. She has picked up his device between conference calls and felt the earpiece warm, even hot. A microwave signal sent from earth into outer space and back again, Route One to the human brain. That said, if he's using the mobile as a shield against her, surely it's poetic justice that thoughtlessness might catch up with him in the end.

Losing Brendan to radiation is not a scenario she dwells upon too often. She can't imagine him more withdrawn than usual, drifting away under morphine, confusing dreams with reality and the pair of them still unable to reconnect, a twinkling of atonement glaringly absent from his unticked bucket list. Not the most fulsome *adieu* imaginable but under afternoon drizzle in their Nobber mansion she often feels she has lost him already.

A captain of industry, he likes to proclaim, keys bouncing off his belt like the commercial pull of the outside world, his nautical lodestar making him feel important. If the boatyard is a conduit AC for any life force he still possesses there's not much left in the tank afterwards. She can't tell any more if he cares. Says he does but she suspects he's full of it.

Last Sunday she watched him shaving in the mirror, the cordless humming quietly as it skated his jowls. She saw his mobile illuminate on the dresser but said nothing, just handed it to him when it stopped. A missed call. Mopping his neck with a towel he raised an eyebrow at 'no caller ID' on the screen and asked why she didn't answer it.

'Could've been important,' he muttered, blowing bristle off the shaver.

'Probably the White House,' she replied. 'Want to ask you about China.'

That's when he resorts to hurt silence, nodding slowly in a mood of high offence.

'If it's important enough won't they ring back?' she countered as a peace offering, mustering more reassurance than she felt he deserved.

He threw on Old Spice like he was slapping himself in the mirror. Both hands, both cheeks. Stretched some facial muscles in what might pass for a smile in Bulgaria. Then he was on his way. No goodbye kisses any more, though they were downgraded AC to a walk-by peck long ago. Even that is all ancient history, though she can hardly be accused of overdoing encouragement.

He parks the Range Rover nose out every time. Faces the sensor gate so it's ready and waiting for the next makey-up emergency. Don't think these things pass her by. Each fresh crisis, a too-complicated-to-explain hitch on some river-related escapade he's devoted himself to. Whatever! Scrambles for his wallet, fights his way into that burgundy corduroy jacket – his favourite, though a little snug these days – scans the room last-minute and half-jogs to the door, don't-wait-up-for-me (love), no smoke without fire and all that.

All this hurly-burly running on the spot ramps up like migraine, a whirlwind of fuss and urgency on grounds that are unconvincing – even irrelevant – to her. Whatever state he knows she is in appears of little interest or consequence. Brief exchanges such as these are usually brought to a swift close by the fading jangle of keys and an assured click of the hall door. Going through the motions in this way Irene is grateful for the economy of small mercies, big fat radials spitting gravel in their wake.

'I'll leave you in peace,' he offers as a blessing.

His deliberate misuse of this phrase irks her. He knows damn well there is no such thing, not here. From behind security gates in their County Meath home what he really means is he wants away.

'A fireman wouldn't slide down a pole faster than you,' she observes.

He has no time for analogy.

Day-to-day in Nobber can sometimes feel so un-lifelike that at times she feels she landed a bit part in a very mediocre TV soap. Were this the closing scene from this afternoon's episode she would be left standing in the hallway, facing out

19

to set in motion the scheming cogs. And from this position she would remain, ready to peer into the middle distance had he not blocked it off by closing the door.

Regular viewers watching Brendan's hasty departure would never mistake Irene's doorstep stare for vapidity. Soap devotees will tell you that the purpose of insult, real or imagined, is to plant longer-term seeds of revenge. A ratings-friendly harbinger of what's to come.

– 4 –

B rendan doesn't like these fights. He didn't mind them at the start because they might clear the air and, afterwards, they'd make up with a good ride. Passion, as the man says. But now he'd prefer skip the whole rollercoaster altogether. Wears him out so it does. Cross words flying in every direction – the kitchen, the living room, the bedroom. He notes with some disquiet that lately she's taken to standing in front of the TV during *The Sunday Game.*

At this stage he wouldn't even class the bog as sacred ground. Last week she followed him into the toilet during a full-blooded argument so he now resorts to turning the key. He does not regard locking the bathroom door as extremist; he'd call it crowd control.

If she is ink, he is blotting paper.

Things had been bad enough ever since the calendar went AC but following the good sergeant's bad tidings the idea of their home doubling up on grief meant misery wholesale under one roof. He wondered if his wife went back to bed or crashed out on the settee. Maybe she took a sleeping tablet or gulped painkillers, none of which ever did what they say they'd do.

It's not something he could talk about. Not to Gary or to anybody connected with the job. And that's where his meaningful world exists – work. He had discussed the home situation at length only once with a stranger on a barstool in Kells. As his companion drew from a packet of savouries, a slow procession of pints and multiple chasers led to a rather frank exchange of views.

'Don't want to put you off your peanuts but I can't do a good, clean dump when I'm sitting on the throne,' ventures Brendan. 'Not when I'm getting an earful through the keyhole.'

'Hah?' replies his companion, blinking in disbelief.

'That's a fact. You shouldn't have to concentrate on nature but your head does be melted when you've got a call from the wild the other side of a locked door.'

'You mean you can't even do a shite?' sympathises the stranger, eager for clarification. 'I'm telling you if you were a Yank you'd be onto your lawyer straight away.'

'Ah no, Horse. I'm not that way inclined. But sometimes it feels like being under fire every waking hour and there's no basis whatsoever for the half of it.'

Bolstered by the stranger's confession of a dalliance with the local postmistress, Brendan did admit to taking fresh precautions with his other half.

'I don't even leave me car keys on the table any more in case she'd hide them.'

'Go away.'

'Ah, things have changed. "Oh, there you go," says she, when I make me move. "Running away – *as per usual*!"'

'Awaytafuck!'

The stranger nodded with the solemnity of someone digesting multiple scenarios, not all of them palatable.

'Where do you go so?'

'I've no plan. No plan at all.'

'You need a plan.'

'I mean, get out of the house, head for wherever – sometimes the workshop and other times out on the job, *mar dhea*. Doesn't matter! Zap the ole security gate in advance like it's the last fence in Colditz. I mean to say, it feels like a getaway but it's not like it's all been thought out in advance.'

They sip, crouching at the counter.

'Did you ever see *The Italian Jobbie?* Not that modern version – the original. Now *that* was a plan.'

Brendan would not be drawn into discussions about cinema or motoring advertorials for a spunky new sensation from 1960's British Leyland.

'You didn't see it, no?' persists the stranger, his mind unspooling celluloid.

'Nah.'

'Sure them boyos ended up hanging off a cliff,' he laughs. 'Nifty drivers in their Minis, flying across rooftops what-have-you, leaving the *Eye*-ties in a tizz. They're virtually home and dry but doesn't the getaway bus take a bit of a spin on this mountain road. It's a big bloody drop! So they're crowded together at one end and all the gold they've pinched slides down the other, putting the whole enterprise in the balance.'

'So what happened?' asks Brendan disinterestedly.

'D'you know I can't remember. All I'm saying is, soon as they have it in the bag doesn't it all go pear-shaped! Come to think of it, you can overdo the oul planning.'

'Don't I know it, hah?' replies Brendan, unsure as to what he is agreeing with. He nods to the barman for another. 'It's not like I'd be at this crack normally, not in the daytime. Better off being busy, doing something.'

'Isn't this doing something?' grins the stranger, peering into his Powers. 'Hafta drain the spuds.'

Brendan watches the stranger step down unsteadily, draw breath and walk purposefully to the gents. He pictures his wife at home, barefooted behind security gates. Chances are she's in her dressing-gown, her feet slapping off warm tiles. Chances are there's a Chardonnay on the go.

In fairness, she did come up with a really good proposal the other week to overhaul the criminal justice system. She proposed that anyone found guilty of premeditated murder should be put into a cell for twenty years plus. On a pre-arranged date far, far into the future, let the victim's family come to the jail. Let *them* decide. And let the prisoner see them standing outside, holding the key.

The stranger returns. He tells Brendan not to worry; the world will probably end soon anyhow.

'I won't lecture you but, if it doesn't,' he adds, pausing to belch, 'maybe the pair of ye need to try that other business – counselling. Not for me now but . . . *coping mechanisms*, isn't that what they call it. And they say these things work both ways.'

'Is that so?'

'But then again, your other half has to *want* to be helped – as well as yourself. Tis no use otherwise.'

Brendan suggests Irene's coping mechanism involves going through him for a short cut. She'd prefer that to paracetamol any day. Him getting home from the marina – barely in the door – like a hair trigger to remind her of everything that's gone wrong. He wonders if it's chemical or does the menopause involve a forwarding party? If Irene finds herself struggling with the universe five years into this, why not make that his fault too?

'I've got me own mechanisms, that's what gets her. Put the head down, keep moving, throw meself into the job, what-have-you. Of course she can't resist having the odd little dig over that too.'

'Little digs is what women do. Well, wives, anyways.'

'"*That's all you care about, the bloody job*." If I got a penny every time she said that.'

'Ah you're goosed one way or the other,' consoles the stranger, picking himself off the stool for an unexpectedly urgent return to the gents. 'Fuckin' prostate,' he adds by way of explanation.

Brendan twirls a beer mat on the counter. Before this latest bombshell from the sergeant he thought of telling Irene she'd want to buck up. As things stood there was no way back for them. Good luck to conversations, to laughter, to feelings, to fancy dinners on the company card. Even make-up rides were a thing of the past and, truth be told, he wasn't minded enough to miss them.

– 5 –

After Flanagan's social call this morning she thought she'd share the good news. It took a few attempts, as per usual, before Brendan picked up. He told her he was in a meeting but she could hear him driving. These stupid little games!

She is not one for long phone conversations. Neither is he – unless, of course, it's business-related. This time though, she wished the call didn't end quite so abruptly. It was like she got rudely elbowed aside by a dial tone, the remainder of a long day yawning before her. She must have dozed off for a couple of hours. Thought of phoning him again when she woke up to see if he was on his way – pretty unlikely – or if he'd wrapped the Range Rover around a tree. But why bother dialling?, she asked herself. He wouldn't answer either way.

It's late afternoon at the villa. She has no real appetite these days. Makes a pot of coffee when she gets up and that usually does her. She's not a supermodel but her dress size has dropped from 14 to 10 in five years. The last time Agnes was over she suggested her daughter was wasting away. At least Mother would worry, she sighs. Brendan wouldn't notice if she went on hunger-strike and ended up looking like Kate Moss.

Maybe it's a good day to start smoking again.

Her father died of lung cancer when she was in college and everybody presumed that's why she suddenly gave up cigarettes. But that wasn't it at all. She just lost interest. Trying to look sophisticated, puffing away, just seemed, well, silly.

Irene finds a pack of 19 Silk Cut Blue she bought down the village last week. Got them for distraction, nothing more. Arriving home she tore off the cellophane and removed the gold wrapper. She actually had one between her lips before realising she had no way of lighting up. Not with a ceramic cooker and coal effect fireplace fed by natural gas. She can't remember the last time she saw a box of matches – for some reason they used to be called Friendly. In a flash of inspiration she got the car keys and sat into Sylvia, turning the engine to pop the lighter.

Drawing deeply to make sure it catches hold, she makes for the back garden to sit where she usually sits: Cathal's seat.

Cathal was twelve.

There is no denying her mother was deeply upset about losing her only grandchild. Absorbed it all without saying too much. With a professional undertaker at her side Mother joined their pitiful gathering in Portobello, adding to November greyness her own unhelpful brand of quiet despair. Myles had to go back after a couple of days – solid citizens reliably expiring in Salisbury – and, under the weight of a suffocating silence, all readily agreed it was better Agnes went with him.

The first weeks AC are blank. Irene simply can't recall them. When her father died it was only family and friends; with Cathal there was a steady stream of strangers calling, phoning, writing. It felt like they were under siege in Lennox Place.

Everybody wanted to convey how *desperately sorry* they were for her trouble. A scrawl of handwritten envelopes – *THE GOGARTYS (some where in Dublin)* – like people wanted to join the parade and be part of the action. The postman's bag stuffed to over full, his daily walk doubled up in collective mourning. They were deluged with Mass cards, sympathy cards, long letters and short notes.

> *Dear Irene and Brendan,*
> *You don't know me but . . .*

Irene gave up reading them. Bouquet followed bouquet into the compost bin. Did she appreciate such intrusion? No, she did not. Brendan made himself scarce. Away to work don't-you-know, even though it was off-season for leisure craft so he could easily have cut the week back to three days.

She stopped answering the front door and, to Brendan's dismay, used a hammer and screwdriver to make a few DIY adjustments. Callers would approach the stippled glass, preparing to announce themselves. Then, confusion, a furtive mime show when they discovered the doorbell had been neutered, their hands waving around in silhouette.

It went on for days, maybe weeks. From an armchair in the unlit hall – or sometimes hunkered into a corner of the kitchen – she would watch gargoyle faces press against the glass like they had a right to stare in. She didn't have the energy to roar at them but if they were living in Texas, Irene would have dropped down to the local supermarket to pick up a semi-automatic and plenty of bullets.

These strangers would usually hang around for a few minutes, then drop a card on the doorstep or leave flowers – she'd nailed the letterbox shut. They'd slope off disappointed, swindled out of a front row seat to misery and a good story for the pub.

Maybe it was the central heating but she began to feel like there was no air in the house. It surprised her how quickly shop flowers can rot and stink the place out. The perfume of unwanted gifts. She'd toss them in the sink and Brendan would bin them when he got home. One morning there was an infestation of flies. She sprayed the house with air freshener – which does not smell like it sounds – and splashed disinfectant in the passageway where the rubbish was stored.

Still they kept coming. She closed the windows, which made it even stuffier. She prised open floorboards but found nothing. When she saw a couple of flies nosing around the fireplace she rattled the grate with a poker. Scores of dirty great bluebottles appeared all at once, the swarm zigzagging like violin bows, a dizzy shapeless orchestra crashing one after another against the living room window. Irene had to cover her mouth for fear of swallowing one.

There was at least a hundred of them and she immediately grabbed the Nilfisk from under the stairs, sucking them up within minutes. The oddest thing was how sluggish they were, not like ordinary flies at all. They made no attempt to get away. Grimacing, she removed a squishy bag from the vacuum cleaner and dumped it.

She was going to ring Brendan and tell him about the plague but curiosity distracted her. She pulled at the fireplace, levering it loose with the screwdriver. The draught guard gave way, soon followed by a loud sigh of black soot. It startled her when a small feathered body dropped into the grate like a prize toy in an amusement arcade, its white plumage blackened so she didn't recognise it straight away as a magpie.

Normally she would be horrified by the sight of a dead animal but she found herself picking up the bird and holding it close. One of its small dark eyes stared ahead, the other was closed. Its chest had an open wound dusted with soot. It got trapped in the chimney and must have injured itself trying to get out. She wondered how long it had been there.

One for sorrow.

She remembered reading somewhere that magpies pair off for life, the same as swans. Irene walked out to the front gate and from the edge of the path she heard cawing from up high. Its mate, watching forlornly from a chimney pot nextdoor. She couldn't bear its cries and begged it to stop. Only when she threw a stone did the magpie take off, retreating loudly to a higher perch. A neighbour's Venetian blind shimmered back into place.

She placed the bird on a white linen tablecloth like an offering, its dark tail beautiful and surprisingly long. Some feathers had loosened during its struggle so she did her best to put its coat back in order. Everything was perfectly still but for scores of larvae incubating in its open carriage. She shook the scrubs onto a napkin which went into the bin. A long, shiny dark blue feather fell to the floor. She tucked it under her hairband. Touching its charcoal beak with her lips she made a silent wish for the little creature's soul and another for its bereft mate.

Taking a trowel from the shed she dug a shallow hole out the back garden and, there, unrolling the tablecloth as a wrapper, laid the bird to rest. Its mate was nowhere to be seen but might have been watching from distance, piecing together all the tragic clues like the clever birds we know magpies to be. Tears trickled down Irene's sooty face leaving smudge tracks. She could think of nothing but this little creature trapped, crying out in panic, unable to find a way out of the darkness it suddenly found itself.

When Brendan came home it shocked him to find her so dishevelled. She had forgotten about the blue feather in her hair. In between sobs she told him about the little service. He didn't know what she was talking about until he saw a small patch of upturned soil beside the daffodils. All that remains. Brendan put his head in his hands as if he'd been struck in the face, turned slowly and shuffled inside.

– 6 –

He'll have to wait for The Big Day. The day McGeedy gets out.

Truth be told, Brendan has gone through this scenario so many times you could tell him it had already happened for real and he'd believe you. God knows how it's going to pan out but right now that's not his concern. He has to do this; otherwise it'd eat him up from the inside and he'd be no use to anyone.

McGeedy turned the Gogartys' world upside-down five years ago and here he is again, turning them inside-out once more. The good sergeant said they have a right to know the release date but can take it no further than that. The perpetrator has rights, said he in Garda-speak. He's *constitutionally* entitled to his privacy and to his freedom. So all Brendan knows is some time on Tuesday between 10 am and 2 pm. No more, no less.

Having to stomach the idea of McGeedy set free halfway through his sentence is enough to give you the sick. Brendan didn't want him to get out at all but what say has he in any of this? He's only a dead boy's father. That's all.

Cathal obviously couldn't speak for himself so his parents were asked by the judge to make a victim impact statement. Irene wanted things said but was in no fit state to say them. Brendan approached the witness stand, slight tremor in a small sheaf of handwritten pages. He just didn't want to let his son down. He saw McGeedy's partner scuttle away with that cursed baby just before he started. Typical! Then he quietly told the court about the Gogarty family blowing bubbles in Lennox Place and how one man came along and destroyed their future.

He made it clear to the jury that things would never be the same. 'Never' was forever. And now, five years on, it felt like everything he told the court that day was forgotten. Their pain, he realised, had a sell-by date. 'Impact' obviously means here and now, at least when it comes to victims.

You can wrap it up in Garda-speak to sound like it makes sense but all he can see is the justice system desperate to roll out the red carpet for this toerag. And the cherry on top? The Gogartys told they better take all of this lying down or it's them who'll be in bother.

At first, Brendan didn't know what to do. His head clouded over, his thinking fuzzy like a bad signal on the wireless. He called three local TDs and each of them said they'd get back. Didn't hear from two of them and the third rang him yesterday around lunchtime to say there was nothing she could do. Priceless, hah? Well there's three party coffers that won't be getting a contribution from Gogarty's Marina Ltd next time they come begging.

Not that he'd depend on them anyways. He figured he was better off going scattergun. So he wrote to the Taoiseach. Not a sausage. Ditto the Minister for Justice – sure why would he want to get his hands dirty? Couldn't reach by phone the Governor at Arbour Hill. Brendan was told they don't talk about 'individual cases'. Maybe if he rang up to offer their star gardener a part-time job they'd be chirpier, full of the joys of spring and the restorative power of justice.

Got nowhere with the Prison Service or the Probation Service either, so nothing for it but to drop over to Rathmines and ask for Sergeant Flanagan.

'Ah, Brendan,' said the good sergeant, guiding his visitor into a side-room like he's about to hear confession.

With no one bothering to even return a call Brendan was already under strain from getting the absolute runaround from Billy to Jack. He could not believe the scumbag was about to get out. Someone was responsible, even if it seemed pretty obvious nobody was. Was there nothing could be done to overturn the decision? Get it reversed, like? Sure who in the name of God wants to let a madman loose?

'Like, put yourself in my shoes, sergeant. They're bending themselves backwards over that little bollox since Day One. And when you try folly up, you get nowhere. Nobody cares. You try ringing someone and all you get is *Greensleeves* – if ever a song was going to send you around the twist that has to be it.'

'Will you have a cup of tea?'

'I've run out of road,' said Brendan sharply. 'Maybe you could give me a pointer or two. Help, like.'

'Are you sure you won't have tea?'

'Sergeant, this whole thing is a complete joke, y'know. A total and utter shambles. I mean, is there *anything* you can do about it?'

Brendan reckons the good sergeant is probably a decent skin but at the end of the day he's one hundred and ten percent useless. He can probably see the finish line up ahead, working out his pension on café napkins at lunchtime. All his great ideas seem to involve writing letters to morons; besides which, everything the sergeant suggests Brendan had already done.

'It's out of my hands, Brendan,' he repeats for the umpteenth time.

That's when Brendan banged the table.

'Right so!'

Flanagan isn't supposed to be another Tom, Dick or Harry. He's supposed to help you – public servant, hah? – except he *is* the same as everyone else. Falling down on the job. Maybe this is one for Dirty Harry or one of them boyos who'll bend the rules to level the playing field. Brendan tells him there's no hard feelings, already turning to go before the good sergeant's eyebrows arch upwards.

'To hell with it,' dithers Brendan under a Rathmines street light, unable to recall where he parked the Range Rover.

If the sergeant was the final straw it did make him think it through from A to Z. Which means now he's planned and prepared. Took a spin up to the city a few days after Irene got that visit. Parked outside Arbour Hill and scoped out the place, noting the granite soaked grey under a rusting necklace of barbed wire. Saw where the deliveries go in and, more importantly, where the prisoners come out. So, he's going to be parked right *there* because he knows for a fact Patrick James McGeedy is going to come out *that* sky blue metal door.

He'll see McGeedy well before McGeedy sees him because he's going to sit in the passenger seat facing *this* way. Then he can pick him up in the mirror good and early. That'll give time to get the Stanley ready. About three quarters of an inch out, no more, so it doesn't catch in the pouch of his hoodie. Then he'll move fast, step out the passenger side, cross the road quickly to make up ground. McGeedy will be expecting nothing so whether he turns left or right won't matter.

If necessary, Brendan will call out his name like he knows him, which, for reasons beyond his control, he sort of does. All friendly, like, 'Hey Patrick!' Or, 'Good man yourself, Paddy!' And when he looks up or turns around it'll happen so quick he'll hardly feel the blade. It'll be across his face, back and forward like a hard slap, forehand, backhand – and if his throat gets in the way, so be it.

He's not going all Rambo when he decides this is something he needs to do on his own. He just doesn't want anyone else involved, especially Irene. And if he finds himself in a bit of bother at the end of it, well . . . if you're up Shit Creek there's no point losing both paddles, is there?

In fact, he has said nothing to Irene. He knows they're supposed to be in this together but, sure, hasn't it wedged them apart? Okay, they're not supposed to keep secrets but isn't it better this way. He doesn't ask that as a question, he's just telling it like it is. Yes, it might take him out of circulation for a while and leave the marina in the lurch but Gary can manage for a few years if needs be. Weighing up serious consequences is not today's priority.

As with previous nights he lay awake thinking it through. He didn't notice drifting off because next thing he's in Connolly Station and isn't McGeedy right there, stretched out on black and white floor tiles. That's definitely him, choking on the Drogheda-bound platform, blood gurgling out his mouth in a fierce loud wheeze.

So it was all going grand on Platform Three. Daily commuters seemed to think they were after walking onto the set of an impressively realistic film set except there isn't a camera crew in sight. Then a young red-haired woman – a uniformed nurse from the Mater – appears from the crowd to try save McGeedy. Brendan has to give her a bit of a smack to discourage her, vaguely aware that hitting an off-duty nurse is probably not a great look.

A few other travellers, led by a young apprentice from CIÉ, try to corner him, dancing around like coyotes. He keeps them at bay with the Stanley pointed out, at least for as long as McGeedy lies there leaking. Then the gurgling stops with one last heave-ho and Brendan knows the job is done. So he throws the Stanley onto the train track for health and safety and puts both hands in the air. The dancing coyotes hesitate, not knowing what to do with him.

He spots a cosy pub the other side of the ticket booth. 'First pint on me,' he announces, willing to let bygones be bygones. 'And sorry about that,' he mutters to the stricken nurse but she's in no mood for conversation. Nor does anybody take up his generous offer.

Brendan, feeling a little rebuffed, sits down to gather his breath, his feet dangling over the shiny iron rail while he waits for the gardaí to arrive. He half-expects Sergeant Flanagan to appear by escalator but before he discovers who is leading the blue charge his eyes open and sees from the bedside clock it's 4.33 a.m.

Now he has to do it all again. Except this isn't a dream – although, in fairness, Connolly Station didn't feel like a dream either. It's not that he's complaining. If this is what it takes, this is what it takes. With a bit of luck there'll be no Florence Nightingale interfering this time round.

He takes up position at Arbour Hill and lets the hours pass by, the mobile on silent. Had to get over early to make sure he got the parking spot he needed. Irene thinks he's at the marina but work today can wait. He hears the phone vibrate but after skipping two calls from Gary he slips it into the glove compartment so he won't be distracted by whoever is looking for him.

No one pays him a blind bit of notice. A spread of *Daily Star* horse racing pages decorate the dashboard to make it look more normal. If you passed twice in the space of a few hours you'd swear he was either a timidly indecisive gambler or the slowest reader in the world.

He thought it would be easy to distinguish prison staff from the scum but soon as someone appears at the gate it dawns on him this isn't going to be quite so simple. Paedos come from the same community as their victims so they probably don't have two heads. There's already been a couple of false alarms with ordinary looking men coming out in civilian clothes. He couldn't be a hundred percent about who or what these people are. Maybe they work inside as painters or cooks or something. Strikes him as a strange place to earn a crust but doesn't it take all sorts?

They dropped McGeedy in there like they do with all the creeps and sickos. They say they have to separate them from the general prison population, especially if crimes against children are involved. Well twelve is a child, no two ways about it. And if you're talking about a creep and a sicko rolled into one, why in the name of God should anyone make a fuss about protecting him?

Even though it's trickier than he thought Brendan has no doubt he will recognise McGeedy straight away. That fucker could hide behind a beard wearing dark glasses under a sombrero or let five years' growth trail Rasta-like down his back. It won't matter a damn because Brendan will see through it all. Is it really five years since he spent day after day after day staring at him in court?

Like, who's on trial here?

No, don't get him started.

Gary leaves another message about road works causing havoc outside the marina but that's not where the action is. Half-eleven now . . . going on twenty-five-to . . . not easy waiting when you just want to get your business over and done with. He's watching his side mirror so intently that the prison gate begins to blur. *Come on. Focus!*

He rehearses the action of the Stanley once again, pulling it fast from the hoodie pouch, sliding the blade in and out, visualising human flesh as its final destination. As far as he can remember it wasn't drawn out like this the other night in Connolly Station. None of this waiting around. That's the beauty of dreams, he sighs. Everything happens on time, clean as a whistle, the job usually done and dusted before you wake up.

– 7 –

Irene never believed in building a shrine to grief but, still, it surprised her that for months she felt the urge to surround herself with every trace she could find of her boy. To reclaim his essence – or at least hold on for as long as possible – she would lay on his bed, inhaling the pillow. Sit on the floor among his things. It was often bright outside when she went up to his room and by the time she made it downstairs darkness had fallen.

Then Brendan would arrive home.

Sometimes lying on the child's bed she wonders if there is a limit of sadness beyond which you can take no more. An absolute. And if there is, has she already passed it?

The obvious alternative came to mind several times. She has a variety of means available – a bottle of sleeping tablets in the bathroom, a razor sharp carving knife in the kitchen, Sylvia's exhaust pipe in the garage. Had she not decided that this would be letting Cathal down she probably would have gone through with it. Resolving eventually not to take such a drastic course she resumed her journey onwards, plodding along in what she feels is an irresolute haze.

Brendan virtually took up residence at the marina. Despite his unwavering commitment to long, unprofitable hours the season then kicked off without discernible pick-up. Nor was there any rebalancing of their domestic routine. Such a peripatetic schedule brought about a gradual suspension of regular meals in Lennox Place. This made little difference to Irene who considered food an optional extra at that point.

Agnes made some half-hearted offers to come over to Portobello and stay for a while but Irene gave equally unconvincing assurances that everything was fine. This was how the Kellys dealt with crises.

Trailing her arm along the banister rail one afternoon Irene went upstairs and opened the door to Cathal's room. Slowly, she unpeeled the football and music posters from the walls. Rolled them up into a cardboard cylinder, taking her time over each item. Every so often she would stop to rest, falling heavily onto his A-Team duvet for short naps. She ignored the occasional rap of knuckles on the front door as she did the phone clanging from the hall.

Going through Cathal's wardrobe she examined his clothes garment-by-garment – his school uniform, a few pairs of jeans – one of which she had neatly patched up at the knee – various jumpers, t-shirts, a Meath GAA jersey, a Puma tracksuit Brendan got for his eleventh birthday. Aside from his socks and underwear, assorted runners and shoes, it was only when she could picture him wearing each item that she could bring herself to pack it away.

She lifted the quilt and stripped the bed. With the help of a screwdriver and adjustable spanner she dismantled the fold-up desk they got him when he started fifth class.

'You have a couple of big years ahead,' they told him. '*Important* years.'

He was an active boy with a pre-teen world of Atari, VHS movies, a deck of cards, adventure books, a Rubik's cube, bits and pieces from school as well as some games and toys he had long outgrown but never thrown out. A magpie-like hoarder like Brendan. An Old Spice presentation gift box rested in a drawer, the same brand as his father. It was unopened.

If they were down the garda station these possessions would be called personal effects. Little clues to an anonymous life, stuffed into a labelled brown bag that sealed at the top so that smaller items wouldn't fall out. Sad, identifying fragments – maybe like spectacles held together with sellotape, a half-finished packet of Polo mints, Bic lighter, travel pass or some such, a few paltry coins. But where do personal effects go if there's nobody to claim them? Who finishes off the Polos?

The Old Spice disappeared into a large plastic crate along with everything else. Sylvia was a two-seater and Cathal's belongings filled its small boot. She wondered about which charity shop to go to – not one nearby because the last thing she wanted was to see her boy's belongings displayed in the window. So she drove to a St Vincent de Paul store in Sandymount. Two young volunteers politely offered to help. Irene asked if they had a cigarette but both were too young and too wise to smoke. She stood back to let them unload the car.

Dublin Bay is particularly shallow on this stretch so the beach is very safe, even when the tide comes in. And when the tide goes out the water's edge seems very far away. She remembered bringing Cathal here as a baby one cloudy summer afternoon many years ago. It was the first time he'd seen the sea. Brendan paddled the overcast shore in rolled-up pants, Cathal in his arms. Mystified and curious, the child slapped and splashed, then put his fingers into his mouth, grimacing at the unfamiliar taste of brine.

That memory filled Irene's mind until she discovered her fingernails digging into her wrist. She put the marked skin to her tongue and walked seawards through puddled sand. Kneeling at a small pool, she spooned salt water with an open palm, leaning back to allow it trickle down her throat. She spooned another mouthful and another until it made her retch.

The young volunteers did not come out when she went back to retrieve Sylvia. Gridlocked by rush hour it was a crawl all the way to Portobello. Sea water had unsettled her stomach. Arriving home, Brendan stomped downstairs to the hall, brandishing her not very mobile phone. She would later laugh at the irony that he had tried repeatedly to call her.

'Where did you put all his stuff?'

'It's time, Brendan.'

'Says who?' he roared, flinging the Ericcson at the wall.

Pieces of red plastic shattered everywhere as the battery slid across the floor. Irene trudged away. She hadn't meant to upset him but was too exhausted to argue. Upstairs, Cathal's bedroom no longer looked the same. The posters left light shadows, the wallpaper patchy where it had never seen sunlight. A bare mattress emptied the room of personality, like a rental awaiting a new tenant.

It took a few days for things to finally calm down. Brendan conceded that their time in Lennox Place had come to an end. Their terraced house, once a happy home but now darkly freighted with memory and sadness. Too much to bear.

Brendan started talking about a 3.5 acre green field site in Nobber, County Meath. Away from it all. Although he had no immediate family locally any more he knew the area well and wasn't he a Royal through and through. Over the next weeks he could get plans drawn up and they could start over. A new house he dubbed *The Villa*. Thirteen miles to Navan, almost the same to Kells. A two-storey Danish design inviting, as the good sergeant would later observe, plenty of light.

Irene went along with it. Her only stipulation was a high perimeter wall. She wanted her own enclosure, less for security than privacy. An intercom gate system and invisibility.

In one sense they didn't leave Portobello. They fled.

Country living was new to her. Black and white moo cows grazing in fields lined by hedgerows. Trees that felt more like shadows. With an unflagging drive to keep the marina afloat, her husband's dual stewardship of construction in Nobber meant he was hardly home at all. He took on the villa as a personal challenge, perhaps hoping that his being so upbeat would rub off on her. But the more effort he invested, the less she felt part of it.

She knew it was childish, even selfish, to remain so uninvolved but how could he expect her to be enthusiastic about anything?

As it started to take shape he'd want its progress to enthuse her. They would drive out from Portobello for him to showcase small details, like the exquisite tongue and groove finish adorning the timber deck. He drew on an impressive array of carpentry skills he'd left behind since going full-time into boating. The villa was his pet project, almost like a peace offering. She could appreciate the workmanship but could not pretend it meant anything. Our family got smaller, she mused, and here's our house, getting bigger.

Completed nine days ahead of schedule Irene hoped Brendan would slow down, maybe even relax. Everything had been so hectic she just felt like sleeping. She didn't object to his gang of builders gathering in the kitchen for a few celebratory beers but did put her foot down at a full-blown housewarming. She was never going to pretend that they had moved out of the city by choice.

And so the villa, still unnamed for no good reason, boasts three *en suite* guest rooms in case friends ever stay over. This is yet to happen. Apart from making a very occasional dinner – she's not such a bad cook if she could shake herself – it has to be the most immaculate kitchen in Ireland. She can safely say the kettle, the coffee-maker and the toaster all work fine but every other appliance is practically untested. When they first moved in Agnes gave them a beautiful Haviland bone China set for eight as a housewarming present. No surprise, it's still in the box.

As a result, any meet-up might take place in Navan or sometimes up in Dublin. Or that's how it used to be. Couples they used to meet socially seem to have fallen off the face of the earth. She knows that one-by-one they could no longer handle her division of eternity into a BC/AC dichotomy. Even good friends melted away. Already at the end of their rope they'd broach it with a preamble like, 'We know it's very sad and all Irene but it must be seven, eight years. You have to move on – can't you let it go?'

She could see these nervous appeals coming from distance, giving her time to regard the tablecloth or fix a stare upon a light fitting overhead. She'd let them finish out, after which they would anxiously await her response:

'Actually, it's four years, seven months.'

The truth is Irene grew as weary of talking as they grew of listening. These people – closest friends included – did not understand. How could they? She would drift out of dinner conversations and somebody would invariably try to haul her back in. A mercy intervention to keep her *present*. But if the chatter was property prices or investments or holiday breaks or Gaelic bloody football she was already gone. She'd sip more vino, refill her glass quicker than everybody else, try to laugh at appropriate moments and wait for her conjuror husband to make the bill disappear.

She admits that occasionally she tipped over on these soirées. Last stop was usually TJ's for a nightcap she could do without. The Gogartys usually ended up arguing – probably my fault, she admits – which led to her being unofficially delisted from hospitality events in the boat trade. It's easier that way.

Such a serious restructuring of the Gogarty social calendar did not keep her awake at night. At one stage, Brendan remarked a little pointedly about invitations drying up left, right and centre; by now she considers it a blessing he is rarely asked anywhere *plus one*.

Agnes and Myles have visited Nobber a few times but never actually stayed at the villa. Agnes prefers to book into a posh guest house outside Kells. Then it's a meal out or a rendezvous on neutral territory so that when a truce is finally declared they can safely disperse into the night. It might all feel a bit lame but their half-heartedness is reciprocal.

Irene has to admit that despite her mother's repeated hard sell of 'a beautiful spare room with your own bathroom' the Gogartys have yet to cross the channel to Salisbury. Predictably, Brendan draws on work as an excuse and Irene can't summon the energy to go it alone.

Her mother remarried after seven years of widowhood. She says Myles, who she refers to as *my Englishman*, is good to her. She says she's happy, happier than she's ever been.

'Happier than you were with Dad?' asked Irene, sometimes unable to resist an unnecessary jab.

Far from easing off Brendan maintained his pursuit to become the busiest man in Ireland. And so Irene became queen of this unnamed castle. The kitchen looks out on the back garden, which is a big open lawn with bushes and shrubs around the edges.

The fountain was a finishing touch. Brendan's idea. Irene thought it sounded pure kitsch until he showed her the water feature he had in mind. Marble stone with four angels, one in each corner, water bubbling out of their little trumpets. Alongside a wooden bench with a brass plate dedicated simply to Cathal. By night, it could be illuminated by a light switch in the kitchen but Irene doesn't trouble herself with that. Water is just something to listen to – besides, who wants to see angels poke out of the dark?

Daytime is better. Quietly babbling, flowing, sort of peaceful when you sit by it any time of day. She finds it pleasantly comforting, even graceful. A calming sound without beginning or end.

– 8 –

He catches the squad car in the rear-view mirror. Three grown men stuffed into it like a scene from *The Benny Hill Show*. The car prowls slowly up the street and lines up alongside his Range Rover, Sergeant Flanagan filling the front passenger seat. Arbour Hill is wrong side of the river – he's southside and this is northside. Shouldn't he be over in Rathmines? Through rain droplets Brendan can lip read a clear instruction: 'Go home.'

Brendan feels caught red-handed even though he hasn't done anything yet. He's totally flummoxed by the sergeant showing up. He goes to roll down the window but the electric controls won't work when the engine is off. Stretching across to turn the key he glimpses in the side mirror two men coming out the blue gate. A short haired man on the right and a stockier figure on the left, wearing glasses and a denim jacket, red football bag slung over his shoulder like he's going training. McGeedy. That's him! A hundred and ten percent!

Then all his planning goes haywire. The Stanley is in the pouch of his hoodie but he's in such a hurry it fumbles beneath the driver's seat. Reaching frantically along the floor he slices his finger. When he swings open the passenger door it bangs against the squad car and there isn't enough room to squeeze out. Flanagan warns him again to leave it be – leave *what* be?

The target is right there. Within Stanley distance. He has to move quickly now but the squad car has him wedged in. Clambering across front seats he skips out the driver's door only to find the law blocking his way.

McGeedy must hear the commotion because he looks around. He clocks Brendan right enough because for a split second fear contorts his face. It's nearly worth it for that alone. Except a split second is no way near enough for him, not by a million miles. Brendan is here to do damage, real damage.

As soon as he goes for it one of the young gardaí grabs hold of both arms. Brendan has a notion that these boys in blue might take the place of the red-haired nurse in his dream. If he's going to get to McGeedy the whole lot of them might have to kiss the Stanley. Okay, they may be doing their duty but, can't they see, so is he!

He wrestles free and McGeedy breaks into a run. Brendan stumbles from the kerb and takes off after him but one of the recruits hand-trips him like a rugby schoolboy and the other lands in on top. The big goon just sits there, like Brendan is a bench in the park.

'I'll get you!' wheezes Brendan, sucking for air. 'I'll fucking get you.'

McGeedy doesn't stop to look back. He hails a passing taxi. It's a yellow one, like the driver thinks he's in New York. McGeedy jumps in the back and is driven off. Flattened against the tarmac Brendan is practically shaking with rage.

'Get off me, you fat prick!' he sobs.

He sees McGeedy steal one last look from the back seat before the taxi turns the corner. Flanagan walks over and tells the young bullocks to let their prisoner go. They ask if they are to make an arrest, clearly keen to do so. 'Public disorder sergeant,' suggests one, earnestly. Flanagan shakes his head.

He extends a hand to pull Brendan to his feet but Brendan doesn't want the big mucker's help so he stays put.

'Garda fucking síochána,' he says, studying his bloodied finger. 'Why is it ye always protect the wrong people?'

He can't help it but there are tears streaming down his cheeks. Cheated and defeated, he's some specimen so he is. Didn't he make a promise to his young son – on oath – that he would even things up? Yes he did. And did he keep that promise? No sir. McGeedy walks away scot-free *again*; aided and abetted by our so-called justice system. *Again*.

A joke? Don't get him started.

He has let Cathal down, simple as that. Not for the first time. How can he even say sorry? If there was a manhole nearby he'd crawl into it and never come out. The boys in blue are supposed to be on duty but they stand awkwardly in fresh light drizzle, their hands pocketed in a mockery of regulations. Brendan watches the pair of them shamble back to the squad car. He swears if they're not scarlet with embarrassment they should be.

He can feel skin burning where his chin grazed the asphalt. His hand stings. The knee of his pants is sticky from the tarmac, like chewing gum. There's a rip in his hoodie.

'Go on home Brendan,' says the sergeant. 'Look after Irene.'

Flanagan retracts the blade. It must've fallen out during the scuffle. Regarding it like he has removed bullets from a loaded pistol the sergeant hands the Stanley reverse-ways to the man on the kerb and says no more. Brendan pockets it, sucking blood off his finger. He runs a thumb through the hole in his hoodie and waits for the squad car to leave.

A young mother – about twenty, if even – passes, pushing an empty pram through damp air. It's not actually empty, it's just there's no child in it. She's wearing an orange Adidas tracksuit and imitation Reeboks. Two plastic Tesco bags hang from the handlebars and a five-kilo bag of spuds sits in place of a baby. She takes small steps but is a fast walker all the same, leaning forward, hair glistening, her mouth tight in semi-grimace and eyes fixed on the path ahead.

It's all over bar the shouting. Brendan wipes his face against his sleeve and does one big sniff to stop all the smaller sniffles. His nose is runny, his eyes teary. Rising from the kerb he hobbles to the Range Rover. Blood now streams freely from his cut finger. He finds tissues in the car and wraps it loosely, soaking up the flow.

Arbour Hill is quiet again and there's not a sinner about. The phone vibrates in the glove box. Irene, again. Five missed calls. He leaves it be, wondering where those tears came from. He's not one who cries easily. He reaches into the pouch, the Stanley cold in his hand, the blade gliding in and out, out and in.

– 9 –

Irene guessed she was grinding in her sleep again because on the morning of The Big Day she woke up with a toothache. She lay on her back, facing upwards.

'Four years too soon,' she told the ceiling.

She went to the kitchen and took two paracetamol. Looking out at the garden she switched on the fountain and began to think, as she often does, of their time in Lennox Place.

She pictures the stainless steel sink where she used to bathe the child, airy suds bubbling up and popping against the kitchen's back window. The carpet where he first crawled; the buttercup wallpaper he helped pick; his bedroom with a brightly coloured globe lantern; pencil rulings on the scullery wall, each inscribed with a date to record his inexorable ascent over twelve years.

Often, when Brendan got home from work, he'd take his son up to the canal to feed the swans. Cathal was full of chat – even BC, Brendan used to say he enjoyed those evening excursions more than any holiday. Looking back, great times.

Irene loved the redbricked terrace from Day One and they made it their own. Even gave it a name: *Avalon*. It may be a small thing but the villa does not inspire the same affection and is yet to be christened. This mansion all to ourselves, she reflects. After three and a half years it still doesn't feel like home.

The garden calls her.

Just as well she didn't bin those Silk Cuts although once she got her hands on a lighter she should've known she'd go overboard. Stretched out lengthwise on Cathal's seat she listens to the birds and smokes five in a row. Purposeless really but mildly pleasant to sit by the fountain and feel somehow occupied.

There are days she wonders if her husband might be having an affair. She hypothesizes whether the man she once loved – reconstituted as a plumper, grey-topped version with hairier ears – could attract another woman. It's not that she'd claim they have an 'open relationship' where each of them is a free agent with a night pass to excitement. Nor would she want to learn about him having his cake and eating it, as per gory details furnished long-lens by some diligent private dick.

In truth, Irene could not describe Brendan as fling material even though she wouldn't be the first to get that wrong. Heavily thumbed editions of *Hello!* at the hairdresser's in Kells were proof positive that even gormless paunchy eejits could seduce the youthfully more photogenic.

One thing sure, ciggies kill your appetite. She couldn't face dinner tonight but picked up something pre-packed from Supervalu for Brendan. She hardly knows how to use their very fancy Neff microwave but after twiddling a few buttons the rotating carousel started to unfreeze a Chicken Kiev with mixed veg and three croquet potatoes. She's not convinced microwaved food tastes as cooked as in a normal oven, but Brendan doesn't complain. That's probably one of few things between them that hasn't changed.

Towards the end of a regrettably unremarkable day she sets the kitchen table for one. It looks funny, sort of sad. The chicken was done – well, *hot* – so she just left it in the microwave and put cling film over it. Nothing reminds you of hospital food as quickly as a dinner plate under cellophane.

It's well past seven and still no sign of him. Brendan stopped giving notice of his ETA ever since he became a Captain of Industry. 'No point saying,' was his usual refrain. 'Sure, you never know what's going to crop up.' Over time she lost interest in the twin mysteries of commerce and commuting. At this stage she's not even consistently angry. Over time, it just means they do their own thing and leave plans, expectations and the clock out of it.

If her husband was going to do the dirt she couldn't decide whether she'd rather he come up with one decent adversary – *an affair* – instead of trying to replace his nearest and dearest with a string of sluts. As far as she could make out that's what it could boil down to; a serious competitor or Brendan grabbing it wherever he can.

She thinks of Fiona, who landed in the marina from college two years ago. 'Great to have an extra pair of hands around the place,' explained Brendan, when pressed.

'Great pair alright,' replied Irene, tartly.

'Sure aren't we getting her for nothing – and the customers seem to love her.'

In between being mentored by Brendan and ogled by Gary, Fiona ended up doing bits and bobs around the place. A work placement module as part of some diploma in tourism. Top marks for a toothy smile. Strawberry blonde, firm boobs, hockey-thighs and fourteen years younger. A possibility, alright. Liked the work hard/play hard routine with Brendan and Gary, although she lost a bit of ground at an end-of-season party that ended with projectile vomiting and tears. Proving yourself on the job should never involve tequila.

Irene swears, rather unconvincingly, that she wouldn't care if her husband unearthed something meaningful elsewhere. Or that he may still be capable of bringing happiness to someone else. But these unhelpful imaginings quickly coalesce into bleak conclusions that leave her even further adrift from everything around her.

She tries his mobile again and it goes straight to message minder. She had called several times earlier today and he never bothered ringing back. She's beyond caring about his bad manners but this was no ordinary day. This was the day McGeedy was getting out.

Brendan's head was in the sand, as usual. Give him a work project that involves planning and bureaucracy and he'll cut through obstacles like they're not there. A master at getting the job done. A finisher. But her husband was not a man to go into battle with. If you're talking something a bit rougher on the edges, maybe a bit of pushing and shoving, a bit of steel, possibly a physical altercation, well you'd be better off drafting in someone else.

He even left the house earlier than usual this morning. Which put him conveniently missing in action *before* she could bring to his attention the significance of the day. She knew road works outside the marina had him stressed out lately. Maybe fussing over that made him forgetful. It's a thought she soon dismisses, however, realising he knew exactly what he was doing. Making sure he got away before she could remind him of his cowardice.

The mobile phone is custom-made for such a man. Plenty of room to hide. She tries again. It rings a few times. No answer. Fidgety under the cherryless blossom she texts *Hello???* Lights another cig, knowing her husband isn't going to get back to her. Even if he did, he'd deliberately leave it too late. McGeedy already scot-free, probably out on the razz somewhere, celebrating.

Time trickles by and her mood blackens against a cloudless sky. Water plays from the four angels. Bees hover around the honeysuckle. Will it always be like this? She chides herself for asking such a daft question. Of course it will! How can anything ever change if Cathal isn't coming back?

She recalls one afternoon a few months ago. Lying on the settee, feet tucked under her. Refilling her wine glass she happened upon a TV documentary about Africa. It followed a pride of lions in the wild, all cuddly and quite lovable until they went hunting. Fuelled by hunger, they identified grazing antelope as potential prey.

She found herself repulsed and enthralled by the pride working in tandem, moving in for the kill until one antelope was savagely felled, helplessly writhing through its last moments under a dusty cloud of claws and teeth. Two others escaped with bite injuries. Stunned by the speed of the ambush they stumbled from the open plain into camouflage where they could lick their wounds.

Irene unfolded her legs and leaned forwards, watching the dazed pair limp through high grass.

'Fuck sake,' she said. 'That's us.'

It was this latest twist that really got to her. Whatever tedious rehearsal and re-rehearsal of *motive*, whatever the sequence of argument and rebuttal, she recalls that a guilty verdict was finally arrived at. Years later all that *talk* gets casually tossed aside. The Gogartys, their emotions still raw, are last to know. Favourable treatment for one; a lurid farce for others.

Systems made by man were not to be trusted, she decides. Irene saw justice as no more than a showy and lucrative charade, process and procedure dressed up as phony convention. The legal system a pretence of wisdom melodramatically represented by a gavel, a cape and a chalky wig. The Gogartys had suffered an injustice that could not be remedied. The best they could hope for was restoring some sense of balance but that would only be achieved through supernatural force or – a better bet – personal retribution.

So this should be a day for action. She wanted Brendan to come with her down to Arbour Hill and wait at the prison gate for McGeedy. Let him know the Gogartys don't forget and that he would never get away with what he did to their boy. Shame him to the core. And if McGeedy as much as smirked she'd tear his eyes out.

She indulges these thoughts until they chug along under their own steam, nagging her, needling her. Soon as that animal was let loose he was probably helping oul biddies cross the road. Then, wait till you see. The minute the cameras are gone he'll shove them under a double-decker for sport.

Prodded by the harder edges of grief she staggers to the edge and back, loathing the self-pity that makes this drama all her own. She and Brendan felt strongly that McGeedy should have got way more than nine years. Maybe a small validation to hold onto, inscribing into public record his role in their destruction.

She now realises, had he got fifteen it still would have felt deficient. Never enough. A longer sentence could not do much to fill the hole, never mind ease their pain.

Her chain smoking continues in a cloudy stupor of anger and protest. Not because nothing could make this right but because it feels like everything is against them. The whole system falling over itself, fretting that the person who did all the damage should be afforded another chance. Everything geared towards him getting to live again, even though he took Cathal's life and ruined theirs.

She wants Brendan to show up. To present himself. To be counted. But the man who should be her staunchest ally has gone AWOL. He's probably wading through riverside mud, ignoring the world around him. When you're a Captain of Industry, renting out a boat is obviously more important than exacting justice for your murdered son.

She knows there's a half bottle of vodka in the cabinet and a few baby tonic mixers in the press. It's all there. But today she's not bothered. Instead, she waits for her husband to come out of hiding, feeling bitterness and despair spread through her like cancer.

A pair of injured fucking antelopes.

She hears him pull in at ten to eight. She goes inside to reheat the microwave for 2:45 minutes and slowly pours a glass of milk for the lone diner. The front door closes quietly. Brendan skulks through the hall like a thief.

'Sorry, got delayed,' he says, not sounding sorry at all.

'Is your phone broken? I rang you a thousand times.'

'It's been hectic, Irene.'

'There's a plate there for you.'

'Thanks.'

'You know McGeedy got out today. Or did you forget?'

He gives her what she calls that lost look.

'No, I didn't forget.'

'I rang you because I wanted you to do something. Instead, he just gets out and walks free. Like we don't care.'

'I need a shower.'

Imagine, that's all he has to say for himself. A shower. Very brave altogether. She's not bothered to ask about the cotton bandage wrapped around his finger. Let him give the carousel another whirl when he comes down but, really, she feels like tossing the plate out the window. He takes a mouthful of milk, wiping away the creamy moustache above his lip. He turns for the stairs with a tired end-of-long-day fake sigh. The microwave dings.

'Brendan?'

'*What!*'

'Your sleeve is torn.'

– 10 –

Gary is out in the yard explaining to Antonio and his Neapolitan brood how the eight-berth works. Their English is as limited as his patience.

'Not understand,' says Antonio for the umpteenth time. His wife and five children are getting restless.

'Lookit, I'm only the mechanic here,' shrugs Gary at the end of his tether. He asks them to hold on a minute and makes for the office where he finds Brendan lost in some sort of reverie.

'Boss, shake a leg.'

'Hah?'

'This isn't my thing – you better look after it.'

Brendan wishes Fiona was here. It's what she was good at. He doesn't feel like playing host but Gary has already disappeared into the workshop and pulled down the shutter. He gathers himself, tries to brighten up and greet the customers with an expansive, open-armed Italianite gesture – *Prima volta in Ireland?*

He tells them that when you're out on the water it's all about the red buoys and the green buoys.

'The red boy and the green boy?' repeats Antonio's daughter, puzzled.

But Brendan finds it hard to concentrate. All he can see is McGeedy jumping that taxi and Templemore's finest holding him back. Flattened against the ground, crying like a baby; the sergeant withholding the Stanley like you'd deny a wailing child a soother. Even thinking about it a day later Brendan nearly feels sorry for himself.

When Brendan says it would give you the sick he's not exaggerating. Yesterday he had to pull in at the side of the road outside Abbeyleix, convinced he was about to throw up. He didn't, fortunately, but still doesn't feel great and isn't convinced his tummy has settled yet. Too much acid.

Having ignored Irene's calls through the day he knew she would be on the warpath when he got home. Of course, he could have left her an early morning voice message to cover all eventualities. Tell her not to worry; that he loved her and, whatever might happen next, he was doing it for her and for Cathal. She would see he was the sort of husband and father she wanted him to be.

But he chose not to. How could he reassure her when he didn't know how it was going to pan out? He'd have to keep it vague and that sort of talk would only confuse matters. As for bringing love into it? *Steady on, Horse . . .*

Sure enough, she had a right go at him for overlooking McGeedy's release. Brendan leaned against the kitchen sink like a punch bag. He just couldn't face recounting his thwarted plan without putting the entire fuck-up under one dirty big spotlight.

He waited until Irene returned to the TV room before he came back downstairs. Sat at the table, picking at a plate of garlic chicken she'd microwaved. With all his comings-and-goings he should be used to eating on his own but he still finds it a bit strange to hear cutlery rattling off a plate to the ruminant crunch of your own chewing. He wonders if she deliberately chose chicken. A photo on the fridge caught his eye – Cathal's holy communion. With his neat grey suit and a giant white rosette, proud parents standing behind. The three all smiles. He stared at it and stopped chewing. He couldn't taste a thing.

'He say "boy"?' enquires Antonio's wife.

'Hah?'

'You say "boy".'

'Not "boy", Senora. *Buoy.*'

'Is same, no?' says Antonio.

So it's true – great minds *do* think alike! She wanted them to go to Arbour Hill together to confront McGeedy. Of course, had the Stanley done its job the Gogartys would have found themselves in a very different position. Down the station Irene would be hysterical about him going off on a solo run and keeping her in the dark.

He understood perfectly why she was upset but there was nothing he could say to make it better. He couldn't tell her that he did exactly what she wanted, that his instincts and her wishes were in fact the same thing. Before, of course, it all went pear-shaped.

Had everything worked out he would probably end up behind bars for murder, their semi-nuclear family now reduced to one. Irene in solitary, at home. The prospect of jail did not actually bother him. Maybe it would have been a break from everything. A sabbatical.

The big drawback would be a court case with notebook-wielding reporters and a scrum of TV crews jostling for position. Opinion writers from the Sunday papers would start pontificating from self-raised moral peaks. One or two might descend on the marina workshop – *where the boatman snapped* – to catch Gary unawares for some background colour.

Did the boss have a bit of a temper?

Did he ever talk about his son?

They might even have tracked down Fiona in the Algarve. She'd love that – and she'd be good for photos.

Is it true he used to buy you tequila?

Given the circumstances, you could probably expect the court to show leniency to a stricken father gone temporarily berserk. After which Brendan would have been an exemplary prisoner, maybe even helping out fellow inmates in the woodwork room. Surely some prison governor would then slice and dice his jail sentence the way they do for all them that's on good behaviour. Isn't that how the system works?

Taking the law into his own hands would have been a price worth paying except that's not where things are. It's been a washout. Gary won't need to lock himself into the workshop. Fiona can go back to Portugal if she likes. Their employer is not a firebrand and definitely not a hero. Every great plan under the sun fallen asunder and absolutely nothing to show for it. He feels like an amateur burglar, nabbed up a shaky ladder *before* breaking in.

The Neapolitans are confused. They discuss in rapid detail the reckless ambition of adventure in a country where there is no sun. Where the boat's open deck will get no usage because of constant rain. The energy of these exchanges and the breadth of disharmony suggests they now believe their excursion to be a mistake. The father, Antonio, looks a little crestfallen.

Brendan can't quite imagine McGeedy sitting in these nights, babysitting. Or giving his so-called partner – if she lets him in the door – a night off. After all he's put her through? Not at all! He'll be swanning around the city somewhere, gone to swill suddy pints and toast his liberty. Maybe we'll have to wait for the *Sunday World* to catch up with him smoking his brains out in some Amsterdam brothel with all the other hard men. Or wherever he is enjoying freedom, his rights and entitlements.

'Okay, okay!' he announces, dismissing McGeedy from his thoughts for five minutes. 'I will show you. Watch me. Not talk. Just look.'

He hands out life jackets and starts the engine. From the marina the cruiser sweeps through reeds into the Shannon's deceptively strong currents. The Italians are becalmed. This is what they came for. They see cows graze in the fields of the river plain. Some plod to the grassy bank to drink, rude globules of water dripping beneath their hairy chins. The children point and whoop in delight. Antonio learns basic navigation and, taking the wheel with grim concentration, smiles nervously at his wife. His daughter takes a photograph. The younger children shout in alarm when they feel he is getting too close to the river bank.

'Papa!'

'Okay, okay! The red boy and the green boy, sí?'

'That's it.'

Brendan retakes the wheel to turn back for the jetty. The holiday is saved. Sometimes he thinks it'd be a lot simpler if he didn't run his own company. Working for someone else he could stick to fixed hours without having to eat, breathe and sleep the job.

Standing under the shower last night Brendan didn't feel much better than he had in Abbeyleix. He turned the spray to cold but had no sensation of water temperature changing against his skin. Towelled into fresh clothes. Even had to spin a yarn about catching his hoodie on a nail in the yard but luckily Irene was too out of sorts to give a damn. He noticed she had taken up smoking again for some reason but that was her own business.

Chicken.

The mansion in Nobber is big enough but the TV volume was up so high that laughter trailed from the hall. He couldn't tell if it was a sound effect or real people but every joke got a rise and every five minutes a bigger gag brought the house down. The rhythm of organised mirth. Irene sat in front of the telly but found none of it remotely funny. Brendan had seen her wear this expression before. A formless, unhappy detachment.

Relieved not to lose Antonio's booking Brendan is glad to call it a day but not quite ready for home. He pulls off the M7 at Mountrath and finds a bookie, one of the only places open other than three pubs and a chipper. He puts a few quid down, doesn't win a penny and does not care. The nags – or was it dogs? – pass an hour or two.

The young fella wasn't even three when Gogarty's Marina Ltd came into being. Brendan grew bored of steady work as a chippie. Saw his future elsewhere – on the river – and took the plunge. Borrowed when interest rates were double-digit, using their first house in Portobello as security. The first years were very tight but things gradually evened out. Sometimes, Irene quips that her main contribution was to allow him to remortgage their family home in the hope that 'boat people' could mean visitors to Ireland from places other than Vietnam.

His mind vacant as he walks up Church Street Brendan zaps the SUV with the remote, hops in and starts her up. Stopping at the bookies was no more than postponing things. He drives the last miles heavy with dread. Irene is so burdened, so consumed with pain that sometimes he wonders if she enjoys it. He once put it to her about getting help. Offered to pay and all.

'Are you saying I'm crackers – is that what you're saying?' she shouted. 'Help is the last thing I need.'

'I'm just saying you could talk to someone.'

'That's priceless coming from you,' she steamed. 'You who talks to the world and its mother and says nothing.'

The deejay announces to the world yet another boyband so Brendan switches to Kildare FM. He doesn't usually listen to chat radio but his head is already fried by sunlamped teenagers devoted to the deep and meaningful. The programme is half way through when the interview goes all quiet in a way that makes him curious.

'Just so angry, Caroline. With everything,' says a woman.

'That's it,' agrees a man, who Brendan presumes to be the woman's other half. 'Because, really like, what did our little girl do to deserve this?'

The presenter asks about the impact on their relationship. The couple laugh in a sad way and the man takes it up.

'Things weren't great, to be honest. Were they, Maureen?'

'Absolutely awful.'

'I could've throttled her and she could've throttled me. Well maybe not throttled . . .'

'I wouldn't have ruled that out Dermot.'

They both laugh drily.

'We were fierce hard on each other.'

'Tell me about it,' shrugs Brendan, joining in.

'But it was not your fault what happened,' interrupts the presenter. 'Your daughter got cancer. How was that your fault?'

'Well we sort of blamed each other for it,' says Dermot. 'Mad, isn't it? Once we lost Chloe, nothing made sense any more.'

Take the cancer out of it and you'd swear they were roaming the Gogarty mansion in Nobber. The presenter gets them to explain that a cousin of Maureen's went on a pilgrimage and brought back a specially blessed relic for their departed child.

Then friends raised some money and bought them tickets to go on the next trip.

'We're not religious by the way,' says Maureen.

'Far from it!'

'But our friends had gone to all this trouble and I suppose we felt we couldn't say no.'

'So you went?'

'Yeah,' says Dermot. 'To a place where they say Our Lady appeared. It's a small town in Bosnia. A place called Medjugorje.'

'We weren't really expecting anything,' Maureen cuts in. 'Were we? And it felt a bit strange. I don't know what it was but after a few days I just felt a sort of peace come over me. For the first time since losing Chloe. I don't expect anyone to believe me or understand and I don't really care. I just felt, I don't know . . .'

'What do you mean "peace"?' asks the host.

'It was just a feeling that our baby was okay. Chloe wasn't lost or in pain. She's in heaven. And Dermot and I were okay too. It's really hard to explain.'

'Yeah, it might've worked for you,' grumbles Brendan. Ordinarily he would avoid any talk of religious faith – 'mumbo-jumbo' he called it. Happening upon this discussion by chance did surprise him, though, as one not given to superstition he would hardly read too much into it. Except there was an honesty about this couple that he found quite compelling. He stayed with them. Attempting to broach pain in private wasn't exactly his thing and the very notion of doing so in public horrified him. That they should bare their souls in this way for no personal gain was impressive, even if it made no sense.

'Sure, why would you?' he asks aloud, wondering how the husband got on. The presenter pipes up like she's reading Brendan's mind.

'And how about you, Dermot?'

'It took a few days because, at first, to tell you the truth, I was wondering what in the name of Jaysus are we doing here,' sighs Dermot. 'But, like Maureen says, something *did* happen.'

– 11 –

About a month later Brendan booked it. Then he told Irene.

'You have to give it a chance,' he began, which put her on guard.

McGeedy was already out five weeks so she was in no mood for a romantic getaway. You couldn't even drag her – well, maybe you could – to the Big Apple for a shopping weekend.

'Where?'

'Like a time out – they call it a pilgrimage.'

'Have you lost the fucking plot Brendan Gogarty?'

At first, she really did think he was joking. She trailed off to the kitchen to make a pot of coffee but it was just an excuse to leave the room. Brendan followed her.

'It's not what you think. People like us go there – I heard them talking about it on the radio.'

'What people are like us?'

'People who have lost kids.'

'Aaaahhh, so that's what we are? People who have lost kids . . .'

'It's a place called Medjugorje. In Yugoslavia. Except now they call it Bosnia or Herzegovina or . . .'

'Isn't there a war going on there?'

'Maybe in other parts. It's safe where we're going. I wouldn't take you to a war zone.'

'We don't need to travel anywhere for that.'

He tells her it was some couple from Newbridge talking on the radio. Their daughter died tragically from cancer and all Brendan keeps saying is how un-religious this couple were. 'Just normal people,' he insists.

'Stop lumping us in with them – and will you stop pretending we're fucking normal!'

'Irene, they said it themselves. They were going to throttle each other . . .'

'Well that rings a bell.'

'So they tried Medjugorje as a last resort.'

'What about your precious boatyard?'

'Gary can look after the marina over the while.'

'How long?'

'Twelve days.'

'Twelve days! On a pilgrimage?'

'They say it's more a retreat.'

'So what are we retreating from?'

'You have to give it a chance. We have absolutely nothing to lose.'

Well, that was true. He asked her to think about it. He had to get back to the marina for a delivery but promised that tonight he'd be home before seven. She'd heard that before but his departure was less of a whirlwind than usual. He gathered his keys and mobile phone, stopped to hug her, the brief, tight clutch of a drowning man. A small touch, a flicker of warmth almost alien to her.

She could see he was making an effort. Maybe she would have been less defensive if it hadn't just come right out of the blue. Brendan never took holidays, definitely not AC. On the occasional blue moon she might suggest a weekend break, he always found a way to get out of it. It was hardly worth the effort but, she reasoned, him offering to take time off meant this was serious.

What's more, he had already gone ahead and booked it. She had to admit that her husband had taken the bull by the horns. He was going to deny himself the pleasure of work or tearing off to some GAA kickabout to be exclusively in her company for twelve days. That, by his standards, was a monumental sacrifice.

Hiking for God was certainly not Irene's idea of a holiday. Yet it did strike her how much hope her husband placed on them getting hit by the same bolt of lightning that left two halfwits from Newbridge in a daze. Of course she could say no and let him wander off by himself. But that would be churlish. He had made a peace offering of sorts and she could hardly reject it, especially when she hadn't come up with any alternatives. They were, whether Irene liked it or not, half way there already.

A school friend came to mind. Della got hitched soon after her twenty-first only for her marriage to run aground inside eighteen months. Over cocktails BC, Della once mentioned something about visiting Lourdes. Irene laughed incredulously, asking her friend if the prospect of separation had turned her all holy or something. Della glared at her, demanding an instant apology.

Irene recalled that they did meet up a month after Della got back. Her friend was very solemn about the experience and how peaceful she found the place. Like she was doing her best trying not to flog it. Thing is, she did look a bit better – refreshed even. Sure why wouldn't she? A break in the sun from her soon-to-be ex.

Ordering two more slippery nipples, Irene was ultra careful with her Ps and Qs to declare it 'plain as day' that going away had done her friend 'a power of good'. It also restricted Irene from asking what she really wanted to know – if Della had got down and dirty with another penitent while they were in ecstasy, or whatever it is they do when pilgrims find the Lord.

Besides, with McGeedy now at large she found the idea of leaving Ireland very appealing. Not because there was any real chance of bumping into him but the entire country, clearly run by idiots, felt grubby and tawdry all of a sudden. Nobody could help any more, nobody wanted to.

Irene thought of Della and her seriously steadied ship. Medjugorje couldn't hurt – could it? She went to the living room and pulled their unused world atlas from the shelf. She looked up Bosnia and found a speck. Near enough to Italy and Greece to mean sun, real summer sun. After a coffee and two cigs she rang Brendan. One miracle followed another because he answered straight away. She told him she'd thought about it.

'Well?'

'When do you want to go?'

Part Two

Medjugorje

– 12 –

Getting the green light from Irene was a start. Brendan can't figure out whether it's the Adriatic or the Mediterranean but seeing as they have real summers in southern Europe it'll be a lot warmer than home. Irene isn't quite sure how to pronounce Medjugorje and she doesn't know what to pack. She's searching the wardrobe, pulling drawers open, sliding back hangars – I mean, can you bring a thong when you go on a pilgrimage? If showing a bit of cleavage is a sin of some description most of her summer tops fail the sanctity test. Pressing questions – does everyone fast or can you go out for a proper dinner? Is there a town nearby with a half-decent bar or should they stock up on duty-free? Will they have to sing songs and clap hands on the plane?

She had so many questions swirling around her head she was nearly going to ring Della for the lowdown. She resisted phoning in the end. They hadn't been in contact for years, their friendship whittled short of meaning. A call would arrive out of nowhere and she didn't want Della thinking that, thanks to some drip-drip faith-healing effect, Irene was finally going in search of Jesus. In actual fact the whole idea was a bit embarrassing. She did not want anybody, including Agnes, to know where they were going. Or why. If she had her fill of people's sympathy five years AC she could just as easily do without spiritual guidance.

So they're on their way. Brendan's booking with 'Mother of Perpetual Succour Tours' brings to mind a battery of homicidal nuns at school. In the run-up to departure Irene was liable to change her mind – twice she rang him at the marina to call it off. The only thing for it now was to stop thinking. She doesn't know if they are stupid or mad – maybe just desperate – but she feels Brendan is right in one way (and probably one way only); if something like this could help them, even a bit, isn't it worth the trip? She feels herself fitting into the role of victim-turned-advocate. *If me speaking out here tonight helps just one person etc, etc . . .*

Unsure as to what exactly is in store their only pre-condition was something they could agree on. They drew the line at re-baptism. They will not be taken to a river and dipped like sheep. Praise be. They even had a laugh the other night – now there's one for the diary! – when they realised that if their plane crashes *en route* their parting gift to the world will be for Brendan and Irene Gogarty to be publicly outed as pilgrims. Which is a nice way to describe those who boast about being lost.

On the way to the airport Irene sits in the back of the taxi. Brendan takes the front. They don't say much. It was an early start which meant putting up with the forced jollity of a consonant-shy DJ talking up De Pointer Sisters on de radio.

Yeah, yawns Irene, *I'm so excited too.*

Brendan is also beginning to have second thoughts. It's a punt. No more than that. Seldom has he pushed something for which the strongest argument is, What have we got to lose? He looks out the window, his eye distracted by the driver's taxi licence on the dashboard. Raymond Anthony Dunne is Travis Bickle close up, all beard and glasses, staring at the camera like he hates the world.

Irene leans forward to say the radio is too loud. Travis turns the volume down so low there's hardly any point having it on at all. Then begins the usual holiday probe.

'So where are yez off to?'

'A funeral,' replies Irene and that puts an end to it.

Everything is quiet enough until they hit roadworks around what will be called the M50 orbital, a big roundabout to protect Dublin from barbarians outside the Pale. Some operation, muses Brendan. Earth-moving machinery levelling ground for miles, the site floodlit with early morning teams in hi-viz jackets buzzing around like wasps.

Brendan reckons Raymond Anthony Dunne was glad to drop them off at the airport and get on with his world-hating day. But things do not get any better. The instructions were to meet under the big electronic departures board. Irene says nothing but was staring ahead so intensely you'd nearly hear a crackle. She hadn't been to the airport for years and can't believe how busy it is. A Monday morning in August and Paddies escaping to the heat like migrating birds. Half of the young ones are already fake-tanned so they won't look like ghosts underneath bronze Continentals.

Good luck to them, thinks Irene. *I wouldn't say no if I was bothered, but I'm not and haven't been since . . . since ages.*

They walk to the meeting point. The Gogartys are a bit apprehensive about what sorts of yokes they are likely to be travelling with. The Newbridge couple might have sounded normal enough on the radio but as Brendan and Irene pass through the sliding doors they can't help notice a gaggle of oddjobs idling about, looking more like what Noah's Ark left behind.

Some wear rosary beads. Cardigans are 'in'. Most of the women could be plain clothes penguins. All of them are ridiculously energetic, De Pointer Sisters' early hour giddiness clearly contagious. One red-faced man in a baseball cap is dressed in a shiny blue terylene suit, his trousers hovering an inch above brown leather sandals and cream socks.

'Don't say this is us,' groans Irene.

Anne-Marie, a larger-than-life redhead from Skibbereen, appears. She's the tour leader. Anne-Marie holds high a placard for Mother of Perpetual Succour Tours, presenting it like a road sign for emergency detour. The pilgrims flock around. Pinned to her beige jacket is a smiley badge with a halo. The tour leader is bursting with enthusiasm and has a high colour to match. She lets it be known she is head bottle washer. She'll mollycoddle her charges to death if blood pressure doesn't do her in first.

'If you have any questions, just ask Anne-Marie,' announces Anne-Marie. She speaks loud and fast and repeats this mantra every so often, like she's talking about someone else. Loves the head count too. Goes from one to twenty-seven at a decibel everyone can hear. She's done three counts so far; each time she gets to the end she rounds it off, 'Hands up anybody who's not here!' Brendan knows they might hear this a few more times before the trip is out but already feels that chuckling along with this tiresome gag is being way, way too polite. He wonders how much care and compassion he can take.

To be fair, Anne-Marie doesn't ask anybody why they are here – maybe that comes later – but she handles every pilgrim individually like a fragile parcel and then switches into sergeant-major mode for group announcements. She's got twenty-seven souls to mentor spiritually on this excursion and you can tell it's their neediness that draws her to them. She loves her job and really wants everybody to like her.

Some of the group have definitely ridden this rodeo before. You can tell. Not that there's anything wrong with that. If someone goes to Medjugorje and gets something out of it, why not go back? Same as Vegas or Bangkok. Don't we all return to the places we like? And even though Anne-Marie likes to make everybody feel she's their special friend it's obvious she knows some special friends more especially than others.

As expected, there are more women than men in the group but Irene is surprised at the age range. The Gogartys aren't even the youngest – there's a couple from Portlaoise definitely under thirty, and two girls – hardly twenty-one – from Strabane. Others are a bit older but you'd wonder what has these young ones joining old fogies when they could be getting some action in Corfu.

'Yoo-hoo, gather in everybody,' announces Anne-Marie.

'Did she just say yoo-hoo?' whispers Brendan.

It feels like everyone is back in school – primary school, that is. Anne-Marie goes through flight details like the pilgrims can't read. 'Try to stick together,' she advises gravely, overlooking the fact that most of them are strangers.

'If anyone gets lost in duty-free, look for Gate 23A. That's 23 with an A. With the mercy of God the flight will board at 10.35. Does anybody have any questions?'

A passing group of teenage boys point and laugh at her placard but Anne-Marie doesn't pay them the slightest bit of attention. Irene feels like letting rip because those brats are laughing at the group, which means they are also laughing at the Gogartys. Except, she decides, if it doesn't bother Anne-Marie, why let it get to her?

She hasn't done anything like this for so long that it reminds her of a school trip to Powerscourt. It's been ages since she and Brendan went anywhere. But here, now, instead of going abroad to do their own thing they are suddenly joined at the hip by a bunch of squares. They will be stuck for twelve days with people she would never encounter in ordinary life. She has a sneaking suspicion that someone will unearth a guitar some evening and inflict a Beatles singalong on the Perpetual 27. As far as Irene is concerned, the sandal man and the rosary beaders can go all Up With People but if Anne-Marie thinks the Gogartys are going to turn happy-clappy she's got another thing coming.

Brendan struggles to let the initiation pass without getting all het up. Anne-Marie will test him, that's for sure. He dithers over prices in duty-free.

'We're leaving the EU, aren't we?'

'Ask our tour guide,' shrugs Irene, who is tempted to get a carton of ciggies. Over the previous ten days Irene found her husband considerate, even kind. His stepping away from the job really took her by surprise. She knows he'll have the mobile phone with him so it's not like he's completely out of contact. He'll just have to detach.

Must be that holiday feeling! It's only a quarter past nine when they get through security and shopping so they take a seat at the departures bar. They are surprised to see a few of the Holy Joes down the other end of the counter. Irene asks for a vodka and tonic, Brendan orders a pint. They don't say a whole lot but the mood is steady, even alright.

A diversion like this in Bosnia is absolutely for the birds but Irene is going to try and enjoy it. She was going to ring Sergeant Flanagan to ask if the Arbour Hill release went ahead like he said it would. Or had there been any last-minute hitch, a much-hoped for change of plan? In the end she didn't bother. Out of our hands, she sighs, pledging herself to try to banish McGeedy from her thoughts while they're on 'holiday'.

She sips the vodka and bites the sharpness out of the lemon.

'You okay?' asks Brendan.

'Yeah, fine. You?'

He swallows a mouthful of Guinness and wipes his lip.

'Grand.'

– 13 –

He'd love to say things are looking up but Brendan is beginning to feel like the pair of them are on the run. He felt it earlier, in the taxi. Travis Bickle full of the joys, yapping away about a family skiing holiday in Austria until Irene went through him for a short-cut. It appears the music was too loud, even from the back seat. She really is not a morning person.

What bothers Brendan is that McGeedy has won again. He has, hasn't he? Robbed them blind of their greatest possession and then stuck a poker in their eyes for pig iron. Brendan is quite sure that if he made enquiries in a particular city centre pub he could get likely lads who'd do a proper job for a few quid. Heavies. But once you get into that end of things how do you get out? Like *The Godfather*, who was besieged daily for favours by neighbours and shopkeepers. Some day, inevitably, the Corleone family would knock on a neighbour's door and demand the favour returned . . .

Instead, the Gogartys are running the other way. Brendan's great idea, he concedes, but what struck him in the taxi was you'd swear he and Irene were the problem. Like, following McGeedy's release, they are supposed to get out of his road.

Which means it's them who have to get out of Dodge.

The flight will last about three hours. Boarding the plane is a slow procession. Irene takes the seat in the middle and lets Brendan have the aisle. Gives him a bit more leg room. With each passing minute they wonder why they're going anywhere at all.

Just before take-off they notice passengers all around them blessing themselves. The woman in the next row takes out a prayer card and kisses it. Brendan leans closer to his wife.

'D'you know if she had a black veil over her face you'd press the emergency button,' he whispers. 'Or at least let the airport dogs have another sniff at the baggage.'

'Is it too late to get off?' Irene replies, half-joking.

This is some crack, he thinks. Don't know where they rounded up these hoofers but sure they're probably saying the same about us. Not that there's anything wrong with pilgrims *per se*, but he can tell there's no threat of wild parties breaking out in former Yugoslavia over the next twelve days.

He notices that most of the them whisper when they talk, especially the old dears who seem to treat the plane like a library. It doesn't help that many of them are half deaf so trying to whisper over the roar of jet engines leads to a lot of repetition and blank nodding. It wouldn't surprise him one bit if someone walked down the aisle and started doling out bingo cards.

Irene conks out after half an hour and nestles on his shoulder. He is relieved. It's not like there'd be much by way of conversation but one of them falling asleep takes the pressure off the other. All nice and calm; if you didn't know any better you'd nearly believe everything was hunky dory.

The oul codger at the window seat leaves his baseball cap on through the entire flight. Probably sleeps in it. Brendan notices him sliding his feet out of worn sandals after take-off. Turns out his name is Packie, like yerman the goalie. What's more, he's from Donegal, same as yerman, the goalie. He mentioned something about twin towns or twin towers but that's about all Irene got out of him before she dozed off.

When the air hostess handed out trays – nothing special now, a wafer thin ham sandwich, orange juice, cup of tea and a digestive biscuit – the Holy Joes receive it like it's the last supper. 'Ah you shouldn't have,' says one, eyes popping out of her head. Brendan was tempted to set her straight, like, 'Would you ever relax. Haven't you paid for it in your ticket!'

They land in a place called Split, the same airport the Newbridge couple mentioned on the radio. Getting off the plane they see a tank parked just off the runway – camouflaged, but definitely the real thing. Strikes Brendan as a strange place to leave a tank. He had sort of forgotten Yugoslavia was on the evening news regular enough at home. Blonde reporters in body-hugging flak jackets saying how complicated the situation was. That the Balkans was living up to its reputation as 'a powder keg,' whatever that means.

In fairness, Brendan wouldn't pay too much attention to who was shooting who but now that they're here it all feels a bit different. If Anne-Marie expects the Gogartys to defend the Catholic faith at gunpoint she should have said so before they left Dublin.

Traipsing through the airport terminal Anne-Marie tells Donegal Packie to stop taking pictures of the tank. Someone asks her about the war and Anne-Marie says that the Croats are Catholic, the Serbs are Orthodox and the Bosnians are Moslem but in all her time coming to Medjugorje the only fighting she personally witnessed was when an Offaly woman and her husband from Cahirciveen had a barney about the five-in-a-row. That gives the pilgrims a laugh and everybody feels a bit better.

They spot a couple of young soldiers lounging around the airport, bored senseless. It's definitely strange walking through armed military like this. Inside the terminal, policemen with guns try to separate a couple of barking dogs. Truth be told it doesn't feel like much of a war zone. If there is a front line and soldiers are being sent to it, Brendan reckons these recruits landed themselves a very cushy number. Acting all macho with a planeload of Holy Joes, for God's sake . . .

The Gogartys fall in step behind a pair of sisters, Julie and Kathleen, from the midlands. The sisters have been over here a couple of times before so they know the ropes. Medjugorje veterans. They're so blasé about it all you'd swear they grew up under curfew in Kilbeggan. Marched right off the plane to collect their bags and straight on through customs without batting an eyelid. Nothing for it but for Brendan and Irene to follow.

'From where you come?' asks the immigration officer staring at Brendan's passport.

'I don't know why he bothered asking,' mopes Brendan after being cast aside. 'He was no more interested – turns out he'd never even heard of Meath.'

Irene didn't get the same grilling at all. A uniformed official just stamped her passport straight away and didn't ask a single question. 'D'you know,' adds Brendan, 'you wouldn't want to be too paranoid in these oul Commie countries.'

Anne-Marie is ahead of the posse, taking up a position at Arrivals with her placard held high. She reminds Brendan of the fella who stands behind a goal at GAA matches with a homemade billboard advertising Jesus. The pilgrims gather round, a few stragglers taking up the rear. Anne-Marie does a head count and is puzzling over twenty-six like a lottery ball is missing when Donegal Packie, the suit and sandals man, comes through with rosary beads tight in one fist and a bag of duty-free wrapped around the other.

'And Packie makes twenty-seven!'

'Aye,' nods Packie, wondering what all the fuss is about.

Someone asks about changing money in the airport but Kathleen whispers a secret from Fatima that they would get a better rate on the main street in Medjugorje.

'Well,' says Packie. 'Saved us a few shillings, rightly.'

They follow Anne-Marie and feel the heat as soon as the doors slide open. It'll be shorts and t-shirts soon as they get to the hotel. Maybe even a swim if there's a pool. There's no sign of the coach so the pilgrims drift over to a shaded part of the terminal. Newcomers have no cash to hand but one of the regulars has some local money. She picks up a few bottles of water and is happy to share.

Anne-Marie starts getting all flustered and tells the Perpetuals a thousand times she's going to complain 'in the strongest possible terms' to the bus company because the whole itinerary is now up the Swanee.

'Ah relax,' remarks Brendan, fanning himself from a cool spot in the shade. 'I'm sure the Blessed Virgin will wait for us.'

The Kilbeggan ladies throw him a dirty look, burning a 666 into his forehead. Irene doesn't see the funny side either. Brendan has to remind himself he's among believers here, which means for the next twelve days there's a lot of things you can't joke about.

Let them have it their way, he shrugs, switching his phone to a Croatian network. As long as they don't make me a target for conversion.

– 14 –

Faruk, a burly lad with a curly crown, swings into view half an hour late. He doesn't see it coming but he's hardly out of the cab when Anne-Marie savages him. Irene marvels how she manages to do so without cursing once. She already grasps that the Perpetuals are not big fans of bad language. 'Suppose there's no need to eff and blind when you're from Cork,' suggests Brendan.

Anne-Marie does another head count but she's too stressed to finish off with her favourite joke. They pile onto the bus and Irene grabs the first free seat beside Rosemary from Cavan, another veteran with more holy medals around her neck than your average Russian general. Brendan is left stranded in the aisle.

'It doesn't matter where we sit,' says Irene crossly.

Dismissed like a slow-witted servant he moves down the bus and slides in beside Packie. The Donegal man reminds Brendan of a little fella who used to run the snooker hall in Kells. Has his own quiet-spoken way, the Boston Red Sox cap planted on his head like it's surgically attached. Without being asked he tells Brendan he's from Stranorlar.

'Stranorlar and Ballybofey is twin towns,' he explains, which is news to Brendan, although it's not what you'd call earth-shattering information. Turns out Packie has not yet been out this way either.

'Same as that,' says Brendan.

No sooner have they left the airport than Anne-Marie wants to thank God for getting them here safely. Brendan was going to throw in a shout for the pilot but after his joke flatlined at the airport he wisely decides to keep to himself. Anne-Marie taps one of the Kilbeggan ladies to do the honours and lead the chanting. Packie knows the Rosary right enough, mumbling away to his heart's content. Brendan doesn't know the words but finds himself tuning into a soft, whispery Donegal accent praying. Easy on the ear, in fairness.

From what Irene can see, the countryside is beautiful. It'll soon get a bit dusky but John Hinde could have rolled down the window and snapped an entire collection in five minutes flat. The road trip takes three hours, up along the Adriatic coast and then inland over mountains. Grass on the hills burnt brown. It's sticky enough for an August evening. Way too hot for cows or sheep, which might explain why there are none.

It's full steam ahead on the Rosary and the Perpetuals are giving it socks. Irene finds herself lassooed by a set of rosary beads. Not much she can do to defend herself so she lets one of the Kilbeggan sisters straighten the noose around her neck. She feels like a young brownie getting her first girl guides' badge. Turning around, she catches Brendan's eye. He can only smile and close his eyes under Packie's sibilant hush.

Not that there is much time for dozing. After an hour and a half they hit the border crossing out of Hrvatska, better known as Croatia. A customs guard walks through the bus like he's taking it personally. The Perpetuals only arrived in his country and now they're leaving – they'll hardly be asked to fill out questionnaires for the Croatian Tourist Board. Passports are checked and returned. Then Faruk drives half a mile along another country track to take them into Bosnia-Herzegovina.

'Yugoslavia used to be one country,' explains Anne-Marie. 'It's all a bit different now.'

They stop at a red and white barber's pole blocking the road. Soldiers face the minibus from behind sandbags. Apart from a change in the weather it reminds Brendan of a day trip to Belfast, crossing the border at Newry. British troops with blackened faces and small trees growing out of their heads.

Packie takes out his disposable camera.

'Probably not a good idea,' says Brendan.

'Och, just a wee photie,' protests Packie, hesitating.

A serious-looking female soldier boards the bus with a machine-gun slung over her shoulder. Packie puts the camera away. The soldier takes one look and has a word with Faruk. Anne-Marie insists there is nothing to worry about but the more she says this, the less first-time Perpetuals believe her. They have officially left Catholic-friendly Croatia and must now face less hospitable hordes from Bosnia-Herzegovina, which, according to the atlas, is blue and yellow. Except the flags outside have red and white squares which means they must still be in Croatia.

'Where are we, Miss?' asks Packie.

'We're entering Bosnia-Herzegovina,' replies Anne-Marie. 'But we are among friends. This part of Herzegovina is mostly Bosnian Croat.'

She seems to think that this makes sense to her passengers. The Gogartys are none the wiser. Faruk stacks the passports in a neat pile and brings them to a kiosk with one-way windows. The Perpetuals sit, waiting. Quiet chatter on the bus. Then in one of those strange moments everybody seems to stop talking at exactly the same time. The presence of soldiers with guns under the glare of floodlights has some of the first-timers on edge. Kathleen, one of the Kilbeggan ladies, decides to strike up the band. Fine voice she has too.

> *You shall cross the barren desert*
> *But you shall not die of thirst*

To Brendan it sounds vaguely familiar. Others join in quickly, following Kathleen's lead. By the time she gets to the chorus the bus is a choir on wheels. Faruk, Irene and Brendan are the only ones missing the hymn sheet. Brendan doesn't have a note in his head but finds himself joining in quietly before he realises what they are singing. It's more familiar than he thought. The same hymn filled the church when he and five other men carried Cathal's white coffin shoulder high down the aisle to a hearse outside.

> *Be not afraid. I go before you always*
> *Come follow me and I will give you rest.*

He recalls nearly fainting when they got to the church door. It's not a memory he wants to dwell on. Shaking free from such bleak contemplation he glances around the bus. People seem to take heart from singing out loud, for some reason. Like down in the bowels of the *Titanic* where everyone in steerage had a great sing-song after hitting the iceberg.

He can even see Irene's lips moving. She has to be faking it. The Perpetuals reach the end of the song but Kathleen doesn't want to stop. So it's back to verse one and they start all over again. Brendan has already decided that when he gets back to the marina he's not going to mention that they were held at gunpoint. He won't even claim they were in mortal danger. In fact he won't be saying a word to Gary or Fiona about any of it.

Unannounced, the soldier reappears with their passports and scans the coach. All the singing dries up instantly. You mightn't tap her for a dance in the local disco but you wouldn't mess with her either.

'Medjugorje,' she remarks dismissively, shaking her head.

Everyone bursts out like it was the funniest thing they ever heard. Maybe just nervous laughter, who knows. The soldier tosses the passports to Faruk and steps off the bus in a huff. She's not going to shoot them. Not today, anyways.

'Isn't that a good one,' whispers Julie to her sister, all too loudly. 'D'you know Kathleen, I nearly wet myself.'

Faruk restarts the engine while Anne-Marie hands the passports back, one-by-one. The laughter subsides and chat returns, the barber's pole at customs lifting into the sky to let them through.

– 15 –

It was dark by the time the bus trundles into Medjugorje so they can't see much. Had Irene nodded off, she was convinced Rosemary wouldn't have noticed. The Cavan woman has already told Irene everything there is to know – the child visionaries, Apparition Hill, the miracles, the good priests, the bad bishop, the spiritual ceremonies, Cross

Mountain, the food, the weather, the best bureau to change money, where you could get postcards *with* stamps.

This was her fifth visit.

The town boasts one main street and various side streets. A few shops selling knick-knacks and so on. The main drag leads to the church, which is a fine size with two white towers and a big clock. Some of the Perpetuals got a bit excited and started taking pictures, the flash rebounding unhelpfully off the coach windows.

'That's the basilica of St James on your right,' marvels Anne-Marie. 'Oh don't worry about photos. You'll get plenty of time to see it in daylight.'

It looks like any country town back home except for an alarming shortage of pubs and the appearance of sprightly young priests on walkabout. That and the heat. Irene is ready for a shower, a large vodka tonic and silence. Nobber already feels days ago.

Anne-Marie reads out the accommodation list so the Gogartys are in with Rosemary, Kathleen, Julie, Packie and a retired couple from Kilkenny. Their residence – Pansion Regina – is only five minutes from the centre of town. They will soon find out that everything here is within walking distance. The rest of the Perpetuals are distributed between three other guesthouses.

Pansion Regina is in complete darkness when they arrive. A power cut across this side of town. Anne-Marie cheerfully tells them this happens all the time but Marijana, the owner, is highly apologetic, handing out candles like a scene from Dickens. Kathleen and Julie have stayed here before and they just can't tell her often enough that all this inconvenience is absolutely no bother whatsoever. They're so OTT, Brendan wonders if the electricity going off was all their fault.

'Aren't these things only sent to test us,' smiles Kathleen.

He's feeling tested enough already.

'Breakfast served between eight and nine,' announces Anne-Marie, shifting into sergeant-major mode. 'Mass in English is at ten, so we'll pick ye up at 9.30 sharp. Don't forget to re-set your watches now. Medjugorje is one hour ahead. That's one hour!'

The Gogartys are in Room 4. Marijana gives them a key and lights the candle. Up the stairs to the left. The corridors are pink. In a previous life – or BC, at least – Irene could imagine this being good fun, a bit of an adventure; right now, it's a drag. The room door doesn't even lock. Basic enough, nothing fancy but clean, in candlelight at least. Two single beds, one pillow each. A bible on both bedside tables. A crucifix on the wall. No ashtray and Irene is ready to kill for a vodka.

'Can't find the mini-bar, Brendan.'

She says it for a laugh before he breaks the news. Seeing as they were coming to a holy place he felt a bit self-conscious in the airport and decided not to buy any duty-free. Irene retorts angrily that he can offer up all he likes but he doesn't have to haul her every inch of the way. She shouldn't have left it to him. Why didn't she pick up a carton of ciggies *and* a litre of Smirnoff herself?

'Where do they hide the bathroom?'

'I think we passed it,' he says quietly. 'Other side of the stairs.'

'Ah here – not even *en suite*?'

She goes down the corridor but finds the toilet occupied. Irene was never quite over the moon about this harebrained idea but she's quickly losing the will to live. She returns to the room where Brendan sits at the end of the bed, bouncing off the floor like a mattress salesman.

'Firm enough,' he says.

'You sure know how to show a girl a good time.'

She pulls a shuttered door that leads out to a small balcony at the back of the pansion. The door sticks noisily before she jerks it free. Two dusty plastic green chairs and a small table overlook a litter-strewn car park. Room to sit out at least. A scrawny ginger cat picks its way along a high concrete wall. Another settles in nearby bushes. This does not feel tropical or even remotely continental. More like a dumping ground for strays.

'Brendan?'

He follows her out. She can see an outline of the whole town in darkness, which is precisely how she feels herself.

'Room with a view,' he says, pretend-chirpy. 'We'll see more when the electricity comes back.'

'Are you serious about being here for twelve days?'

'That's the package.'

'That's not a package; it's a sentence.'

She searches her bag for ciggies and sits, exaggerating a sigh for Brendan's benefit. He looks surprised when she lights up. She takes a few drags expecting him to finally ask why she took up smoking again. He says nothing and is bitten by a mosquito. They love his blood more than she does right now.

'Someone forgot to build the swimming pool,' she notes.

With hopes of a vodka tonic all but disappeared Irene would settle for a shower and gladly wash her hair. But with the power off there's no hot water. She'll be lucky if she gets to spend a penny. There's not much more to say really. It's all quiet on the balcony. She detects paint peeling from the wooden rail. She presses it hard and her middle finger goes through rot.

'Not to be leaned against.'

Irene drifts inside and collapses on her bed. Brendan stays out on the balcony. She sees him sit back in silhouette, his hands cupped behind his head. He lets out a shout when he's bitten again. Slaps the back of his neck. Too late.

His mobile phone kicks into life with *Eye of the Tiger*. Rummaging in his jacket, he checks the caller before answering. It's Fiona. 'Missing you already,' teases Irene.

It's a compact Nokia 232 and Brendan's pudgy fingers hit the button to receive. Tells her it's no bother calling so late but doesn't mention they are a full hour ahead because he's in southern Europe on a pilgrimage with his wife. Irene wonders what other details are omitted, realising that both of them took an undeclared vow of *omerta* about this trip. A mosquito has a quick nibble on his ear. He swipes at it after feeling the draw of blood through the sting.

'Yugoslavia,' he repeats. 'Yugoslavia! Twelve days . . . go on so.'

Irene's eyes have adjusted to the darkness and she turns to face the ceiling. She imagines Fiona, not long back from Portugal, is inconsolable. Why couldn't he bring her with him? She knows these are just playful notions following the trajectory of her fading spirit. *Well, if she could see the pair of us stranded in this monastery those tears would dry up quick enough.*

Brendan finishes up the call and snaps the phone shut. His shadow fills the doorway. Irene notices he doesn't name the caller when he reports back to base.

'Parts container stuck in Rosslare.'

'This a working holiday?' she asks.

He lets out a long slow breath and returns to the balcony. The church bells from St James ring out. She hears Brendan smack his neck again, harder this time. Just when her eyes have grown accustomed to the dark the room lights up, power returned.

– 16 –

At four in the morning Brendan finds himself standing on the bed, a white bathroom towel coiled into rope. He's poised, dead still, then springs to flick a mosquito perched on the wall. Crushing insects into dark red blotches is a simple pleasure but not the quietest form of revenge.

'What are you at?' grumbles Irene sleepily.

'They're eating me.'

He has hardly slept a wink. Woke up full of marks and lumps where blood suckers had run amok. He considers them the most useless creatures ever invented – *I mean, what do they actually do?*

And just to rub it in, they're not bothered with herself.

So she gets all the shut-eye she wants thank-you-very-much while these little fuckers have an all-nighter on me.

He'll need cream and repellent or it'll be blue murder for the next ten nights. His fingers and ears are so itchy it's not funny. One got in underfoot and crawled right between his toes for a bite – yeah, even there! Despite all this blood-letting he's first down for breakfast. The others are already sitting at a communal table, buttering toast and yapping about Mass.

'As long as it's in plain English,' declares Packie, trying to scrape one last dollop of marmalade out of an empty jar.

'No, the other Masses are in different languages,' explains Rosemary, who acts like an unofficial information centre for first-timers.

Julie arrives, a little out of breath. She has big news.

'This morning will be very special,' she announces. 'Father Connellan will celebrate our Mass. He's the parish priest in Strokestown.'

'Visiting priests are invited to say Mass in Medjugorje,' adds Kathleen, giving the Kilbeggan ladies a competitive edge in the newsflash department.

'Father Connellan said he was humbled to be asked,' Julie assures the table. 'He says it's an honour.'

'Well seeing as he's one of our own, at least we'll be fit to know what he's saying,' agrees Packie. 'Just a shame he's not from Donegal.'

It's hard to know why, but when Irene appears Kathleen and Rosemary immediately fuss over her something shocking. She might have got forty winks-plus, but Raymond Anthony Dunne was not the first – or last – to discover that Irene is not a morning person. Even so, they want to pour her juice, butter her toast, choose her cereal. Brendan knows from experience that all she wants to do is sit with her coffee and ease quietly into the day but he spares them advance warning and allows the spectacle to unfold.

'How did you sleep, love?' smiles Kathleen.

'Grand.'

Marijana arrives with fresh tea and coffee. They are told to help themselves, which they do.

'A bowl of prunes will keep you regular,' Packie informs the room.

'Marijana, where can I get cream for mosquitos?'

'They bite you?'

'They love me. That's the problem.'

He's wearing shorts so the evidence is on display. His legs look like pizza.

'Isn't that a terror,' says Packie, more curious than sympathetic.

'Yes, you find *ljekarna* in centre,' nods Marijana. 'Anne-Marie will say you.'

The Kilkenny couple simultaneously check their watches while others hurriedly excuse themselves. There's loads of time but nobody wants to be late. Packie calmly pours himself another cup of tea.

'That's a brave heat out there,' he says, adjusting his baseball cap. 'I don't bother with all that sun screen business, factor 30, factor 40 what-have-you. Just keep the sun off your wee head, that's what I do.'

Irene sips her coffee, a picture of isolation.

'Do you know that's why pigs roll about in muck? So as to avoid sunburn. Oh aye. Pigs is very smart so they are but don't ask me what factor muck is.'

'Is it not a bit warm for the suit?'

'Don't you go fretting.'

'But a shirt and tie? You'll be baked.'

'Haven't you enough on your plate with your mosquitoes and whatnot.'

They hear the blast of a car horn outside. It's the minibus.

'That boy is five minutes early,' says Packie, finishing his tea with one loud slurp.

He touches his forehead in a blessing as he rises. There's a holy stampede down the stairs, followed by an unholy scramble for the front door. Irene listens to it all, both hands holding the cup, elbows on the table.

'Worse than the January sales,' she says.

The guesthouse empties quickly. Outside, voices babble over the running engine. Father Connellan can expect a lively reception from the partisans.

'Everything is okay?' asks Marijana, making one last check.

'Grand, thank you.'

The Gogartys are alone again. Brendan watches Irene place her cup on a matching ceramic saucer.

'How's the coffee?'

'Fine.'

'They were talking about an Irish priest saying Mass here this morning. Big excitement.'

'Why don't you go?'

'Me! What about you?'

She reaches back, stretching high.

'The sun is shining and I'm going to lie right under it. I might read a few pages of my book or I might not. A nice, lazy day. So why don't you go do the praying and leave me to work on my tan?'

She has her mind made up. Her face is neutral but there's a very clear told-you-so in that look. Your idea entirely, it says. He flogged it to her on a nothing-to-lose basis so that's what she signed up for. All she was asked to do was come along, which she did. Not an obligation in the world but to show up.

She's right, in fairness.

He leapt; now, he's looking.

Brendan doesn't particularly want to go to Mass on his own but sitting out sunbathing would bore him to death. No updates on Rosslare from Gary or Fiona while he's dawdling over breakfast in Bosnia or Herzegovina or whatever you call it. Not for the first time he wonders why he brought them here. Wouldn't he be better off in county council offices back home banging some heads over pig slurry seeping into the Shannon?

He takes a sup of tea and finds the cup empty. He reaches for the pot but there's nothing in it. Marijana has disappeared so there's no chance of a refill. He hears the minibus rev up and finally pull away but it doesn't get too far. After a loud hiss of brakes and a spit of hydraulics, they hear the slap-tap of footsteps hurrying their way. Anne-Marie standing red-faced in the doorway mumbling 'twenty-five' and a pair of Gogartys in her sights.

– 17 –

The Kilbeggan ladies have definitely taken her on as either a charity case or a pilgrim challenge: Project Irene. With Kathleen continuously dropping hints about spirituality maybe she feels the agnostic from Nobber might be lured away from the dark side. When the Rosary broke out on the bus yesterday Julie was shocked to see Irene beadless. She emptied her handbag and draped around the non-believer's neck a spare set she keeps for emergencies, the way a motorist might pull jump leads out of an untidy boot.

Why, wonders Irene, didn't I open my mouth and hand them back? I could have argued that faith is a private thing. Could've said something about personal space. Then again, protest is not always an option. Like the one-way discussions over breakfast at Pansion Regina which Irene stays out of for the most part. Kathleen is persistent, you'd have to give her that. But if she keeps pushing it for eleven more days Irene can't guarantee she's going to keep her trap so politely shut.

Meanwhile, she notices Brendan seems to have struck up with the old goat who sat beside her on the plane from Dublin. Packie from somewhere in Donegal. The pair of them talking GAA *ad nauseum* about what county won what All-Ireland in 19-whenever. Brendan can tell him all about his collection of match programmes, going back to when he was six and his Dad took him to Páirc Tailteann. That will keep them going for a few days. Once they get started Irene finds herself zoning out, as the Americans say, but she'd be the first to admit she's zoned out most of the time whether Packie is there or not.

The man has been wearing his blue terylene suit since they got here, complete with shirt and tie. Brendan keeps asking is he not baked in it. Half-baked, more like. The furthest Packie would go was to take off his Aran cardigan the day after arrival. Irene wondered if he had more than one shirt or if all his shirts were identical, the way people set in their ways often buy a lifetime supply of the same garment. Packie ended the mystery when he told her he rinses his shirt and socks at the end of each day and dries them on the balcony. She didn't ask about his underpants.

It was his nephew who brought him the baseball cap back from Boston so he wears it all the time. Got used to it 'parked on me head'. Sometimes he swops the sandals – which Brendan calls 'Jesus boots' – for a 'mighty' pair of black Reeboks. He never married – Irene did ask – but has a bit of a glint all the same. Leggy young ones pass by in micro skirts and she sees Packie's eyes watering. He can't blame dodgy cataracts every time.

She was going to ask him if he's a leg man or a boob man but she doesn't want to embarrass him. He's harmless for God's sake. Which is one thing most of the Perpetuals have going for them: harmlessness. They're a decent enough bunch but she can't think of anything she has in common with them. Irene was expecting herself and Brendan to be grilled about what brings them to Medjugorje but thanks be to God that's one friendly interrogation they've been spared.

To date at least.

Irene reckons she's been at wilder Tupperware parties but this morning took the biscuit. All set to lie in the sun after finishing her coffee save for Anne-Marie to storm in with a bee in her bonnet and round them up like escaped convicts. You could put it down to the tour leader's force of personality but if Irene was honest she'd blame herself for being such a pushover.

She noticed Anne-Marie was cute enough to let the Gogartys board the coach first and take the full brunt of saintly opprobrium. Hot and bothered by this momentary delay the Perpetuals were all revved up about their first Mass, nervously checking their watches. The church is a whole three minutes away.

'Twenty-six, twenty-seven,' triple-checks Anne-Marie one last time. She sounds triumphant. 'Hands up anybody who's not here!'

Irene watches Rosemary fold a woollen scarf on her lap.

'Cashmere?'

'Oh, it's for the blessing,' explains Rosemary. 'Mammy isn't so well at home. Cancer of the throat. They ask for special items to be presented at the end of the Mass so I'll get this blessed. Might give her a lift.'

Irene told Rosemary she'd light a candle for her mother. The Cavan woman appeared genuinely moved by such a small gesture. She took Irene's hands and there were nearly tears in her eyes. It might sound a bit OTT but Irene didn't know where to look.

The Gogartys haven't been to church since God knows when. They don't know when to sit or stand or whether to sit or kneel, so, squashed into a pew with all the believers they just take their cue from everybody else. Apart from all this positional fussing, for Irene, the best thing about Mass is nobody knows when you've zoned out. The Strokestown priest gives a sermon about the rights of the unborn and says every pregnancy is a gift. 'That's right,' nod Julie and Kathleen, both fervent and childless.

It surprises her to see Brendan join the queue for Communion. The choir sings while she watches him receive the host on his tongue. He comes back, hands joined in prayer, looking quite reverential. Quite fanciable, she had to admit. He kneels beside her in the pew with his eyes closed, head buried in open palms. Really concentrating like a true penitent. Irene had to say she was impressed. She thought she'd try a few Hail Marys of her own when she heard a strange buzzing sound. Brendan broke away from his devotions to sneak a look at a text message received on silent. He should have been ready for a sharp elbow in the ribs when he started composing a reply.

At the end of the service the priest asks the congregation to raise items for special blessing. Rosemary takes the scarf out and holds it high, like a soccer supporter declaring undying allegiance to a corporate franchise. The priest throws holy water from the altar in their general direction. Rosemary doesn't mind that they aren't even within spitting distance. Her eyes are closed tight as she makes a private wish. Then she blesses herself, puts her beads to her lips and folds the scarf, smiling. Irene finds it all a bit hokey but Rosemary seemed very pleased with the whole thing.

Anne-Marie stands outside the basilica under a Perpetual Succour umbrella.

'Is she always holding things up?' asks Brendan rhetorically.

There's a constant flow of human traffic around St James, inside and out. People walking slowly in ones and twos or lighting candles, praying intently. Or just sitting there like they're waiting for a train but not too bothered whether it's coming or not.

'Yoo-hoo!'

Irene notices Brendan drift away, glued to his phone while he paces the footpath. Working himself into a bit of a lather by the looks of it. She shuts him out. The nerve of him, begging her to come here and now he's all bluster on the blower, talking shop. *Plus ca fucking change.*

'Let's go to the shaded area behind the trees,' commands Anne-Marie, leading the way.

'Wonderful sermon,' whispers Kathleen, falling into step with Irene.

'Wasn't it?' lies Irene.

'And very important. The unborn can't protect themselves.'

Irene was going to say some of the born don't have it too easy either but she lets it pass. She realises Kathleen wants to mould her into somebody else but in a strange way she's flattered by the attention. Anne-Marie waits for the last of the stragglers and there's a lovely breeze under the trees.

Everybody is excited because the Perpetuals will be doing stations of the cross tonight at the basilica. Anne-Marie won't keep them out too late because Cross Mountain is to be climbed tomorrow at dawn. And if that doesn't float your boat, there's always Apparition Hill on Thursday after the sun goes down. That's when she'll take the group to where Our Lady is said to have appeared.

Some can't wait; Irene can.

The Kilbeggan ladies have already conquered Apparition Hill on their own steam. They don't do half measures, these gals.

'You're getting great value from your trip,' Irene tells Kathleen.

'That's the thing about Medjugorje,' replies Kathleen, ever ready with an allegorical twist. 'You get out of it only what you put into it.'

'Like being microwaved?' jokes Irene, immediately regretting it. 'Okay, I take that back. If Our Lady has a soft spot for this place you've no idea how much I want to feel the love.'

'Then you will,' smiles Kathleen with unnerving certainty.

As far as Irene is concerned Brendan, Packie and all associated fruitcakes are welcome to try the Cross Mountain assault course at dawn. Good luck to them! Anne-Marie can revert to her storm trooper routine but Irene resolves to have a nice lie-in and will definitely give it a miss this time. She's determined to stick to her own plans and to hell with Perpetual Succour.

'Kathleen, do you mind me asking why you and Julie come here?'

'Not at all,' smiles the pilgrim. 'The way we see it, Our Lady took the trouble to come all the way from heaven. A short flight from Ireland is the least we can do. Besides, old batteries need recharging.'

'Right.'

'Everybody has a reason whether they know it or not.'

'No offence now, but you and I are not in the same boat.'

'What do you mean?'

'You and Julie are believers.'

'Oh we are indeed – sure why would I be offended?'

'Because that's you. To be honest, this is not my thing.'

'Of course it's not, dear. But you are here, aren't you?'

– 18 –

B less me Jesus for I am pissed . . .
Packie Sludden was party to the conspiracy, as they say in detective films. But that's a few hours ago. Packie left the scene of the crime around lunchtime and now it's . . .

'Excuse me, what time is it?'

'Ten minutes before nine o'clock. You like another?'

'Sure, why not? One for the *bóthar.*'

Jesus she's a fine thing. Great body. And a lovely smile. You can't ask for much more than that. This stuff isn't bad either. Lighter taste, maybe a bit gassier but not all that different to home. Alright, I admit I've been here a while but what the hell! Aren't we allowed an occasional pit stop? It's not like I didn't do me bit already – sure wasn't I up at half-five this morning! Thirsty work, all this climbing, praying and general pilgrimaging.

'And one beer, thank you.'

'Take it out of that. What's your name again?'

'Tihana.'

'Ah yeah, that's it. Lovely name, Tihana. We don't have anything like that in Ireland – maybe Tina?'

'You say me before.'

'I did, I did. And did I tell you about me collection? Six hundred and four at last count – most of them in mint condition.'

'Yes, you say me. Thank you.'

'I did, in fairness. Sure if you don't follow the GAA it probably doesn't mean that much to you.'

The waitress steps away, taking his empty glass with her. Brendan sits back and looks around. It's only him on the premises, the long, slow unwinding of an early start. He thought of the minibus picking them up before dawn, fifteen Perpetuals in total, including himself and Packie. Anne-Marie did a running commentary with Faruk looking a little fearful behind the wheel – a model of punctuality ever since his evisceration at the airport. The sun hadn't come up yet so it felt quite cool in shorts and a t-shirt before daybreak lit up the valley, sunbeams racing ahead, bringing colour and heat in a way that would gladden your heart. That alone was nearly worth getting up for.

The way Anne-Marie told it, some Pope had a dream about putting a cross up a hill in Herzegovina. Thought it'd be a great idea. Local Catholics got wind of it through some bishop so off they bumbled like the seven dwarfs and built the cross themselves. It all happened when this part of the world was part of Yugoslavia. Despite the fact it was run as a Communist state the plucky locals picked their spot and hoisted it 25 feet into the sky.

'That's no wee cross,' marvelled Packie, insisting on doing the climb in his suit.

The old goat did well, in fairness, smiles Brendan. He swears by his cushioned runners, admitting to anyone who'll listen how his feet can get a bit sweaty in them. Irene had established beyond reasonable doubt that Packie washes his shirt and socks every night; the jury was out on his jocks. A gas man altogether who could not give a proverbial shite about what people thought.

Truth be told, the climb wasn't too bad. Loose rocks and stones on the lower part so you'd want to watch where you are going. You could turn your ankle handy enough. It seemed to start off as a bit of race between Rosemary and the Kilbeggan ladies before Rosemary ran out of puff and got sense. Kathleen and Julie finished joint first.

It took about an hour to get to the top where the scenery was spectacular. They could see the town perfectly clearly in the distance. Brendan could even make out the back of Pansion Regina. From the top of the mountain he thought of Irene asleep in room number 4. There was no way she was going to get up before dawn but he felt it a pity because she would have absolutely loved the view.

Kathleen got the Rosary going at the Cross. The Perpetuals were big into special intentions, which, it seemed to Brendan, was the way things got done around here. There was a railed off area at the Cross where you could kneel and pray. Withered bouquets always look a bit gloomy – though not as sad as plastic flowers – and there was a pile of personal mementos left there. Brendan sifted through them – a single earring, a stripey tie, poker dice, various other things meaningfully deposited by visitors and a rake of Mass cards.

He was sort of curious. Read through the notes and petitions, all written by hand, some of them washed out by rain or faded from sunshine. Some were in foreign languages but most of them just said a name so you'd get the gist. He found himself drawn in by these messages. Felt a bit too private even if they were left there for everyone to see.

'Wouldn't you wonder should you be reading these things at all,' echoed Packie.

Fluttering against the rail, a discoloured Polaroid caught Brendan's eye. It must've been placed there recently enough because it wasn't quite as weather-beaten as the others. It was a hospital picture of a tiny baby boy, tubes coming and going every which way. A screed of thin brown hair like thatch. The baby's eyes were open but distracted and, even though his cheeks were red, his general colour was poor, almost grey.

In the corner of the photo Brendan noticed a newspaper folded on a bedside table. He recognised the small red *Evening Herald* masthead which meant the photo must have come from Ireland. He turned it over. Written on the back it said,

Baby Thomas, RIP. Love always, Mammy and Daddy

Brendan stared at the photo, unable to put it down. He felt a lump rise in his throat. Replacing the Polaroid he rested it under a bigger stone so it wouldn't blow away. Said a prayer too for all the good it would do. Sure what chance did that little fella ever have?

'Hai, wouldja take a wee photie, Brendan?'

'No bother.'

'Make sure you get my good side now!'

They took it handy coming down the hill and Faruk got them back to town just in time for Mass. No sign of Irene at the service, oddly enough. Maybe it's a day of devotion to the tan. Packie wanted to change money. Brendan was already sorted with German marks and a few US dollars but said he'd go along. Packie pulled out a Thomas Cook traveller's cheque for £50 sterling. It had been a while since the teller saw a traveller's cheque but she finally cleared it and gave him a wedge of Croatian kuna.

'What am I going to do with all these koohoos?' said a bewildered Packie, holding the notes up like Monopoly money.

They could have gone for breakfast but neither of them were hungry. It was too hot for coffee. They felt like they had already been up the whole day except it was still sunny and bright. They rambled down the main drag and noticed Tihana dusting down chairs outside what resembled a pub. A taste of home.

'Too early?' says Packie, mischief in his seventy-something eyes.

So they detoured for a couple of bevvies. Packie is not a big drinker, but Brendan finds him a pleasant travelling companion. Easy going, like. Neither does he ask too many questions and is happy to let the silence sit. They were having a nice relaxed time when Packie remembered he was supposed to go to confession. Said he wanted to go back to the guesthouse first for a lie down and after that he'd get rid of all his sins. The only other option was to lighten his load by getting rid of all his sins first and then have a lie down.

'Och, the priest would smell the drink off of me through the wire box,' he reflected gravely, choosing Option A.

'You go on ahead so. I'll folly on.'

'Are you sure you want to stay?'

'Yeah. Yeah, I'm sure.'

The previous night Packie had knocked on the door to Number 4 with his duty-free Powers Gold Label and three paper cups. A fella you'd hardly look at twice in a crowd can be full of surprises. Brendan went downstairs and got some ice from Marijana. They had just the one because of the early start ahead but other than an occasional mosquito dropping by for a refill it was nice to sit out and shoot the breeze. Irene, Brendan and Packie on the balcony, chatting.

Brendan stayed on at the pub, half-hoping that sinless Packie, complete with a clean slate, would drop back after he'd finished all his bits and bobs. Three slow-paced beers later and no sign.

Maybe he got a heavy sentence and that took the wind out of his sails.

So, okay, he's had a few more since. Irene will probably have his guts for garters but Brendan has already lined up his defence. He didn't do it alone – well, didn't do all of it entirely alone. She can't give him that holier-than-thou look, not today. After all, who climbed Cross Mountain? And who did not? Not him either who didn't show up for Mass. When he considers what is becoming quite a long day he realises he hasn't seen his wife since leaving the guesthouse before dawn.

Suppose I could try a bit harder.

He lifts his beer, observing its flow by tilting the glass at a variety of precarious angles. With the perspicacity of a day's drinking under his belt he tries to figure out this whole pilgrimage lark. Isn't he an entrepreneur for God's sake? Setting up Gogarty's Marina Ltd from scratch took courage. Energy. Perseverance. Knowing deep down that it would work. Faith!

The only difference setting up a pilgrimage site is the starting point. Faith here meant belief in God. That's where they parted ways. Hard enough to pull everything together to make a business profitable; quite another thing altogether if you're reporting to a project manager you can't even see.

Which is exactly how Medjugorje appears to him. Like you join a conversation with somebody who isn't there – in effect, talking to yourself. The Perpetuals do it from morning to night. He has never seen so many people so intensely self-engaged for such long periods. Time was when that sort of behaviour could get you certified. The trick is you just call it prayer and Bob's your uncle.

Medjugorje has enough novenas and rosaries going round to make sure nobody is left behind. Special intentions to beat the band. Is that what it means to be a pilgrim? But what of it – isn't everyone just asking for favours? The other week Brendan was ready to cut McGeedy open with a Stanley knife and now he's under a big high cross, seeking what – forgiveness?

He knows what he'd like to pray for. Better luck next time.

He feels the dread rising within so he tries to break the cycle of McGeedy-orbited thoughts. He shouldn't be getting worked up when he's supposed to be chilling out. Ever since the court case – and that's neither today nor yesterday – he's under doctor's orders to take it easy. To mind his blood pressure – relax, like.

'Jesus,' he mutters aloud, 'How do you do that?'

You could argue this trip is a time out for his mental health. Granted, it's not your typical holiday and he wishes the Kilbeggan sisters would stop going on about *working with God*. Brendan reckons he works 51 weeks of the year. Shouldn't a trip to the Med – or is it the Adriatic – be time off?

Maybe he's overdone the relaxing part today but can't he put that down to medical advice? Irene wouldn't be too impressed but sure, what's the odds. He tries to remember the waitress' name – Tatiana, is it? No doubt about it, she must work out regular to keep in that sort of shape. Ten out of ten to the girl with long black hair, whatever her name is. He's never gone offside but now he's not so sure. If this one wanted to take him home right now he has to admit he could be persuaded.

Hate to let you down now Tahina but there'll be no gymnastics on the kitchen table tonight. It'll have to be a well-sprung couch or an orthopaedic mattress.

He's not trying to introduce health and safety to passion but he put his back out loading a boat a few years ago and it hasn't been the same since. Gets the odd twinge at the wrong moment.

So, Tinahina, you'll have to settle for meat, spuds and two veg. That's me. Fast and furious from Nobber. I won't keep you waiting.

'Goodnight,' she says.

'You're away?'

'Yes, I finish now. If you want another beers, Ljubo will get.'

And off she goes into the night.

Playing hard-to-get so she is, decides Brendan, raising his glass. *Sure in the name of Jesus amn't I the only customer here? Maybe it's just as well, all things considered. The pubs here probably have a strict policy for staff: Don't shift pilgrims.*

He takes out his phone and sees it has no bars at all. Don't talk to him about reception in these parts, not to mention the fact that there's probably a container still stuck in Rosslare. *Gary should've had that sorted – cat's away, mice fucking around what-have-you. Which reminds me, this phone needs recharging. Battery's nearly dead.*

It's hard to beat outdoor pints but he wouldn't really be one for lone drinking. In the face of imminent condemnation, possibly even a lynching from the half-rotted balcony, he returns to setting out his defence.

Irene, before you hang, draw and quarter me, let me say this pit stop was totally unplanned. Spur of the moment. Are you going to shoot me for showing initiative? Besides, it started out with a pair of us. After losing a man overboard I might have stayed on a bit longer than intended. Otherwise, I'd say we had a grand day seeing the sights in Medjugorje.

The only drawback is that Polaroid. A recurring vision of the dying baby up the mountain. He hopes the photo didn't blow away and the stone was heavy enough to keep it in place. As Brendan sits alone on the terrace he can see clearly the little mite's face.

'You like another?'

'No, Ljubo, thank you. I'll saddle up and let the horse take me home.'

It's time to go. He thought Irene might pass this way at some point earlier in the day – he's not exactly hiding in the bushes! She used to like the odd bevvy herself, though she's more vodka tonic than beer. Or Chardonnay, by the bucket. Who knows – if she dropped by and he wasn't too far ahead she might well have climbed aboard for an alcoholic catch-up.

But now, when there's so much the two of them can't talk about, what would be the point? And it's definitely harder to stick to the rules when bevvies are involved. Under a feed of pints the built-in bleeper – the one that keeps your thoughts in check – switches off, temporarily kaput, so anything that enters your head takes the M1 straight out your gob. All that is fragile and unspoken, intentionally hidden away and put out of reach, gets pulled down into the open and ripped to shreds.

Mr and Mrs Gogarty used to do nearly everything together; now, they spend most of their shared hours apart. It's hardly a secret that their cocktail sessions AC inevitably went awry so all in all it's probably better Irene went sunbathing today instead of praying. He really doesn't want to find her up waiting for him tonight at the guesthouse, all primed for a big serious chat when all he wants to do is sleep.

They've had them before, chats like that at times like this; Brendan would readily tell you they led nowhere. One would get louder, the other quieter; a general rise in temperature usually ending in a slammed door and separate sleeping arrangements. Bumpy nights to pass through uneasy, restless hours, an inescapable fugue. The morning would begin with a peace offering – a cup of tea silently placed by the bed. A sugar-free token of love. If their row the previous night had gone the whole nine yards the only good thing was neither of them could remember all the things they regretted saying.

– 19 –

For Irene, Brendan texting in the church said it all really. Having decided they needed help he signed them up for twelve days of penance. But just when they're holding out for deliverance he can't stay off the phone. Now he's gone AWOL and she's left at the guesthouse, waiting around like a fool. She notices his phone charger on the bed. That, if nothing else, will bring him back. She pulls it from the adaptor, goes to the balcony and hears it fly through the bushes.

She replays the day it in her mind. This morning before dawn he and Packie went off with a few other early risers to climb that stupid mountain. Afterwards, Kathleen and Rosemary said they saw him at Mass. Packie told her Brendan helped change some money and the pair of them had a bit of a ramble around town. Says they had a coffee up the road from the basilica.

That's six hours ago!

She doesn't know where he is and she's not going out looking for him. Maybe he met somebody he knew – some wandering Irish pilgrim who follows the GAA. Or he could be in a bar up the town but drinking alone is not his style. She paces the room, lights a cig and sits out, resting her feet on the unpainted rail. The car park doesn't look any better lit up. A mangy stray picks its way along a glass-pointed wall.

She'd had a wander around town herself this morning. The Perpetuals are a hungry lot, tucking into corn flakes and toast, even in this heat. Irene doesn't usually eat in the morning anyway so she decided to skip breakfast and avoid recapture by Anne-Marie. Couldn't face the lot of them babbling on about the wonders of Cross Mountain and telling her what she missed. To hell with that.

She stopped off for a coffee and a croissant in a nice café near the post office. Was tempted to send a postcard – *Hi Della! Living the dream!* – but went off the idea. There's no hurry in Medjugorje and it really has the feel of a country town. Tractors rolling down the main street, trailers loaded with vegetables, that kind of thing. Millions of pilgrims have passed through here but the town isn't really set up for tourism. Maybe that's part of the charm although some of the locals insist it has changed beyond all recognition.

It was pleasant enough just being on her own, away from everybody. Strolling over to the basilica she lit a candle for Rosemary's mother in a small grotto at the side of the church. You'd hear chirping in the trees, birdsong in harmony with the choir inside.

Taking a seat at the back of the grotto Irene watched a young mother walk in with a pram. A local woman, no more than mid-twenties and very pretty. She stopped to light a candle and retreated to a pew. While she knelt to pray she rocked the pram with her free hand. The baby was as good as gold. It was all so simple and so beautiful Irene couldn't take her eyes away. As the woman blessed herself she looked up and caught Irene staring. It was a bit embarrassing but the young mother smiled shyly in recognition as she left the grotto.

Irene stayed on and tried to pray. She really did try. But not for the first time she found things don't always go as hoped. If they did she wouldn't even be here right now. She should be at home planning Cathal's eighteenth birthday party. Eighteen! On the cusp of adulthood.

She pictures the curls he had when he was born. A sort of light blond that turns red when the sun catches. Even as a little boy Cathal didn't want them cut. Irene was happy to leave it, especially when Brendan started going on about his son looking like a girl. Granted, it did get a bit long so they agreed that before his first day at school he'd go to Jimmy the barber for a trim. Irene brought her son – his first haircut – where he sat nervously on a raised wooden board across a cherry red leather chair.

Jimmy was a cheerful, thin man in his late sixties who always wore an old-fashioned white shopcoat. He tied a blue nylon sheet around Cathal's neck and gave the whole spiel about looking the part. Jimmy turned and winked at Irene to show he was doing his bit for parent-support. Irene didn't like the feeling they were ganging up on a four-year-old so she didn't respond. Cathal's eyes darted about, the nylon knot loosening around his throat as he followed the barber's steady movements.

Jimmy plugged in the electric clippers and ran the blade up Cathal's left temple. The first blond curls fell onto the blue bib and then billowed to the floor like autumnal blossom. The clippers ran to the crown, Jimmy squinting closely as though he was a bricklayer eyeing up the straightness of a new wall. Irene watched more curls tumble to the tiles and then saw Cathal's mournfully brown eyes stare at her though the mirror, big tears welling in silence. It made her feel mean and cruel. She caught her breath as her heart lurched, telling her boy all too quickly how handsome he looked. She knows that sometimes she speaks too fast. Can't help it.

Cathal faced the mirror and let the barber plough on, shutting his eyes tight till the finish. He said nothing when Jimmy held the mirror up to his shaven head.

'There you go,' says Jimmy. 'Big boy now.'

Irene lit another candle, unable to stifle the image of Cathal in that barber's seat, his curls falling to the floor in slow motion.

Despite residual pangs she prefers to think of him like that instead of how they saw him at the end. Tries not to imagine his last minutes but it's hard when you've heard the coroner's report in full. Five years later and she's still sick to the pit of her stomach.

She watches the candle burn to the wick. All gone. Praying is not easy, not for her. Taking the long way back to Pansion Regina she made her way slowly down side streets. Given that sense of direction is not one of her strong points, it pleased her to find a way back, however circuitously. She wouldn't say she felt lighter or better but seeing that young mother gently rock the pram was the highlight of her day.

There was a soft knock at the door. She thought it might be Packie bringing more whiskey.

'Come on down, Irene. We're having a cuppa.'

Kathleen, like a drug dealer with teabags.

'I'm alright, thanks.'

'Waiting for him won't get him home any quicker, love. Come on – we always bring a supply of Barry's from home.'

Reluctantly, she goes downstairs with Kathleen. There's a gaggle in the kitchen and they start fussing over her straight away which makes Irene regret once again being so easily persuaded. She resolves from here on to stop giving in.

'Do you take it strong or weak, Irene?' asks Julie, pouring tea.

'Medium is fine.'

'Kimberley or Mikado?'

As ever, they're all discussing the weather. It's going to be hotter again tomorrow. Might even be a thunderstorm. Some famous cellist from Florence will accompany the choir at eleven o'clock Mass. Confessions in the afternoon and a much anticipated evening climb up Apparition Hill. Irene knows they are trying to be kind the way they talk about everything except the missing pilgrim. She feels like screaming.

'Top-up anybody?'

The front door slams loudly. Brendan staggers in and pauses in the hall. She hasn't seen him this drunk for years. He peers in the doorway like he doesn't see her.

'Tis yourself, Brendan,' confirms Packie.

Brendan grunts and stumbles on, heavy-footed, up the staircase. The door to Room 4 opens and shuts.

'Now,' says Kathleen with a smile that conveys nothing has happened. 'Who's for a hot drop?'

He's snoring by the time Irene goes upstairs. Lying on his back in his jockeys, dead to the world. A warm breeze passes through from the window. Other strays have returned to the back yard and are engaged in a loud feline dispute. Irene stands in the centre of the room, puzzled by her husband's uncharacteristic display. She goes to the balcony and lights up, the mewling of cats punctuated by midnight bells at the basilica.

– 20 –

'Have you seen it?'
        'What?'

'The charger! I'm 100 per cent sure I left it plugged in.'

Brendan doesn't say anything about his late return. He has a bit of a head and sunlight beaming through the window does not help. He maintains he is not hallucinating when he repeats his claim about the missing accessory. He's certain he left it in the socket. Maybe the cleaner took it. His phone battery is about to clap out and he's still waiting for Gary to get back to him.

Irene throws her eyes to heaven and goes down to the breakfast room. Brendan checks under the bed again, tossing sheets and pillows. He turns the room upside-down but the charger is well and truly missing. An absolute mystery. Then the Nokia dies. Lovely!

Of course he overlooked putting the repellent on last night so he's paying double for his sins. His legs and arms are blotchy again and shocking itchy. He knew Irene would give him the cold shoulder for his unplanned detour. Anticipating an equally frosty reception from the breakfasting Perpetuals he makes his way downstairs, one self-conscious step at a time.

Irene sits by the window. She's keeping her powder dry, reckons Brendan, whose hangover-encrusted mood is wearing thin. Marijana brings them tea and coffee. The Holy Joes tiptoe around the table like the Gogartys are a minefield.

'Does anybody have a charger?'

'For what?' says Packie, who seems to be the only one listening.

Brendan holds the phone aloft.

'Och, not them there things,' says Packie. 'Sure why would you want everybody knowing where to find you?'

Turns out the man from Kilkenny is the only one in the group who even has a mobile and he says he left his at home.

'That's not much use to me,' says Brendan, resisting the urge to explain why he needs to be contactable at all times.

Pansion Regina doesn't have a normal phone, never mind a mobile charger. Marijana says the main line got cut off months ago and it's too expensive to repair. As for mobiles, they're for business executives and UN representatives.

'You are big businessman in Ireland?' she laughs.

All the Holy Joes want to talk about is Mass and tonight's odyssey up Apparition Hill. Even the veterans are excited, their breakfast babble full of earnest promise. Irene sits with a coffee staring into the distance. Brendan's head is splitting so he lorries into the orange juice.

'You needn't think I came out here so you could make a show of me,' she says finally, taking her coffee to the patio outside.

Instead of going by coach they will walk to St James this morning. Irene tells Kathleen she'll go with them. Nobody asks Brendan. He's a one-man leper colony. They gather in the hall and Irene joins them. Brendan pours another juice.

'Are you right there, Brendan,' says Packie. 'Sure the walk'll do you no harm.'

The Kilbeggan ladies lead the way and Brendan takes up the rear, joined by Packie. Brendan has downed four orange juices but his mouth still feels parched. His head is a dull throb. He picks up a straw hat on the way because the temperature is already climbing. Going to Mass feels like martyrdom, especially when all he wants to do is go back to bed.

'I told Irene we stopped for coffee,' Packie confides. 'Coffee is all I said, in case she asks.'

'White lies don't count, Packie.'

'Do they not?'

'I stayed on a while afterwards and had a few more. Truth be told, I'm feeling it now.'

'Aye.'

'Were ye all up when I came in?'

'Aye.'

'Was I bad?'

Packie doesn't reply. They shuffle into the church, glad for a sudden coolness in the porch. Hat off, Brendan dips fingers in the font and lets holy water trickle across his forehead. He stifles a belch. From where he stands, Rosemary, Kathleen and Julie in a nearby pew remind him of the Munster front row. Irene, the smallest of the four, could be scrum-half. Packie squeezes in beside the couple from Kilkenny.

The priest is foreign – not Irish, at least. Croatian, guesses Brendan, which means he's not foreign at all. They do the collection – in the heel of the hunt doesn't it always boil down to readies? – and he discovers he's left his wallet behind. Says he'll catch them next time, if there is a next time. Irene follows the Kilbeggan ladies to Holy Communion but avoids glancing over on her way back. His throat is still dry but the headache is easing. He'd love a Club Orange or a 7-Up. He'd even settle for slug of tepid tap water for Jesus' sake.

At the end of Mass the priest says he'll do a blessing. Everybody gets to their feet and Brendan watches them raise personal items like offerings for sacrifice. Rosemary has a scarf packaged for her mam although Brendan remembers she had it blessed the other day. Suppose spreading the bet can't hurt, he figures. The Kilbeggan ladies are foostering around for miraculous medals, never averse to taking a punt on divine intervention.

Irene rises slowly with them, her head bowed. From the back of the church Brendan watches her carefully remove her necklace. As far as he can make out she's in some sort of trance. Irene presents the necklace aloft in the general direction of the altar.

'Kathleen's mumbo-jumbo finally got to you,' mutters her husband.

If blessings were Irene's thing, so be it. Except he happens to know they're not. And there she is, wedged among the believers, offering it up. Professing magic words from the altar the priest lobs a bit of holy water at the congregation before wrapping up proceedings with the sign of the cross. The show is over.

Irene refastens the necklace and sits down. The Perpetuals turn to embrace each other, warm with enthusiasm.

Of course it's not the necklace; it's the locket. The memento inside. A smiling baby photo of Cathal under a sprig of his golden hair. Brendan has always found it hard to grasp why she carries it around with her. Without wishing to be macabre or maudlin it does feel a bit strange to him, even a little weird. He's careful not to mention it, even after a few bevvies, but the thought of it makes him shiver.

He nips out, ahead of the faithful. The glare in the front courtyard would blind you. He bends the hat's rim down over his eyes but can feel perspiration bubbling on his brow. He's really thirsty but Anne-Marie draws everybody over to the shaded area for a pep talk. Irene is chatting away like ninety with the Front Row. He never thought he'd say this but he wonders is she becoming a stranger? Maybe after years of pushing each other's buttons this could be the beginning of the end. His other half, spirited away by a sect.

Well you're the one who brought her here, he reminds himself. 'Yoo-hoo!'

Anne-Marie has good news and bad news. The big announcement is that there is a good chance the Perpetuals will meet one of Medjugorje's visionaries in person tomorrow afternoon. The visionary, a local woman, will tell them what she saw all those years ago and how it completely changed her life. It's not set in stone but Anne-Marie is very hopeful.

'She'll do her level best to make time for us because she knows Our Lady has a special place in her heart for Ireland.'

Some of the veterans under the canopy are beside themselves with joy. Rosemary has tears in her eyes. Brendan is wondering how come the Blessed Virgin is so hot on geography. How does she even know where Ireland is?

Packie raises his hand.

'What's the bad news?'

'Thank you, Packie, for bringing us back to earth. I know everybody was looking forward to Apparition Hill this evening but I'm afraid there's a serious thunderstorm forecast so we'll have to postpone the climb.'

'Sure, what's a few drops?' retorts Kathleen, supported by a general murmur.

'Thunderstorms here in summer are extremely heavy,' counters Anne-Marie, her voice stiffening. 'As you know only too well Kathleen, they're nothing like our little showers at home.'

There's a rumble in the distance that makes them think the storm must be well ahead of schedule. The noise gathers and the older pilgrims cover their ears. They'll have to admit Anne-Marie was not exaggerating. Then a thunderclap, like an explosion. Two specks tear across the sky.

'Must be F-16s,' says the man from Kilkenny. 'NATO.'

Knowledge sometimes comes from unexpected quarters.

'Them's fast wee planes,' ventures Packie, squinting into the clouds.

The Kilkenny man says they just broke the sound barrier and that's what the big bang was.

'Did you say NATO?' asks Brendan.

'Fighter planes. American-built,' he replies, obviously a bit of a planespotter. 'They can do up to 1,500 mph so they're not going to match the Soviet MiG for speed. Doesn't matter anyhow when NATO control the skies.'

'Well, we won't worry about any of that,' decides Anne-Marie, who clearly has more pressing matters to deal with.

'Are you serious about postponing the climb?' falters Rosemary, looking a little shell-shocked. 'That would be a total disaster.'

Blessed are the meek for they're the dangerous ones. Kathleen, who Brendan suspects has already turned his wife's head, bypasses Anne-Marie altogether and makes a direct appeal to the faithful.

'Hands up those who want to go!'

The pilgrims revolt with a big show of hands. The tour leader immediately realises it's a battle lost.

'Well isn't that faith in action!' she says with a sour smile that reminds Brendan of Margaret Thatcher during the IRA hunger strike. 'Don't come back to me when it pours from the heavens.'

'We won't,' beams Kathleen triumphantly.

'Front of the basilica so. We'll leave at half-eight.'

'Thank God,' sighs Rosemary, blessing herself.

Brendan desperately needs a drink but first he wants to speak to Irene. She's making even more plans with the Kilbeggan ladies and when he interrupts their confab she turns with a what-do-you-want look in her eyes. The sound barrier has truly been broken.

'Want to go for a coffee?'

'No time,' says she.

'We're not meeting till half-eight.'

'Eleven o'clock Mass is starting.'

'Haven't you just been? Anyway, that's in Italian.'

'What do you want, Brendan?'

'All this holy stuff. It's not you.'

'How do you know what's me!' she says hotly before regaining her cool. 'Your idea, remember? We're not all here for the beer you know.'

He stands aside and lets her pass.

The electrical shop in Medjugorje does not do phone chargers. Nobody does. He finds a telephone kiosk where you can make international calls. They operate it using a meter which he's sure can easily be rigged. It's going to be a rip-off either way so this is no time for long conversations.

The inside of the cabin is an oven and Gary sounds like he's in a badger's sett eating a bag of Tayto. But, thankfully, all is well. From what he says they got the container released from Rosslare and the parts have been delivered to the marina. Everything under control.

'Fiona says you're in Yugoslavia.'

'Well, yeah.'

'What's it like there?'

'Ah, it's different.'

'Give us the number of your hotel.'

'It's not really a . . . look, I'll give you a shout in a couple of days. In any event I'll be back Monday week.'

He hadn't wanted to tell Gary exactly where they were going or why. Mention of boarding the pilgrim express would prompt too many questions.

'Going to get cut off. Good luck!'

He pays and wanders back up the main street looking for a shop. The same waitress stands with a menu on the edge of the path, alluring passers-by. She's every inch the vision she was last night but Brendan has a lot on his mind, in fairness.

'Good morning,' she smiles, bright and bouncy.

Relieved, he sits where he sat yesterday, purely out of habit. *If she's this cheerful I mustn't have made too big a show of myself.*

The headache is nearly gone and he's tempted to pick up where he left off, hair-of-the-dog being a good enough excuse.

'You remember my name?'

'Tina.'

'Tihana. Again beer?'

'A large glass of cold fizzy water, please, with a slice of lemon. And a coffee.'

'Coffee, sparkling water with lemon,' she repeats.

Brendan sits back. Did he just imagine that? His wife holding the locket above her head? Just as well Cathal was their only child because if he had a brother or sister Brendan fears they'd see Cathal every day. They'd be reminded by mannerism, by voice, by posture, by movement, by smiling, laughing, eating, even sleeping and, truth be told, it would be too fucking much.

It's not that they planned it this way – though seeing as Cathal came along within a year of them getting together you could hardly say they planned it at all. Irene always says it had to be Salthill and he's inclined to believe her. She understands these things better than he does.

That bank holiday weekend was their first getaway, Bonnie and Clyde heading west without the guns. Brendan got the loan of a car from a fella he was working for at the time. Drove through a bit of a downpour – granted, it was October – but they couldn't give a toss. Gave them every reason to ignore the seaside attractions and take shelter in their not so salubrious B&B.

They arrived on a Friday night, out the prom near the big diving board. A widow in black – more like a tribute act to Peig Sayers – kept them at the door in lashings of rain to confirm they were married. Yes, they said, trying to keep straight faces. The *bean an tí* glanced at Irene's ringless finger, financial calculations going through her buttery head. A long weekend late season and it pissing from the skies, her re-carpeted B&B full of empty rooms. All factors in young love's favour. Peig knew she might go directly to hell for taking in sinners but if she didn't put them up, she'd be down twenty quid.

'Ye have to pay in advance,' she nodded.

So for the next two days they'd address each other as Mr and Mrs Gogarty whenever Peig was around. There were no other guests. Back in the room they went at it like rabbits. The only time he remembers getting out of bed was to run down for fish and chips and on Saturday afternoon nipping into the casino for a twist on the slots.

Irene won a £5 cherry-laden jackpot and that paid for a few pints. Then back to the B&B for what they told Peig was a late afternoon nap. For such a springy mattress they thought they were quiet enough until reminded by Peig's firm rap on the door that other people – imaginary guests, more like – were trying to sleep. Mrs Gogarty was mortified. Of course she got the gids which meant the cold shoulder over breakfast next morning. When they went to return the keys Peig told them she didn't want them back.

It's not like they had too much opportunity at home. If either had a free house the furthest they'd get was dry humping for fear of someone walking in. Otherwise, a snog under a tree, bit of a grope in the back row at the flicks – they once tried a loveseat in the Green Cinema but when the house lights came on they thought they'd happened upon a Roman orgy.

Anyways, Salthill was the beginning of Cathal. Young lovebirds stuck indoors for two rainy days. No pill, no condoms, sure they'd figure it out as they went. Feel your way, like Braille. Brendan admitted he was no expert in the sack but you wouldn't need a bald head and an unwrapped lollipop to figure out that one of his quick and early withdrawals might not have been quick or early enough.

Packie shuffles along the far side of the road and peers at the sun under his trusty Red Sox visor. He waves over. You can tell the heat is getting to him but the terylene suit is his ensemble for all seasons. He could easily be persuaded to have a proper drink and almost looks disappointed at seeing Brendan served mineral water and coffee. He may not be one to take the lead but is clearly willing to be misled.

'Maybe 'tis a wee bit early,' he ponders. 'Och, I'll have same as that so.'

'Coffee, sparkling water.'

'Aye.'

'With lemon,' adds Brendan, coming back to life.

'Grand wee spot, hai? They're talking up this storm something hectic.'

'Ah, that one Anne-Marie loves a bit of drama.'

'You'll not let me go on me own.'

'I hadn't really thought about it.'

Brendan dips a lump of sugar and watches the coffee seep through.

'Och, they say the Blessed Virgin still appears regular.'

'Oh yeah?'

'To them that sees her.'

'The blind leading the blind, more like. Apparition Hill, scene of the crime.'

'Och, you'll not prove it one way or the other. Faith,' says Packie, 'that's the boy.'

– 21 –

Irene goes back to the basilica to hear Mass in Italian with Kathleen and Julie. There's a heavenly Florentine choir and the cellist's performance is so beautiful, so heart-rending that it brings her to tears. Sometimes music says it all.

It's not that suddenly she started believing in the Gospel According to Kathleen & Julie. She finds them genuinely kind and considerate. Decent people. Simple as that. And, for God's sake, isn't it nice to have a laugh! It's hardly a surprise that as soon as Irene decides to make an effort Brendan is off sulking like a baby. Couldn't he, just once, go with the flow . . .

When he suggested they go for coffee after Mass maybe it was to apologise for his carry-on last night – if he can remember any of it. Brendan is not big on acts of contrition so she wouldn't hold her breath. At this point she doesn't know where he is or what on earth he's up to. He can do what he wants. She is his wife, not his keeper.

So the climb will now go ahead early evening when temperatures get a bit cooler. As tour leader Anne-Marie was clearly miffed at being overruled when she tried to cancel it. Then she saw she simply had to concede – most of the group would have gone whether the tour leader led them or not. Irene is actually looking forward to it. She has already heard all sorts of stories about how climbing the hill can affect people in a positive way. She wonders how it might affect her.

In fact she is beginning to feel a bit silly for having put up all this resistance in the first place. Even if Our Lady doesn't show up in person tonight Irene feels a faint hope that it could be something special, even wonderful. She is open to the possibilities. If it could mean feeling any better afterwards she is definitely open to it!

Hundreds of people mill around the church courtyard through the afternoon. Kathleen and Julie say something about confessions being heard so Irene tags along. Sure why not? In for a penny, in for a pound.

A number of priests sit out, each with a sign indicating whatever languages he can hear all the bad stuff. It looks strange to see people having their confession heard out in the open. Not that you can listen to what anybody is saying but it's just Irene remembers from many years ago such a private act being carried out behind closed doors.

She hasn't done this for so long she wonders if she'll remember what to say. Will she get the order right? Bless me Father for I have sinned . . . Kathleen tells her there is nothing to it and absolutely no reason to be afraid.

'It's just you and God. The priest is only there to help.'

'Oh I don't know. It's been years.'

'Won't it all come back to you?' says Kathleen.

'Like falling off a bicycle.'

The trio choose a priest near the grotto. He's young and slightly heavy. Mid-thirties, she guesses. His sign includes little flags for Croatian, Italian and English. It's more old school than the open air suggests but she finds herself growing a bit nervous in the queue. Like a schoolgirl trying to recite lines for the class play.

'Bless me, Father, for I have sinned . . .'

There's too much ground to cover. Maybe it would be better to skip to the main action. She hasn't killed anyone which, if you include her husband, is pretty good going. She hasn't coveted anyone and doesn't think she has been coveted – and if she was, well they could have let her know.

Oh God, she mutters . . . *I can say I told a few lies, I suppose. Seems like tiddler stuff compared to . . . the faithful here, saving up all their sins and getting great value.*

The priest looks Italian. Must eat a lot of pasta. Irene wonders about his life experience as a qualification for the job. There are plenty in line after her, men and women of all ages from different countries. She is tempted to walk away but decides that maybe it is time to face up to things.

She lets Julie and Kathleen go ahead of her. They arrange to meet up afterwards on Main Street for a post-penitential ice cream. Obviously the centrepiece of the entire pilgrimage will be tonight but now that they've decided to fess up as a sort of palate cleanser, Irene wishes she could think of something more substantial from her past. Just one proper indiscretion. But like what?

My name is Irene Gogarty. I'm hundreds of miles from home because my husband wants us to turn our lives around. Things haven't been great since we lost our twelve-year-old son Cathal.

That's five years ago. The man responsible for all this has just been let out of jail so I'm afraid we're a bit out of sorts. We'd like to make sense of it all, I suppose, try come to terms. That's about it – but, Father, if you don't mind, can we leave forgiveness out of it for now?

Kathleen steps away from the confessional after almost ten minutes. It's hard to imagine her having any Grade A sins to tell. She passes Irene a secret smile of encouragement. Confessors here must get into the nitty gritty because Julie takes just as long to unload. Irene steels herself. The priest fans his face when Julie stands to go. They pass a sisterly glance. Irene takes a deep breath and steps forward.

It's a lot different to what she remembers. First of all it's not dark, it's very bright. The priest sits in front of her and there's no grille to slide back. A box of tissues rests on a low table, some crumpled in the bin.

'*Buongiorno.*'

'Hello.'

'You are from?'

'Ireland.'

He opens his hand as a gesture to sit.

'Bless me, Father, for I have sinned. It's been ages since my last confession.'

'How long?'

'I don't know. Maybe twenty-one, twenty-two years.'

'That is a long time.'

'It is.'

'There is no hurry.'

'Well there's a load of people waiting after me, so . . .'

'If you have not visited Christ for twenty-one years, I think they can wait.'

He pours water into a plastic cup and hands it to her. Part of her cries out for a vodka and tonic. This is all very different, that's for sure.

'Thank you . . . should I say my sins? I'm not claiming to be a saint but it's hard to remember.'

He nods.

'I threw my husband's phone charger into the bushes.'

'Take your time, please.'

She takes another deep breath and blows out slowly. Feeling any apprehension go with it she pulls a tissue to wipe her hands.

'Father, I don't know why I'm here.'

'At confession?'

'Medjugorje.'

'It is a very special place for the Blessed Virgin.'

'Yeah I know. My husband booked it.'

'Maybe we should start at the beginning.'

'Yes.'

'Do you believe in God?'

She sips from the cup and feels water travel down her throat. A church bell rings across the basilica. The priest narrows his bushy eyebrows as he waits for an answer.

'I don't know.'

The young priest sits forward, joining the tips of his fingers as a steeple.

'But you want absolution for your sins.'

'Yes.'

'Why do you come?'

'To start again, I suppose.'

'You say you don't know why you are here. Or if you believe in God.'

'Well there's no point lying, is there?'

This isn't the answer he is looking for. Irene doesn't mean to be awkward but she knows she's being prickly, sniping back. Speaking too quickly, blurting out answers. Whatever it is, the young Italian leans back, as though hopeless cases are outside his terms and conditions. He opens his hands, palms upwards like a question. Confused, she shrugs, shaking her head. He brings her confession to a close and blesses her in Latin.

'Is that it, Father?'

So much for saving those who waver. She steps back to make way for the next imperfect soul. Julie and Kathleen, certified believers with a clean bill of health, got ten minutes apiece. Irene is out in three. Why argue the toss with a steadfast agnostic when more deserving sinners are waiting patiently in line?

The priest has given her no penance at all so she's free as a bird. That's not how she feels. For whatever reason she'd like to talk to Brendan. She decides to take a raincheck on the ice cream and leave the sisters be. Maybe they want to compare sentences. She makes her way through a long queue of penitents and wonders if it's too late for that coffee.

– 22 –

What Irene said got him thinking. She is giving the pilgrimage a chance and here he is, ready to buckle at the first fence. Well that isn't entirely fair – didn't he climb a mountain yesterday? But he admits she does have a point. So he walks over to St James basilica and lights a candle.

It's been a long time since he did this. Truth be told, he doesn't know why he bothered. He says a short, jumbled prayer – the Our Father meets Hail Mary – but his mind is blank. He goes through the motions, just tricking around with a set of words, fairly surprised himself that he can recall snatches of anything at all.

Soon enough he runs out of road with the holy yap. He rambles around town in the afternoon sunshine, then heads for Pansion Regina. Marijana is hanging out washing so he offers to hold the basket. Which makes her laugh.

'You are not businessman. You are gentleman,' she says, peeping around a bed sheet. 'Now I make you coffee.'

He tells her there is no need but she insists. He potters around the living room as she puts the kettle on. He'd settle for instant but they do it differently in Bosnia with small copper pots flame-lit like an old style percolator. Nosing around the sideboard he sees a framed black and white wedding photo. A younger Marijana, thinner in those days.

Like the rest of us.

Happier too.

Like the rest of us.

A moment from his own wedding day comes to mind. At the hotel as they got out of the limo Irene's left shoe fell off. With a bouquet in hand she stumbled unsteadily against the car, free arm on the roof for balance while hopping on her good foot. He can see her head thrown back, laughing deeply. Collecting her shoe he knelt before her with a grin, presenting his thigh as a resting place for her bare ankle.

'Milady,' he said, triggering another round of giddy fun. Back when their life together produced a soundtrack of laughter.

He looks at Marijana's photograph again, her betrothed with a curved moustache, stern-faced, as though bothered by the camera.

'Where is your husband?'

'Mostar,' says she, with a sad sort of face. 'Fighting in army.'

'I heard planes flying over yesterday. Otherwise, you wouldn't know there was anything going on.'

'NATO,' she shrugs. 'No fighting here in Medjugorje but very bad in Mostar. Many people killed. Also Stolac, Caplina . . .'

She pours the coffee. Strong-smelling in a small cup. He can tell Marijana didn't want to mention the war and now she can't stop talking about it. Her husband dodging bullets while she takes breakfast orders from visiting pilgrims. He guesses Marijana would rather be left alone but then feels like he is abandoning her when he asks to take his coffee up to Room 4.

Brendan sits out on the balcony where the warm air is heavy. It's a far cry from Peig's Salthill hideaway. Thinking back to that stuffy B&B is like remembering when they were someone else. Could've done with a bit more time than they gave themselves. Seeing as they had never read the parenthood manual it took a while to realise that things all happened a bit too quickly. He wouldn't like anyone to get him wrong now – he was pure thrilled when the little fella came along – but he now wonders how ready they were.

He was twenty-one, she was nineteen. Both of them had lost a parent by then. When Brendan told his father that Irene was pregnant he remembers his dad lit the pipe and said he was after getting himself into something he wouldn't be able to get out of. His mother, a gentle soul, would have been kinder. She would have fawned over her only grandchild something terrible and happily spoiled the boy to death had she got the chance.

Brendan never met Bill, Irene's dad, but a true gent by all accounts. The pity of it was that the two parents who passed away would have cared a lot more than the two left behind.

Irene was nervous about breaking the news at home so they arranged to sidetrack her mother before dropping the bombshell. They took Agnes to the Royal Marine Hotel in Dun Laoghaire. Fancy afternoon tea to soften the blow.

Agnes was still out of kilter over losing Bill and she took their announcement with the same foreboding she tuned into the weather forecast. In fact, she said nothing except to ask the waitress to bring a pot of hot water.

Just in case Agnes suspected Brendan was going to do a runner they explained to her that they planned to get married the following year. What's more, Brendan promised to find a place for them to live so they would be all ready for the new arrival.

'I see,' nodded Agnes. 'I see.'

Irene had no interest in going back to college. She wanted to mind the baby at home, wherever that may be. Meanwhile Agnes would be living on her own in a three-bedroom house in Chapelizod. She preferred it that way and never gave them the option to move in temporarily. It was Dublin, 1975. Unmarried, Brendan and Irene would be first-time parents. They'd have to live in sin somewhere else.

Not that it mattered in the end. Brendan was making regular money as a chippie but they knew things were going to be tight enough. Irishtown was small but grand. Irene, for some reason, always called it Ringsend. A terraced house. The downstairs flat. They got by and within a few years they made the big move to Lennox Place, Portobello.

Cathal's big entrance seemed to knock Irene back. Not in an immediate way but for a while she lost a bit of fizz. Minding the baby could leave her beyond tired. And easily upset. Brendan would come home and lift the young fella overhead, rejuvenated in the role of daddy playing helicopters. With Irene's energy already flagging her patience was equally short. Even after the baby was off to sleep Brendan couldn't surprise her or wrap his arms around her or nuzzle her or make her laugh the way he used to.

Bit like the way it is now, he reflects.

Their rabbit days were over, until further notice. No chance they'd be locking themselves away in any weekend B&B for the foreseeable. Hard going, fatigued by sleeplessness. For something so commonplace it was strange, in retrospect, that nobody ever talked about it. With a remnant of pride Brendan reckoned the three of them did as well as any makeshift little family in the circumstances.

Afternoon sun prickles his skin so he goes inside and flops on the bed. He dozes off and on, feeling groggy, his tongue bitter with the aftertaste of Bosnian coffee. Irene arrives back from town. She's also tired from the heat. Falling onto the bed she flicks her flip-flops to the floor.

'I went to confession,' she says with a yawn.

'What – why?'

'Thought I'd clear the slate.'

'What did you get?'

'He wouldn't give me the all-clear until I signed along the dotted line.'

She lies back and closes her eyes. Both are quiet for a moment.

'I hope you know all this talk of thunderstorms is completely over the top,' says Brendan.

'Showers can be heavy here in summer, that's all.'

'Ah yer wan is a bit of a drama queen.'

'Are you coming on the climb?'

'Yeah, suppose.'

'Oh,' says Irene, eyes reopening. 'Alright.'

– 23 –

The group meets up at St James just before half-eight. The sun is beginning to set but you can feel the town baked from the heat of a long day. It looks like most of the first-timers have taken Anne-Marie's fire and brimstone to heart. They're so fully waterproofed you'd swear they never saw rain back home.

If the world is about to end it's like the Perpetuals have the inside track. The sight of Packie coming out of a souvenir shop with a bright yellow poncho brings a smile to Irene's face. It's wrapped tightly in plastic and he looks a bit puzzled at how to unpack it.

The Front Row and other Perpetuals are kitted out with climbing sticks and bottles of water. Ever since Jack Charlton went on about it last year at the World Cup in America Irish people seems to have become obsessed with dehydration. No one bothered telling the pilgrims that even after sunset it won't be particularly cold out here, whether it buckets down or not. Nobody is taking any chances – except the Gogartys, of course.

From the basilica they start walking along a path that winds through local vineyards at the back of the town. The soil is rust red and rises as dust that leaves everybody's shoes covered in ferric clay. The walk begins to stretch the group out into a thinner line. Irene is up near the front with her new besties, the Kilbeggan sisters.

Julie presumes she found confession 'cathartic' and Irene isn't bothered to put her right. But, as Kathleen and her confessor pointed out, the specifics are not particularly important. Irene is here. This is a special place so, gathering all her strength as a grieving mother, she resolves to put her heart and soul into this. Put it down to auto-suggestion; all you have to do is open your heart and let the holy spirit flow through.

Brendan hovers around the middle, waiting for the Kilkenny man to catch up. He wants to hear more about these fighter planes and this lad obviously knows a thing or two about aviation. Instead, he gets Anne-Marie, her Perpetual Succour umbrella deployed as a walking stick. She seems to have recovered from Kathleen's ambush.

'Did you not bring anything, Brendan – not even a poncho?'

'Living on the edge, Anne-Marie.'

'It is forecast. Don't say I didn't warn you.'

'In fairness, I could not say you didn't.'

They stay in step.

'I love this walk,' she says, surveying what Brendan would agree is a grand route for a stroll. 'These fields haven't changed over the years. Do you know they make their own wine here? Plum brandy as well.'

'Must give the brandy a whirl.'

'As long as you're able to handle it,' she adds in a way that tells him she has spies all over town. 'How are you enjoying Medjugorje?'

'Well, like you'd say yourself, it's not something to enjoy.'

'Is it what you expected?'

'In fairness, Anne-Marie, I didn't know what to expect. That's the truth.'

'And Irene?'

'Oh she's taking it in alright. In her own way.'

Reaching the foot of the mountain they gather in a semi-circle. You can tell that Anne-Marie has given this spiel a million times before. Down to names, dates and pregnant pauses, she has it off by heart, told with the conviction of a door-to-door saleswoman. But this faith-laden pitch soon overloads Irene's low threshold for blather. She doesn't care about the history lesson and asks herself why in God's name is she so keen to climb a steep hill in Bosnia.

She doesn't know what she's waiting for. Maybe God or the Blessed Virgin will enter her soul and make everything okay. Heal her broken heart. They say that's what can happen to people who climb Apparition Hill. These are facts – or so they say. Sort of facts. All these stories of people who were at death's door coming to Medjugorje; within days their tumour clears up – miraculously! No obvious medical explanation for any of it. Doctors and specialists in clinics all over the world struck dumb by what they see, X-ray machines immediately despatched for service and possibly overhaul before legal letters start flowing in.

Irene is not the gullible kind yet she finds no reason to doubt any of this. They say miracles *do* happen if you believe. Or maybe if you're lucky. She can't tell why the Vatican is still iffy about Medjugorje. Rosemary says the Blessed Virgin visited in 1981 when Yugoslavia was still a Communist country. And Communists, as the history books say, are devout atheists. So, according to Rosemary, the Vatican didn't want Communists running off with Our Lady. That's the main reason Rome would never give Medjugorje the green light.

'Commies don't deserve miracles!' laughs Brendan when she re-tells the story back at Pansion Regina. 'That's not very Christian, is it? Anyways, Yugoslavia isn't Communist any more – actually, it's not even Yugoslavia.'

If going up this hill tonight makes her feel any better – or does her any good at all – she'd call it a miracle in its own right. That might not make headlines in the *Meath Chronicle* unless they put Before and After photos of Irene on the front page. Captioned: *Before miracle* – maybe an unflattering CCTV shot of her being ejected from TJ's; *After miracle* – Irene Gogarty beside a candle, smiling beatifically with full rouge and lipstick. At peace. It may not be in quite the same league as stopping cancer or healing brain tumours but it'd mean a lot to her.

She reckons Brendan feels he has to do the climb because, even if he's lost a bit of enthusiasm since Dublin airport, wasn't this whole trip his brainwave? Or else he's just trying to make amends for his drunken performance the other night. If she was being perfectly honest she doesn't blame him. She can't say it out loud but there are times she feels so fed up she wouldn't mind going out and getting shitfaced too. Might even be a bit of crack if they did it together some time.

They used to do that in the early days before fun went out of bounds. The thought of it makes her feel like she's talking about different people, different lives. The first few years with Cathal were tough enough but, once things settled down, days rarely passed without a laugh or a cuddle.

Obviously their world has since changed. If by some chance they did venture out together, AC, and you added booze to the equation, you could be sure it'd end in tears. They have it down to a fine art. Tearing strips off each other for sport, bringing up favoured old arguments. Weak spots held in reserve as special targets. After twenty-one years they know every short-cut to each other's deepest wounds.

Still, she's genuinely glad Brendan is tagging along and not moping around Pansion Regina. If spiritual lightning doesn't strike her tonight she would settle for it to stun her husband as a runner-up prize. Hold the *Chronicle* front page for *his* Before and After photos. She finds it difficult to imagine Brendan smiling beatifically – unless Meath won the All-Ireland – but if either of them is a little bit happier after this, wouldn't it help? Instead of holding each other down, levelling one another inch by inch, blow by blow.

She can't believe she's getting excited about the climb. They are standing around waiting for the lecture to finish and she just wants to get started. She feels jittery, impatient. Her feet start tapping. She wishes Anne-Marie would hurry up.

' . . . and the children were afraid but they came back on the third day and Our Lady spoke to them. She gave them a holy message: Peace, peace and only peace. Which is why Our Lady is revered here as Mary, Queen of Peace.'

'What language was Our Lady speaking?' asks Packie.

'She spoke to the visionaries in Serbo-Croatian but they also heard her speak Latin.'

'Be the hokey . . .'

The Kilkenny woman wants to know what the Blessed Virgin looked like. Anne-Marie is ready for this one.

'The children described her as a young woman of incredible beauty. She wore a long grey dress with a white veil and a crown of twelve stars. Sky blue eyes, long black hair and rosy cheeks. When she appeared, it was as though she floated on a cloud.'

It sounds to Brendan that when the tourist season calms down Bosnia should enter Our Lady into the Rose of Tralee. He's tempted to catch Irene's eye but can see she isn't in the mood for him acting the can. When she gets into that frame of mind he wouldn't fancy being the one to stand in her way.

Anne-Marie, thank heavens, winds up the talk.

'This is often a highlight for pilgrims to Medjugorje and I know you dearly wanted to do the climb tonight. When our pilgrims speak as one, The Mother of Perpetual Succour Tours has to listen. And as your tour leader, I take that responsibility very seriously. Just be careful on the rocks. Even when it's dry, they can be slippy so take your time. The Blessed Virgin will wait for you.'

At last.

The Perpetuals all have their rosary beads at the ready. When Anne-Marie fires the starting gun it's no surprise that the Kilbeggan sisters lead the charge. There's a stony path worn up the hill but the rocks are loose so you have to pay attention. Kathleen is up the slope like a gazelle and there's no way Irene would be able to keep up with her. Devotion can make an Olympic athlete out of middle age.

The hill sub-divides into stations of the cross. They will say the Rosary as a group so at each station whoever is first (Kathleen, inevitably) will have to wait for whoever is last (Rosemary, usually). Irene pulls from her pocket rosary beads Julie gave her and selects the first bead as they start the ascent. She is open to the experience, her plaintive heart gaping so wide that the breeze itself could blow right through it.

– 24 –

It is unquestionably the main event – unless, of course, the visionary shows up tomorrow and plays a stormer. Brendan considers it a good yarn about kids playing up the mountain when Our Lady came out of the clouds. He has to resist asking why no one reported a UFO. Anne-Marie tells every twist and turn with such gushing sincerity – Our Lady walking on air! – that the Skibbereen redhead must believe all this stuff herself. She has to! Otherwise, all's Brendan can say is he'd hate to meet her across a poker table.

The Perpetuals are definitely up for it. He sees that Rosemary has a special stick to lean on and is seriously out of puff each time she comes to a stop. If this was a race you could have novelty bets, something like the Grand National where you can throw a few quid on which nags will have to be put down by the end of it. One thing sure – if Rosemary gets a heart attack up here they'll never be able to carry her back. Might have to wrap her in ponchos and roll her down the hill.

Brendan found it enjoyable enough chatting with Anne-Marie on the walk through the vineyards. She could talk for Ireland, he reckons, but her preaching leaves him cold. Considering she wanted to call off the climb he has to hand it to her; she saw the writing on the wall. Denying the devout front row tickets to the miraculous can enflame the meekest pilgrim.

He chides himself. He's not here to pick holes, even if she is overcooking things now, just like she tends to when forecasting weather. She told the Perpetuals how scarified the kids were at first when they saw the Blessed Virgin. Sure, why wouldn't they be, he muses, especially if she was walking on air . . .

Fifty years earlier a few locals in Medjugorje were clearly ahead of the posse. Knowing that Our Lady would be dropping out of the clouds – they *knew;* they just didn't know *when* – they erected a 25-foot high wooden cross to mark out a landing spot for her on the rather unimaginatively named Cross Mountain. With the navigational aid securely in place you could say their job was done. Then, five decades later than advertised, she shows up on Apparition Hill. Half a mile away!

He thinks of the Allied soldiers parachuting over Normandy on D-Day only for one of the paratroopers to get caught on the steeple of Caen cathedral. Maybe Our Lady wasn't great at reading maps. Maybe it was foggy that day. If she landed where they asked, all she had to do was wait for some barefooted Yugoslavian shepherd to spot her on Cross Mountain. Then she could make a big entrance into town without scaring the shit out of the poor kids.

Whatever the reasons behind her losing her bearings it means that Apparition Hill is the big cheese in Medjugorje and Cross Mountain is very definitely Number Two. You wouldn't blame the men who erected the cross for being a bit put out by Our Lady overflying their well-crafted marker. And had she landed on Cross Mountain instead of Apparition Hill the town would surely have kept them in plum brandy for the rest of their days. *They'll think twice next time they're asked to build something for nothing.*

Brendan knows he is still in semi-disgrace himself, like the black sheep on the fringe of a very woolly flock. Half the pilgrims are giving him the cold shoulder over his late night bevvies and a clumsy entrance he doesn't quite remember. What if I was walking on air, he wonders. Would they talk to me then?

Now that the Perpetuals are lined up for the big event they would think he's taking the mickey if he starts querying why Our Lady landed in the wrong place. Nor does he feel it's the right time to moan. He feels an occasional twinge in his back but feels he's already drawn enough attention to himself. Better off saying nothing and suffer in silence. When they reach the first station the field has lengthened out. To give Rosemary her due, each time they saddle up she is ready and willing to resume the climb.

Brendan can see that Irene is off doing her own thing. It's like he has become invisible. As though she came here alone. He notices she's wearing the rosary beads Julie gave her. When they approach the next station he offers his hand to help her through a tricky gap. But she pulls back, determinedly. Obviously wants to go her own way. Solo. So she can say she's doing this for herself, by herself.

Everybody seems to be getting in the mood at altitude. It's full-on prayers at each station. He is amazed to see Irene mouthing the words. He knows she doesn't know the Rosary but she's carrying it off here better than karaoke night in TJ's. If she can pull off a show like this, how, he wonders, can you tell which of the Perpetuals isn't faking it?

Packie is holding his own. No surprise he's in his favourite suit and trusty Reeboks. Okay, he lost his nerve on the weather warnings, the plastic poncho stuffed in his jacket pocket. He must feel a bit stupid carrying it around on such a glorious evening but Brendan does his best to stop annoying people for a while.

Other pilgrims come down the hill as the Perpetuals ascend. They make stops for long slugs of water, like camels. Brendan, semi-curious, keeps his eye out but does not spot anybody walking on air. And when the Perpetuals reach the fourth station they have to wait for another group – Polish speakers – to finish up praying before Kathleen and Julie kick in with a refrain. Same happens at the fifth station, which is just a bit much. It's like teeing off for a decent 18 holes only to get stuck behind slowcoaches who won't let you play through.

There aren't any bins up the mountain so they'll have to bring all their empties back down with them. He doesn't see any toilets either. Brendan doesn't claim to be a Holy Joe but he wouldn't be too comfortable peeing on a holy site. Never mind a Number Two. That said, when you have to go, you have to go. God forbid it comes to that but if it does, Brendan hopes Jesus would understand; naturally, the Virgin Mary would have to turn away.

Rosemary is visibly glad for rest stops but Brendan can see she's getting her second wind. He's ready to change his bet. She'll finish strongly, she could yet even place well. By the sixth station Brendan has stopped thinking about all the reasons he should not be here. He concentrates on the climb. A steady path, the next step. Idle conversation has dried up around him. There are no unfunny jokes, no insightful comparisons between Medjugorje and Ballinspittle. Everybody's thoughts and intentions have withdrawn into private space, harnessed by the physical challenge of the stony ascent. He wouldn't boast but it dawns on him that he is giving this a real go. He even throws in a few partial Our Fathers and Hail Marys but draws the line at miming the Rosary.

Each time they pause at a station he gathers his breath. When Rosemary sees he has brought nothing with him she passes over a water bottle. He unscrews the cap, swallows gratefully and hands it back.

'Thanks.'

Rosemary's face is flushed red but she is no longer a point of ridicule. Her resilience now impresses him and he realises she will probably reach the top before he does. Perspiration trickles down his neck and mats his shirt to his back. By way of distraction, the sun is slipping steadily from its zenith. It hangs suspended like a big orange tennis ball. The more it drops the more the sky floods red. He sees Packie grab a snap with the disposable. One to add to his tank, basilica and sunset collection, something to regale the neighbours back home in the twin citadels of Donegal.

– 25 –

D ust rises in the evening heat.

O my Jesus, forgive us our sins. Save us from the fires of hell.

Lead all souls to heaven, especially those in need of thy mercy . . .

The hill is steeper than Irene expects. Stones slide where she steps so she zigzags a path by looking for bigger rocks on which to place her weight. She wonders how many hundred thousand feet have been this way before her. She fingers the beads as she climbs, listening to Irish accents, adding her own whisper to group prayer. Brendan is hovering nearby but this is a private journey. She resolves to find her own way. Her husband will have to do the same.

The Virgin Mary lost her son so she knows what it's like. They must have a lot in common, plenty to chat about. Irene wants to feel her presence. Didn't she even watch her only child nailed to a cross? Irene's imagination does that for her . . .

Hail Mary, full of grace, the Lord is with thee . . .

The fourth sorrowful mystery, the Carrying of the Cross. When Our Lady appeared to children here a second time it was said she carried the baby Jesus in her arms. Maybe the visionary will tell them more tomorrow. Like Our Lady had a superpower that enabled her to turn back the clock.

Thanks to the baby Jesus getting a second chance at life, it meant all the agonies left behind on Calvary would never be revisited. Jesus – if that was his name second time round – would have a clean slate, a clear run. When this thought dawns on Irene the possibility startles her.

If only I could do that!

She beams joyfully but, like a deep sea diver fearful of reaching the surface too quickly, she checks herself against the neutral mood of the mountain. She cannot get ahead of herself and consciously slows down. Dropping back, the pilgrimage resembles a funeral procession where repeating the same words over and over offers its own comfort. Kathleen likes to tell Irene never to underestimate the strength of prayer. She says you are talking of an almighty power that is limitless when unleashed in a sacred place like this.

'Faith is redeemed,' she likes to say.

And maybe she's right. Irene would be glad to believe as she leans into the incline. The sun has set for another day but her eyes are fixed on angular white rocks beneath her feet. She is conscious of the scent of pine and can hear her own breathing, air caught between her lungs and an ancient verbal formula carrying a plea for help.

'Alright, dear?'

She looks around. It's Julie. Irene smiles and moves on. She doesn't want to be distracted into conversation because you need to be focused and ready if the Blessed Virgin drops by. There's no time to talk. Fifth Sorrowful Mystery, the Crucifixion. Start again, at the beginning.

Hail Mary, full of grace, the Lord is with thee . . .

The ground evens out for a stretch, then rises again. Third Glorious Mystery, the Descent of the Holy Spirit. Mary must be near.

Irene is open, she is ready.

O my Jesus, forgive us our sins. Save us from the fires of hell . . .

There is a rumble far off and Irene feels the first drops. Rosemary reaches for her bag, the Perpetuals' hillside chorus rapidly diluting. At first she thinks it might be NATO planes again but a second heavenly growl, still far away, shakes the mountain air.

'Waterproofs!' commands Anne-Marie, unfolding her umbrella. 'Didn't I tell ye!'

There's a scramble for whatever people have brought with them. Packie pulls out his sealed poncho. He rips the plastic and opens it out. A yellow hood and three holes. It's like climbing into a rubbish bag. He pokes his head through an arm before the Kilkenny woman helps him out.

Kathleen is more concerned about Irene than Irene is about herself. She offers to spread her windcheater like a double cape but Irene doesn't feel the need. Within seconds the rain has arrived, dousing her hair, heavy blobs gluing her blouse to her skin. Brendan soaks it up too but he's used to standing on wet terraces at football matches. A modest flood is nothing new.

Prayers resume, interrupted by another roll of thunder and a crack of lighting. Anne-Marie is a bit nervous about staying out on the mountain. Privately, she tries desperately to recall key clauses in the Perpetuals' insurance cover. Acts of God are not covered, which is a little ironic, but there's really nowhere to hide so they press on. The stones are now very slippery and water trickles down from the mountain top in rivulets. Standing at either end of the saintly huddle Irene and Brendan are already drenched.

Hail Mary, full of grace, the Lord is with thee . . .

It's not chilly but the wind gathers across the mountain to unload rain in sheets. They make it to the last Glorious Mystery and stand before the Virgin Mary, supplicant and ceramic.

Irene is ready. She speaks directly to her.

Hail Mary, full of grace . . .

Our Lady does not answer.

Raindrops collect, running along the statue's nose and ears before dropping to the ground. Some of the pilgrims, including Kathleen and Julie, drop to their knees, oblivious to the downpour. Who knew what deep hopes were brought here by the planeload? Brendan spots one of the Strabane girls wedge a small piece of paper into the stone pedestal. How will Our Lady be able to read her handwriting if the paper gets wet?

Irene is saturated right through. Her fingers rest on the final bead.

O my Jesus, forgive us our sins. Save us from the fires of
hell . . .

The clouds are a mixture of dark and light, hurtling across the valley. There have been so many stories of Our Lady's kind face appearing from the heavens that Irene finds herself glancing skywards for clues. She is ready. Isn't this Apparition Hill! The scudding clouds quickly form new shapes. Irene sees them come together forming a face or certainly an expression – just momentarily – with dark spots as eyes, a nose and mouth. She wants to cry out. But it's not the shy, kind, sympathetic visage; it's Patrick James McGeedy, no question. A thin blue line in the sky recreates McGeedy's smirk when he passed them on his way from court.

She looks around but can't find Brendan. Before she gets a chance to point out what she has seen the clouds tangle up again. The image is suddenly lost, distorting this way and that like a hall of mirrors. The heavens turn grey, the clouds sweep from the east to empty out. Irene reminds herself she is ready but fears that any opportunity may be evaporating.

Our Lady does not look her way.

Irene holds the same upward gaze, her neck fixed at 60 degrees under the statue. Water runs off the plaster like Our Lady has a runny nose. Caught in the wind, the Perpetuals' prayer breaks up into a susurrus of murmurs.

The Blessed Virgin is a no-show.

Irene suddenly steps forward, her hands outstretched.

'Tell me,' she implores. 'Tell me you listen!'

The wind whistles in response, rising slowly. Irene tosses her beads aside. 'Can you hear me?' she shrieks. 'Are you listening at all?'

Brendan breaks free from the group and tries to take her arm but Irene pulls free. Clearly he did not see what she saw. He did not see clouds and did not see signs. McGeedy's smirk was reserved only for her.

'It's okay, Irene!'

'It's not okay – he followed us here!'

'Who?'

'Leave me alone!'

Her husband reaches for her again but she jerks away, slipping on loose stones. She tumbles sideways and breaks her fall with an outstretched arm. Kathleen and Julie wonder if their new friend has lost it. Half a minute passes before Irene finds her knees, a penitent beggar in tableau.

'Do you care? Or are you there at all!'

The Blessed Virgin gazes blankly through the deluge with an unwavering smile. Irene's low, plaintive cry rumbles from within, starting from her gut and gathers force until she simply runs out of air. Inhaling deeply and unevenly she looks up once again to point accusingly at the statue.

'If you care about children give me a sign!' she wails.

She remains where she kneels, in a despondent pool of water. Brendan leans over to pull his wife to her feet but she pushes him away with a baleful moan. He crouches, uncertain about trying again. He steps back and says no more, his head bowed like a wretched sinner.

– 26 –

The bleeding has stopped. Brendan finishes disinfecting her cut knees and puts on the plaster Marijana gave them.

'I don't think we'll be asked back,' she says.

The rain clears and they sit on the balcony, showered and dried. Brendan pours two glasses of plum brandy, local hooch he picked up in a souvenir shop that specialises in ashtrays and crucifixes. It's strong tack but bearable as a painkiller. Irene tries hers and throws a face.

'Where did you get that?'

'Down the town. You don't have to drink it y'know.'

She lights a cigarette and sits quietly. She takes another sip, gazing in the direction of Apparition Hill. Brendan can tell she won't be too bothered if they never return.

'The desperate will find what they're looking for whether it's there or not.'

He detects a bluntness in her voice. Something mean and cruel.

'They need help. Same as us.'

'Ah don't go twisting it, Bren. You say yourself they're so gullible. Sure Kathleen told me she was full of doubts. She does the vigil one night and hey presto! She has a vision. Hook, line and sinker.'

'Where?'

'Walking back to wherever they were staying. Here, probably.'

'But where did the vision appear?

'Oh, who's gullible now?

'Irene . . .'

'Where do you think! Up in the sky. Blue-white light in the shape of the Virgin Mary's face. Oh, blue-white – like Daz?'

'I'd say she loved that.'

'God is good, she said. Well, the jury's still out on that one.'

She stubs out her cigarette and throws it away. Suddenly everything goes dark. Another power cut. It makes no difference, really. Being unseen might even make it easier to talk. Irene lights the candle Marijana left out when they arrived. The flame sputters to life.

'They both said they're going to pray for me.'

'The Kilbeggan ladies?'

'Like adding an item to their shopping list. They're probably still up there, half-drowned, having a good oul chat with the Blessed Virgin herself.'

Brendan doesn't like her tone. He doesn't really know what to say so he tells her things will be fine.

'Would you please stop saying that!' she snaps. 'Seriously, Bren, bringing us here. What were you thinking?'

'I thought it might help.'

'So we came to be found? Get a sign. An answer?'

'It helped others.'

'We are lost.'

She drains her glass, holds it out for more. Ever since they boarded the plane from Dublin he has questioned why he put them through this. What *was* he thinking? He feels the tug of an inward shrug, like he has given up on providing rote answers. He tells her if she wants to go home they can leave tomorrow.

Irene sits pensively and drinks. Then she grabs the candle and takes off. She reappears barefoot in the yard below where she picks her way through wet bushes.

'What are you doing?' he calls from the balcony. 'Irene!'

He's not in the mood for playing games and he wishes she'd stop this messing around. They can stay or they can go. At this point he really doesn't care. He's had enough. He refills his glass. Irene comes back upstairs and places something on the table. He can't see clearly in the half-shadows but can make out the metal pins. His phone charger.

'I was mad with you. Sorry.'

The adaptor is damp. He recalls when turning the room upside-down she never owned up to taking it, even when he asked her directly.

'Look, Irene, what do you want to do?'

She lights another cigarette and inhales deeply.

'Swap places with Cathal,' she replies, blowing out smoke like a long sigh. 'That's what I'd like to do.'

Brendan does not know what to say. He eventually breaks the silence.

'Cathal is gone.'

With the rain stopped it is peculiarly quiet, possibly more so because of the darkness around them. Only then does Brendan pick out small faraway sounds. Had Marijana not mentioned anything about the fighting he would have taken them to be fireworks or a car backfiring. Now he recognises them as small explosions in the distance, maybe mortars.

'Let's rent a car. Get out of here for a few days. Somewhere different. Just get a car and drive.'

'Isn't there a war going on?' says Irene. 'Why don't we drive there?'

'Don't be daft. We can avoid Sarajevo and places where it's kicked off. Head the other way out the coast. Beaches, boats. Go for a swim.'

'There's a war going on and we came here to find peace.'

'We had to try something,' he says, towelling the charger.

She gazes in the direction of Apparition Hill.

'I wonder are the Kilbeggan ladies praying for us. Or have they forgotten.'

'I'm sure they remember.'

'Good for us if they do.'

'And why wouldn't they? They have faith.'

'Good for them,' she says, sounding mean again. 'Because I don't.'

– 27 –

Brendan scours Medjugorje for rental cars but none are available and there haven't been for months. Then he asks Marijana about a leaf-strewn orange Lada in the driveway, which probably belongs to her husband. She says it's been parked up for a long time. When Brendan starts it up the engine backfires and sends birds scattering.

Marijana agrees to rent it to them. She says getting petrol could be a problem but Brendan says they'll take their chances. They coolly ignore the hubbub building among the Perpetuals. Anne-Marie sent them into orbit when she confirmed the meeting with the visionary will go ahead at 4 pm in the shaded area behind the basilica.

'That wee lassie might have something to say,' suggests Packie.

'We'll see,' replies Brendan, feeling a little guilty about leaving his friend in the lurch. Duplicity does not sit so well with him.

That said, the Gogartys are on their way and it feels good to be moving again. The rattle inside the Lada is almost deafening and you can see the road surface through holes in the floor. Brendan calls it classic air-conditioning.

'To be honest I don't know how far this banger is going to get us,' he shouts above the din.

The roads are quite narrow, more like secondary roads back home. They see a sign for a place called Mostar which shows a picture of an old Ottoman bridge. Brendan isn't sure if the bridge is still standing or if it's been blown up. They see other signs for Sarajevo, which sounds very exotic. It could be lovely but any time it's on the news it's dead bodies on the street or ornate Turkish-style buildings in flames. They decide to give it a miss.

The plan, if you could call it that, is they'll keep their distance from the war and see if they can make it as far as the coast. Brendan thinks they should head for Montenegro which, for some reason, is still in Yugoslavia. He says it's cut off from everywhere else, which, to Irene, sounds perfect.

There are hardly any other cars on the road. They see four soldiers in a jeep, then a white station wagon with big UN letters taped onto the bonnet. Half an hour later they pass a couple of army trucks grinding uphill in the opposite direction. Most of the houses have bullet holes in the walls. Some are burnt out. Many look abandoned. Then they come to an unnamed town where every single building is destroyed.

'Don't see too many tourists here.'

'No.'

'Feels like a ghost town. Do you think we should turn back, Bren?'

'It'll be alright when we get to the coast.'

It's frightening to see a place like this. Not one house or shop standing and not a sinner about. A stray pup, a grey mongrel terrier, scampers down the street looking for food. As soon as it hears the Lada coming it runs off, its tail drooped low, the poor, nervous creature hungry and sad.

Their banger makes a terrific racket going up another hill – and there are a lot of hills around here. They have to shout to be heard so Irene chooses not to talk. The handle is broken on Brendan's side so he's getting fried behind the glass even though all the other windows are open.

Irene leans out, taking in the sun. She lets the breeze blow through her hair. Such a summer feeling. She sings loudly into the wind but stops self-consciously. Chugging through another deserted town feels like dancing in a graveyard. They pass red bunting with a skull and crossbones. A warning to stay away.

'Must be landmines,' says Brendan. 'Better not spend a penny in there.'

All these strange sights and so much emptiness to take in. It feels pitiful but it's hard to look away. Nothing but destruction for miles and miles.

'Rosemary has been in Bosnia four or five times. And Kathleen and Julie. I wonder do they have any idea what's going on?'

'Well, in fairness, you wouldn't see much in Medjugorje.'

'Not unless you're a visionary.'

They know they are missing out on the big face-to-face this afternoon. Having said nothing to Anne-Marie before they snuck off they know it will not improve her blood pressure. Reconstituted as a one-woman search party they can imagine her wandering town in an unkempt state, muttering 'twenty-five' to herself like a stuck record. That she successfully produced the visionary for a guest appearance was like presenting the Perpetuals with salvation itself. Only for the troublesome Gogartys to bugger off ungratefully into the sunset.

'She'll never forgive us,' remarks Brendan.

'No.'

In truth, however, they are no longer curious about Apparition Hill. They consider it someone else's miracle.

A couple of hours out of town every car or truck on the road is an army or UN vehicle. It's all so empty. There's nobody walking the road. They don't see anybody working in the fields, no animals either. It only dawns on Irene afterwards – how could you graze sheep if the hills are littered with landmines?

'It's beautiful countryside,' she shouts.

'Yeah.'

'I mean, it'd be just lovely if it wasn't destroyed – wait, what was that?'

He jams on the brakes – no fear of anything behind – and reverses to a brick monument by the side of the road. There's a small flag with red and white squares and a couple of old flowers wilted in a small vase. They stay in the car, observing out the open window like they are on safari.

'Probably a soldier, by the looks of it. Might've got killed at this very spot.'

Irene reads a small handwritten board at the foot of it.

'Andrej Jedvaj. If that's how you pronounce it. Twelfth of the tenth, nineteen ninety-four?'

'Jedvaj? Not too many Jedvajs in Nobber, hah? Born eighth of the eleventh, nineteen seventy-seven.

'Eighth of the eleventh? Cathal was the eleventh of the eighth.'

'November eighth, nineteen seventy-seven.'

'This fella's just one year older.'

She notices Brendan bless himself so Irene does the same. The thought of a boy soldier dying by the side of a country road fills the car with a heavy sadness. They pass another little monument, a clearly marked gravestone with three young faces etched into black marble. They don't stop this time.

'You know, last night there was no blue-white vision for me up that hill. Just yerman's face appearing through the clouds, smirking. Don't ask me why it was his face up there. If anything, it should have been Cathal's.'

She pauses, watching vacantly as the countryside glides by.

'Bren, remember Father Gormley used that phrase, evil let loose.'

'Evil pure let loose.'

'Feels like that here.'

'It does.'

'Why are we supposed to forgive?'

'We don't have to.'

'Good,' she says, relieved. 'The Kilbeggan ladies can have the Blessed Virgin any time they like but if I'm going to have a vision, I want it to be our little boy smiling, laughing. Happy! He has to be happy,' she insists, rolling up the window. 'That's not too much to ask for, is it?'

Hunched over the wheel Brendan drives on without a word, his eyes fixed on the empty road ahead.

Part Three

Montenegro

– 28 –

If you don't count the UK, it's the first time Brendan has ever driven in Europe. A car is a car but it feels different to him, not because of foreign road signs or because he's on the right hand side of the road. He just knows he's not at home.

Apart from the sound of distant shelling you wouldn't notice much out of the ordinary in Medjugorje. But as soon as they leave the city boundary it's a different picture. What war has done to this country! Some places are worse than others but the Gogartys could never imagine the extent of damage in many of the towns they pass through.

They keep going inland for quite a while before there's even a glimpse of the sea. Maybe that's when things will return to normal. Seeing deserted villages and a landscape of such devastation prompts Irene to question whether this is a good idea. Brendan tells her it will be grand. If he keeps saying this he might believe it himself.

After crossing the mountains for several hours they come to the border. Another barber's pole across a deserted road. A female soldier appears from a portacabin like they have interrupted her favourite TV programme. She sees the Lada's registration plate and presumes them to be Bosnian. The driver's window won't open so Brendan springs the door. The soldier jumps back nervously, as though anticipating a weapon in his hand. Seeing raw fear cross her face he freezes apologetically, arms raised. The soldier launches into a tirade of angry remonstration. He hasn't a clue what she is saying but he's clearly in her bad books.

'Eyer-land,' he says, pointing at himself and Irene.

The Emerald Isle doesn't seem to ring any bells with the glaring soldier. She demands their passports and checks the car reg again, takes another long look at them and disappears into the portacabin. Minutes later she reappears and hands back their passports without a word. A smudge on their passports says they have left Bosnia.

'They must round up the sulkiest whores in the entire defence forces and pack them off for border duty,' mutters Brendan.

Same thing two hundred yards later, entering the Federal Republic of Yugoslavia. Conversation is at a premium. The FRY soldier squints at their documents and spits into the dirt. Maybe he was watching the same programme.

A customs officer appears and points at the boot.

'Open,' he says.

Brendan can't find the release button in the car so he inserts the key. A pair of mildewed ski boots lie in the corner, presumably belonging to Marijana's husband. War has disrupted many things here, big and small.

'Go,' says the bored customs officer.

It's hilly for the next hour. Brendan reckons the temperature gauge is stuck because the engine sounds like a high pitched whine. The fuel gauge isn't much better but they'll definitely need petrol soon. The radiator could probably do with a refill too. The first couple of garages they pass are closed but a toothless farmer and his son point to where they can get petrol. Smuggled juice from Romania poured out of big jerry cans, just like unofficial outlets across the border at home.

Otherwise, things look fairly normal. It's reassuring to see sheep and goats grazing, even if the grass is poor. The houses nearby are all intact. No bullet holes here except for someone taking the odd pot shot at a road sign. No big craters in the road or memorials in ditches and not one landmine warning. It feels like they're getting back to civilisation.

Brendan is glad to have cash because plastic doesn't work here. American dollars fill the tank and he is given change in German marks. They are in the right place. The garage shop has sweets and biscuits on the shelf and a fridge full of soft drinks. They get a couple of ice pops and allow the engine to cool down.

Irene sits on a bench, her face tipped towards the sun. Brendan takes the shade. He can't stop the ice pop melting over his hand.

'You're worse than a child,' says Irene without opening her eyes.

After the rad cools he fills it with water and they are ready to go.

'Engine sounds okay,' he decides.

'How long did Marijana say it was sitting there?'

'Don't know. Put it this way, I wouldn't bank on the AA coming to save us.'

And it's true. They are aware – but don't care too much – that if the Lada breaks down they are well and truly goosed. Irene has already christened it, like she does with all her cars. At home when she talks about her RX-7 she'll say something like, 'Sylvia's not herself today' (battery) or 'Sylvia has a sore throat' (carburettor). When they ascend a particularly steep hill in Montenegro Brendan revs it to the point that he genuinely wonders if the engine might blow.

'Lily will get us there,' nods Irene, calmly patting the dashboard. 'She's a good girl.'

The mountains are a bit more rugged this side of the border and you can taste the salt of the sea. This road winds around steep passes where there's virtually nothing between the hard shoulder and a very long drop.

'I wouldn't fancy doing this run at night,' says Brendan. 'Not with brakes like these.'

After several mini-climbs they take a sharp corner which opens out into an expanse of blue.

'Look at that!' cries Irene. 'Is there anywhere to pull in?'

There's a lay-by a bit further on. It's not that long since they stopped for ice pops but sunshine blasting through the driver's side has Brendan half-grilled. Another rest break won't hurt. He follows Irene over to the grass verge where the view is mesmerising. They are so high up the mountains that they can see for fifty, sixty miles. It'll takes ages to get down to sea level. Spaghetti roads below look more like a game of snakes and ladders, the road twisting and turning around each headland, withdrawing further from the sea than you'd expect and then swinging back again.

'Now that's what I call blue,' says Brendan, impressed.

'Turquoise,' corrects Irene, very particular when it comes to colours.

'Like a picture.'

'I wish I'd brought my camera,' she sighs. 'I didn't think taking photos would go down too well on the pilgrimage but sure they were all at it. Even Packie. Amazing holiday snaps to bring home – this is where Our Lady drops by now and again, this one is where I went to confession . . .'

'Give it a rest, hah?'

If they were in a pub quiz – last one was 3 BC – Brendan would have guessed they were looking at the Mediterranean. On the map it says Adriatic. The water is glittering, wherever they are.

'Absolutely gorgeous,' says Irene, taking an imaginary picture. 'Click.'

– 29 –

The land is bare and rocky and anything that was green is burnt brown. All signs of a long summer. The temperature dips as they descend to the coastline and the sun has dropped below the horizon by the time they reach the water. It feels strange to have no destination. Two middle-aged runaways in a borrowed orange Lada.

'When's the last time we did this, Bren?'

'What?'

'Just hopped in the car and drove. Unplanned.'

'Probably the last time I drove a jalopy like this.'

They have driven through so many ruins that Irene is just glad to leave Bosnia behind. She takes heart when she sees a clothes line flapping outside a cottage. Small hints in Montenegro of life returning, the normality of kids playing, two cats sleeping, a mechanic bent over a car bonnet. All these things suddenly mean something.

'Where will we stay?'

'Keep an eye out for somewhere, I suppose.'

It feels different here. In Bosnia it's like nothing could escape being shot at or blown up. Here, things remain untouched and sometimes look as if it's been that way for centuries.

'The Count of Montenegro,' remarks Brendan.

Irene isn't bothered to put him right. The driver's side is now shaded so Brendan is no longer troubled by glare, even though he keeps moaning about being stuck in a glasshouse. As they follow the coastline Irene spots an island monastery in the bay. It's ancient but looks occupied. She is amazed to see two robed monks walk to a jetty nearby to unload groceries.

'Per-ast,' says Brendan, reading a sign with an arrow. 'Will we take a look?'

'Why not?'

She is beginning to like this unpredictability. It's such a change, not just from Perpetual Succour but from everything they've been doing for years. Any time they went away Irene had most days and nights marked off in advance, pre-booked, whether for some local attraction, dinner in a fancy restaurant or tickets for a show. Herded by travel guide recommendations 'for the independent traveller' they stopped letting things happen by chance long ago.

It could definitely do with a full makeover but Perast is very pretty. The shore is white pebbles rather than sand. Small boats roped to wooden platforms. The water laps the edge of the road and the view is lined with palm trees. Brendan slows down to allow a couple of sandalled fishermen carry a repaired net across the road. Others are already on the pier, stacking catch boxes. If you didn't know otherwise, you could be in Italy or Greece before tourism ruined them.

'What about there?' Irene suggests, seeing an unlit neon sign for Hotel Herc.

'Let's have a look.'

They discover that the hotel is full but not with tourists. Corridors are lined with worn shoes placed neatly in pairs outside each door. Belongings piled high on balconies. Broken bulbs have not been replaced, reducing the foyer to semi-darkness. All the guests are refugees from Bosnia and the place is layered with dust despite the efforts of an elderly woman with a straw broom vigorously sweeping the stairs.

A hotel feels so different when its guests are long-term residents. Refugees? More like inmates. Two old men sitting on a window sill are lost in a game of chess watched by a handful of others with nothing else to do.

The Gogartys are told that a lot of the hotels in Montenegro have been adapted in this way. People who lost their families in Bosnia or whose homes were destroyed. There's such a strange torpor about the place. Like everybody is holding out for something, unaware of what they have already given up.

The Gogartys never expected the excursion, never mind their pilgrimage, to turn out like this but it's been coming. Even something as ordinary as getting petrol didn't feel straightforward. Now they don't know if there's anywhere to stay. A local girl with American-accented English suggests they try Hotel St Jovan down by the waterfront.

Built of timber and stone the ceilings at Hotel St Jovan are surprisingly high. A cream, tiled floor at reception feels cool after the day's heat. The hotel restaurant is across the road, literally on the sea, decked out in faded white linen tablecloths. It's not the Ritz but they are ready to take anything. The receptionist says they are full up but the Gogartys are very lucky. They just had a cancellation so there is one room available.

'How much?' asks Brendan, pretending not to be thrilled.

'Seventy-five dollars a night,' says the receptionist. 'Cash only.'

He winces.

'The honeymoon suite,' she adds.

'Does that include breakfast?'

The whole place really has seen better days but they are relieved that their search for a bed is over. Brendan asks to see the room, grumbling something about tourist prices. The receptionist doesn't seem bothered whether they take the suite or not. She walks them to the third floor. The elevator, she says, stopped working long ago. They pass other guests, presumably many of them displaced. A middle-aged couple are arguing loudly, the door to their untidy room left wide open. They don't care that strangers can see and hear them. The receptionist hardly seems to notice either.

She unlocks the suite. The room needs repainting and a few tiles are missing from the bathroom wall. The bed is queen size with the futon circled by glittering love heart chocolates and two discoloured white towels folded into the shape of swans. A bottle of rosé with two glasses sits on the dressing table alongside a very pungent floral display. Brendan sneezes immediately.

The receptionist explains that a newlywed couple were expected from Podgorica this afternoon but they had to cancel at the last minute. A death in the family. The Gogartys act like they are sorry. Taking an opportunity to let in some fresh air Irene opens the shutters and finds the Adriatic sparkling outside.

'We'll take it,' she says.

– 30 –

Brendan does not want to boast but he would like to point out that if coming to Montenegro was a stroke of genius it was his idea. It was, for sure, a bit of a haul over mountains from Medjugorje but if the *Meath Chronicle* is stuck for a filler on Page 5 the Travelling Gogartys could tell first-hand how the miraculous Lada didn't break down after they filled it with dirty black market petrol.

'The old banger did well, in fairness,' he nods.

'Lily.'

'If I see a mechanic around, I might try get that window handle fixed. Otherwise, I'll be like that dog panting on TV – you know, the ad that tells you not to leave pets in a car on sunny days,' he says, fanning himself. 'If I was a mutt, what breed do you think I'd be?'

'Mmmm,' considers Irene. 'Maybe a cocker spaniel.'

'Oh?' smiles Brendan. 'Lovable. Loyal.'

'Long ears.'

Seeing as they actually made it all the way to Montenegro it seems a good idea to give Lily a few days off. Recovery time. Hopefully it – sorry, she – will survive the trip back. Not that they are in any hurry to leave. Hard enough to find a vacant bed here on account of people running from war. So many of them shacked up in what must once have been fancy hotels by the sea.

'Y'know Irene, I'm not saying I know the A to Z of Yugoslavia but it sounds like the main civil war ended a few years ago and now for Round Two they moved all the action into Bosnia.'

'Well, we got sorted for tonight, that's the main thing.'

'Somebody must've died at their wedding or whatever. Lucky for us.'

It was all set up for the honeymooners though Brendan thought it steep enough at seventy-five dollars. It's not the Gresham – except for the price – but the suite is only massive and the sea view from the balcony is icing on the cake. Ever mindful of a bargain he didn't mind pointing out to the receptionist that this pit-stop was not their honeymoon – it wasn't even their anniversary. He made it sound more like he and Irene were on a business trip and they had arrived in Perast under duress.

With an unshakable suspicion that foreign hotels always treated tourists as mugs he doubted that newlyweds from Montenegro would pay seventy-five bucks for one night. He wonders about the other guests who seem a bit more long term. Having stripped any romantic embroidery from the circumstance of their stay he managed to knock the receptionist down to sixty on the basis that they would take it until Monday at least.

In fairness, management had it all set up for a night of romance as long as neither bride nor groom suffered from hay fever. Brendan asked reception to take away the offending bouquet. He also handed back the bottle of rosé.

'A nice touch but neither of us drink that stuff,' he said a little ungraciously. Privately he thought it mildly comical that he and Irene should end up in the bridal suite seeing as only a few days ago they were at each others' throats. Then again, if they weren't ready to kill each other in Medjugorje they wouldn't be here, chilling out in Montenegro.

Sitting out on the balcony he watches village life rub along under sleepy afternoon sunshine. Irene joins him and takes the other seat. She lights a cigarette. He thinks she is in better form. The pilgrimage was worth trying – why not? – but this is more of a holiday *per se*. She's got her book and her sun cream and doing nothing for a few days can't hurt.

'D'you know, if they invested a shed load of moolah here Perast could be like the Riviera,' he says. 'Maybe it was once.'

'It's so peaceful. Strange how the war feels so far away,' she agrees, entranced by a surreal calm rippling to the shore. 'But it's here all the same.'

'Well there isn't much in the shops – that place near the border . . . '

'Where we got the ice pops . . .'

' . . . probably not typical at all.'

He notices that quite a few locals go fishing off the pier. He read somewhere that there's mullet, tuna and mackerel in the Adriatic as well as some strange fish with Montenegrin names. Even the odd swordfish by all accounts. As soon as he finds a tackle shop he intends to pick up a decent rod and show the locals how it's done.

It's only days – but feels longer – since shenanigans up Apparition Hill. Brendan feels that he and Irene are beginning to find their feet. This morning was very leisurely altogether. Breakfast – coffee, boiled eggs and toast – on the balcony.

Then a stroll around the town. A coffee, light lunch, that sort of thing. Leisurely is a polite way of saying lazy.

Irene likes to sit out on the balcony with her book. Brendan gives way, mindful that allowing each other a bit of space is probably a good thing at this point. He goes for a bit of a dander to see where it takes him. The Adriatic is more like a big lake. There are boat trips from the harbour which can take you out to the islands. Another monastery peeks from the bay, which is the second one they've seen alive and praying.

It's not his kind of thing but when you're on holidays don't you do all the stuff you wouldn't dream of doing at home? It's not like you'd find Brendan above in Dublin joining a queue of Yanks for a squint at the Book of Kells. But, if Perast had its own Book of Kells, he'd probably be next in line.

There are plenty of places to eat but not a whole lot of food. Wartime menu, they joke. Wartime prices more like, remarks Brendan. He's not a big foodie but unlike Irene he prefers discovering places by himself. None of this tourist guide mullarkey telling you where to go and what to eat or which epicurean centre some Michelin chef first learned how to boil an egg.

They could wander across the road to the hotel restaurant but it's pretty basic, even sombre. Out on a ramble he spots a place called Vlado's. Even though its rooftop sign seems to be missing half the O it looks reasonably promising. At least it's a cut above what else is on offer. He makes a mental note that they give it a whirl later.

He is surprised when he realises he hasn't bothered plugging in his phone. He thinks about Irene tossing the charger into the bushes. Took ages for it to dry out too. A mad stunt really but he grudgingly accepts he probably drove her over the edge. After everything that has happened he figured it might be a good idea to just pull back completely. So here he is, unplugged.

The battery remains flat as a pancake so Brendan can't get calls. Gary and Fiona wouldn't even have a clue where he is – still in Medjugorje as far as they are concerned. If needs be, he can always find another one of those international kiosks in town to phone the marina. Waiting for Gary to pick up, like a parent apprehensively ringing the babysitter to be told the children have run amok.

For the first time in his entrepreneurial life Brendan is unofficially out of contact. He knows if he recharges the Nokia he'll start to wonder why it isn't ringing. Better off leaving well enough alone for the minute and let Gary stand on his own two feet. Anyhow, didn't the truck get cleared in Rosslare so everything should be under control.

– 31 –

Irene can't believe the stillness. She only realises how calm it is when she drops the book in her lap and doesn't need to hold down the page. Of course the odd storm must blow up here through winter but ever since they arrived she is yet to see anything that even resembles a wave. Surfers must be a rare species in these parts. Even the sea isn't like water at all, more like glass. If someone threw a rock into it the whole picture might crack.

It's very warm for late August. High twenties – they say it even hit 32 last week. Wandering out to the edge of town she finds a little cove where you can lie out. White plastic loungers were originally hired out to tourists but with so few visitors around it's hardly surprising she's the only one on the beach. Nobody bothers to collect money for renting the chairs. It's like they put them out and then threw in the towel.

Irene had picked up a Jilly Cooper in Dublin airport. She read a few of Jilly's before and would be mortified if the author saw her struggling here, one laborious page at a time. Her mind just wanders, floats off and drifts away. She's fully oiled up with Factor 35 and maybe that's what a holiday book is supposed to do, set you dreaming in heat.

She wonders if Jilly Cooper is a real name. Irene could get a *nom de plume* herself but then she'd have to write something, wouldn't she? The book's cover made her wonder does Jilly get it regularly. She saw in a magazine the author was quite a bit older that she imagined. Whether Jilly is her name or not she's written a gazillion racy bestsellers – you'd hardly write about sex so much, would you, unless you had a bit of experience in that department?

She loses her page. That wouldn't have happened in the middle of a dirty bit so it's probably mid-way through a passage describing scenery or the stock market or whatever. Irene is not a writer but she presumes that after the characters get a bit of action you have to pad out the pages. Maybe a couple of historical details about the town where all the fucking is going on. Jilly could probably explain to fans how you can't have non-stop rumpy-pumpy, one steamy scene after another. That you need to give your characters a chance to cool down and your readers time to make a cup of tea.

Irene just can't envisage herself in white jockey pants tucked inside black jodhpurs – never mind the whip and riding hat. She wonders is that what Jilly wears around the house. Even when she's hoovering? She probably has a few maids to do the dusting. Or a handful of swarthy, uneducated teenage boys plucked from the wrong side of the tracks. All smouldering yet respectful and impossibly well-endowed.

'I'm with you on that one,' she says aloud, fending off an imaginary legion of astonishingly handsome young stable hands.

Besides, Irene would say from first-hand experience that education has always been overrated, especially French and Philosophy. College wasn't all it was cracked up to be and she'd be chancing her arm to describe herself as a serious Arts undergraduate. One of UCD's lesser lights is how she usually puts it.

She had just started second year when her Dad died. He was only diagnosed three weeks beforehand so they never saw it coming. And it was those mournful weeks in the autumn of 1974 that would colour her whole memory of third-level. Her Dad was unbelievably calm right to the end. A quiet, wonderfully tolerant man.

Would that some of his patience passed on to me . . .

When he was taken from them Agnes retreated into herself. That process was already underway when mourners shuffled to the door of the family home in Chapelizod. Disappointed at finding no drink on offer they ate all the sandwiches, sniffed at the idea of tea and drifted on up to the Angler's Rest, leaving Irene behind with her mother and an impertinently loud mantelpiece clock. Agnes' solitude was entirely private, which made Irene's grief an orphan. The quiet joys of being an only child.

Agnes' determined withdrawal from family life sucked out any motivation Irene had for study. She missed her Dad a lot more than she imagined and everything loomed ahead like imminent struggle. Then she did the honourable teenage thing and went off the rails. Very easy to do when the idea of reading Philosophy, never mind French, seemed pointless.

A wild and hectic social life ate into her timetable but somehow she made it through second year. She still does not rule out the possibility that her exam results got mixed up with someone else's. A pity, looking back, that she didn't go on and finish out her degree but it's not like she was remotely driven, even bothered.

Put it on my gravestone if you like: Here lies Irene Gogarty (née Kelly), half-hearted in most things she did.

She could blame Phil Lynott, and, at a stretch, Brendan. Because, in a way, one led to the other. Just before Christmas a college friend, Elva Donnelly – a committed Maoist/Trotskyite at the time, won three tickets for Thin Lizzy on Radio Dublin. She kept one for Irene and one for Joe Dunne, another Arts refusenik.

Joe had a bedsit in Rathmines so they brought over a cassette player and a bootleg of Lizzy's *Nightlife*. They thought it was going to be huge – it wasn't – but with the help of Southern Comfort and a small bit of hash the three of them paid more attention to that album in Joe's flat than to anything they did in college.

Feeling bulletproof and ready for the real thing they walked to the National Stadium on South Circular Road. The band had already started when they got there so they pushed past gum-chewing bouncers and surged to the front. It was so loud you could feel guitars vibrate through your body. A beautiful chaos before Lizzy slowed it right down for *Still In Love With You*. Squeezed up at the front Philo reached down and plucked Irene out of the crowd for a slow dance onstage. He was a lot taller than her but in front of cheering fans he kissed her on the lips at the end of it. The cheek of him!

She was buzzing afterwards. With enough in their pockets for one more drink they went on to meet friends at the Long Hall on South Great George's Street. The place was rammed – Christmas sessions in full swing and tons of people back from England. Elva had a sprig of mistletoe in her pocket and it came in handy if they saw anyone fanciable. All great, innocent, dizzy fun. Irene didn't need mistletoe for Brendan. They just got talking. One of those full-on nights where one memorable event led to another and the future seemed gilt-edged, fuzzy, open-ended.

You could tell straight off that Brendan was far too driven to go dossing in university for a few years. She liked his practicality. He was busy installing door frames around south Dublin and proud to be making a living. She used to say to Brendan that if they ever saw Philo walking through town they should stop him and tell him of his crucial role in their history. That he sprinkled a little stardust and let the romance in.

Even though Irene did manage to scrape through second year things were already changing. College life felt increasingly irrelevant and it didn't take too much persuasion for her to defect to the real world. Bit of a whirlwind, really. By the end of the year Cathal was on the way. She couldn't say how difficult the birth was seeing as she hadn't done it before (or since). All she remembers was sweet exhaustion when he was placed in her heavy arms. Eyes closed, a sleeping bundle.

Any notion of further education soon evaporated. She and Brendan found themselves in a rush to the altar. He was earning good money so, after losing her father and watching her mother recede from view, she was glad to have some sense of security. Besides, she was mad about him. That's a detail that usually gets overlooked.

They got married three months later. By then Cathal was her universe and they lived out their happy dream as a miniature family. There were moments she'd nearly be ecstatic and feel deeply fulfilled. Like when she would bathe Cathal in the kitchen sink, listening to his wordless chatter. He would smile up at her. Or she would inhale his soft skin. Alone in her delirium she would find herself teary with joy.

Not that it was easy minding the baby and trying to keep an eye on her mother. The child was full-on; so was Agnes. A strange time really.

Everything was about adapting to her new role as wife and mother. All of a sudden grown-up, imagine! She wasn't ready or equipped and at times felt horribly alone. Giving Cathal all her attention, taking the bus out to Chapelizod and trying to get back in time to make dinner before Brendan got home. Two small saucepans on a gas-fired hob in a dingy Ringsend flat, survival skills from carefree student life transplanted into marigold domesticity.

For the first months it was either a fry or fish fingers, boiled spuds and beans. Or the chipper around the corner for emergencies. Brendan didn't complain. He just loved being the breadwinner. He also loved having her and Cathal to come home to, although she did remember him once giving her a wok for Christmas and, for her birthday, *Angela Comyn's Favourite Irish Recipes*.

'Is that a hint Brendan?'

'Jesus, not at all,' he blushed.

Everything has different meaning when said in a time of laughter.

They were clueless but Brendan was earning a crust and Irene was learning too. By the time they moved to Portobello she could have gone back to UCD or maybe done a course at night but it all seemed a bit aimless. She missed her college friends at the start but when she brought six-month-old Cathal over to Belfield everything had already moved on.

Elva was repeating second year and Joe had dropped out. They were all around the same age but Irene becoming a mother put a generation between them. Student life seemed childish. She was feeding Cathal when Elva and Paudie Lyons got into an argument about Fidel Castro's place in globalisation.

Then the chat moved to big excitement over a midweek vodka promotion. The baby gurgled and threw up on her shoulder. Paudie Lyons said Cathal was obviously in training for the rag ball. Laughing along with everybody else Irene felt very old all of a sudden. She wiped down her jacket, settled the child in the pram and never went back.

To be fair, Elva and a couple of others did show up for Cathal's funeral. They'd seen it on the news. Through the blur of services that followed at Deansgrange it meant something to her that they took the time. Elva looked the same but the others looked far older than the dozen years that had flown by. Irene wonders what she looked like to them. They hugged through tears at the church and she just wished for Cathal to return and puke on her shoulder once more. Faint memories of a student life long gone.

One lifetime later and here she is lying out with Jilly Cooper – you can't really say 'reading' when you've slowed down to a page a day. Yet it just feels . . . calm. Calm*er*. They've been in Perast three days and she has to say she feels the better for it. Don't ask her to explain but it must have something to do with the light. As well as the mountains and the sea. It's not like there's much else to do around here.

Like yesterday, she walked for an hour or so, just trailing along the water when she realised she wasn't thinking of anything. Talk about simple pleasures! The comings and goings of an empty mind. She bought an ice cream and sat on a bench, the water unimaginably clean, looking more turquoise than blue. Dinghies, fishing boats, an occasional yacht, criss-crossing the bay. The receptionist at their hotel ventured that cruise liners might come back this way when the war ends.

'There is no fighting in Montenegro,' she keeps telling them. It is such a lovely setting it takes a while to notice what's right in front of you. Dust covers cars that haven't moved in months because petrol is in short supply. Some of the shops have nothing to sell. Tourist boats have been tied up for so long on the waterfront their bottoms are coated in green slime.

Hotel St Jovan is completely full but the Gogartys seem to be the only ones who come to the dining room. Are we the only paying guests? she wonders.

Groups of men in tracksuits gather at the harbour every day, idling away long hours. Others sit alone staring at the sea. Sometimes she feels like the Gogartys are the only ones with cash in this town. She won't be guilted by luxury though – aren't they spending good money in a place that time forgot?

Every so often you hear one of those really loud planes – NATO jets, according to Brendan. Deafening for a few seconds before a bang like thunder. Breaking the sound barrier, her husband explains, a boy without a toy.

Once they realise you are an outsider – especially a non-Balkan one – any locals in Perast want to talk about mountains and music and food and wine. The way they'd like the world to be. They say what happens in Bosnia is not their problem, even though you can see it is.

A bit like home when every scrap of news from the North came dripping in blood. All of it happening just up the road, same as here. Daytime music on the radio interrupted by a newsflash about a bomb in Belfast or a body found down a boreen in County Armagh. A steady diet of horrors until nobody heard the specifics any more.

Maybe if RAF fighter planes were smashing the sound barrier over Meath it wouldn't have been so easy to ignore what was going on in Belfast, Derry or the border counties. War could be silent, like death. Now everybody at home is talking up this year-old IRA ceasefire, confidently predicting there is no way it will last.

The Montenegrins are much the same really, thinking that if they look away, it's not really happening. Irene doesn't know what the odds are of peace breaking out in the Balkans. Nobody here is talking about a ceasefire; in Perast, they're not even talking about war.

Brendan is somewhere up the town near the harbour. Now that they are doing their own thing they are used to doing very little together. That might be a step in the wrong direction but it feels quite okay. Irene goes for a clutter-free walk; Brendan goes to catch fish. They meet up later for a coffee or a drink at the hotel or occasionally bump into each other on the street, like long-lost friends. Otherwise they set a time in the evening, an unofficial rendezvous for dinner. Nice food, if it's available, some wine and a fabulous view of the bay. It's almost romantic.

They are now able for conversation, which is a start. Tell each other about their 'day' like they are explorers who have just discovered the Adriatic. Not that you can spout on forever about buying an ice cream. It's normal enough that they end up talking about bits and pieces from the past, harmless stuff they have told and retold many times before. The main thing is for them to stay relatively sober and keep away from tired old arguments. At least they are trying.

Yesterday, Brendan bought a fishing rod. When Irene got back to the hotel he was out on the terrace, practising his swing like a golfer. You'd swear he was about to cast a line over passing traffic below.

'Move over lads. Plenty of fish in the sea!' he quipped.

Don't ask him what he'll do if he catches one. She can imagine him in his element, joshing with the locals, bullshitting in a language they don't understand. She reckons very few people they've met in the Balkans would grasp a single word spoken by her husband. She laughs at how he makes no allowance for non-English speakers and wonders how he managed to hook up with locals at the pier. Somehow, she knows they'll all end up having a laugh and she can honestly say she is glad for him.

On the balcony yesterday he looked around with such delight at his latest acquisition – a bargain, naturally – that for a split second she loved him. Not jump-his-bones kind of love but in that instant knowing they have come so far together and he has, sometimes, been wonderful. She would not be lying to say that since they first met – nineteen and a half years now, God! – there has been the occasional moment of bliss.

Still, she has to dig very deep to recall one. Everything that comes to mind is BC. You can't even compare their lives AC. She raises her eyes to heaven when she hears experts talk about the best wine coming last because in their case all the good stuff came first. And after that she doesn't have enough fingers to count out when killing Brendan stone dead seemed the most sensible option.

A counsellor once told her how important it was to 'acknowledge' things and 'own' them. Like reality. 'You can't own reality,' countered Irene, 'but, okay, I acknowledge you are a nosey cow.' The counsellor pursed her lips and suggested Irene was 'not engaging with the process'.

So how about this for reality: Yesterday, when Brendan looked over with that boyish grin dying to show her his new toy, a whole range of feelings flooded through her. She is not making an excuse – or maybe she is – but she had to bury that moment or she knew she'd burst into tears.

'How much?' she asks, not knowing a whole lot about fishing rods.

'Works out about twenty-three quid,' he says, holding the rod like Excalibur.

'Oh,' she answers, adding for no good reason, 'probably made in China.'

Sometimes she just can't help it.

– 32 –

Two local men and a boy, no more than ten, all have lines out down the pier. When Brendan introduces himself it's clear they don't speak English but they admire his new rod and don't mind him squeezing in to try his luck. The young boy holds the branch of a tree taped with nylon and a hook at the end. He watches the two older men closely – one of them may be his uncle or grandfather – and from the assured way he casts out you can see he's learned from them. A serious little man.

'*Anglski*?'

'Irish. Ire-land.'

'Ah, *Irske. Dobrodosli.*'

'Fair play.'

Brendan remembered seeing *dobrodosli* on a big sign in the airport. He figures it must mean welcome. Then he wonders what he'd make of a foreigner arriving into the newsagent in Nobber and whether, if they didn't speak the same language, he'd offer the stranger a *céad míle fáilte* for luck.

One of the men doesn't wear a shirt. He stands around in togs and flip-flops, barbecued to a crisp and not a care in the world. He's been virtually bronzed by the sun. His friend with sunglasses is a little more conservative. He wears a faded Juventus jersey and drapes a blue towel over his head. You can tell this pair are old buddies in the way they're all chat and then go quiet for a while. Juventus produces mandarins from his bag and offers Brendan one.

'*Pomorandze*,' he says, peeling one. '*Mandarina.*'

'Yeah, mandarin. Good man yourself.'

Brendan attempts to find out more about Perast but it's too much bother. All are happier to spare the conversation and concentrate on the fish. Only Tarzan has caught anything. A couple of tiddlers with orange stripes and a medium-size eel splash around his bucket.

'You're doing well,' says Brendan, nodding at his catch.

Tarzan shrugs.

'Is okay.'

'Fair play.'

It's childish he knows but Brendan would love to catch something here, just to fly the flag. Okay, it's not massively important in the great scheme of things – he couldn't even bring the fish home to cook – but Tarzan is showing him up and nothing will scratch the competitiveness of a Meath man as quickly as being shown up. The young boy gets all excited when there's a splash at the end of his line. He pulls in what looks like a sardine. Brendan joins Tarzan and Juventus in cheering the boy as he unhooks it very carefully. He places it in the bucket and then gets back to business.

'Good lad,' Brendan tells him. 'You won't get fat on that but sure isn't it an appetizer?'

The boy takes no notice of the stranger and he's probably right. Juventus lands a bream and Brendan realises he's now the only one on the pier who hasn't caught anything. Poncing about with his brand new rod while the kid lands a tiddler using a homemade branch. Well, this is another story he won't be bringing home to Nobber; the day the Montenegrins outfished the Royal.

But as the afternoon wears on he's less and less bothered. Just kicking back, having the crack. There's no shortage of people knocking around with very little to do. Brendan notices a man taking the sun on a bench nearby. The man has one arm. You would think the missing limb would be the first thing to notice but what actually catches Brendan's eye is the man is wearing a beanie.

People cover their heads with all sorts because of the sun but you won't see too many beanies around Montenegro in August. It looks quite odd. The man looks thin, mid-thirties. He's on his own and, like so many around the town, appears in no particular hurry. Time passes slowly here both for those who are active or, like most, unoccupied. Brendan is fascinated watching him somehow roll a ciggie with his left hand.

The boy bags another sardine and he's made. Tarzan pulls in a bigger eel – which leaves Brendan wincing self-consciously – before they decide to call it a day.

'I'm away, lads,' says Brendan, packing away his fancy rod and feeling a bit sheepish. If this was street football he'd be like the game's worst player who happens to own the football.

'*Ciao*!' says Tarzan.

'*Ciao*,' answers Brendan, feeling Italian.

He wants to get back to the hotel and have a shower. They are going out for dinner tonight and he wants to bring Irene to Vlado's. He's actually looking forward to it. Don't ask him why but this seems to be working out well, doing their own thing, then meeting up in the evening with something, however incidental, to talk about.

He rambles back through town with his rod and parks it on the balcony. His good shirt looks fairly crumpled in the case but maybe he can borrow an iron from reception and take out some of the creases. Make a bit of an effort, like.

– 33 –

While Brendan is down the pier Irene goes for a stroll out the other side of town. She stops for a while to watch a man and his daughter fly a kite on the beach. The strings keep getting tangled up and then the kite nose-dives into the sea. The little girl thinks it's the funniest thing ever, especially when her dad has to paddle out to get it back. He gets annoyed because his pants get wet and that makes the child laugh even more. Irene could have watched them for hours, the innocence of play time.

She knows that Brendan loves to 'discover' a local restaurant or bar on the rare occasions they go somewhere new. Several of the businesses in Perast are closed, probably for good, but he tells her he's found one called Vlado's which he describes as having outdoor tables facing the sea, special fish dishes, not too fussy, not too snobby, no big production over what bread is on offer from the serving tray. He knows each of these would tick a box for Irene. Waiters hovering around with letter openers to scrape crumbs off a tablecloth would send her over the edge, every time.

She makes her way back to the hotel and is surprised to see him spruced up. He's energized, upbeat. It's not like him to show enthusiasm.

'Shall we?' he says, bowing like a Merchant Ivory extra who has just been given a speaking part.

They walk along the waterfront towards the big reveal. Her husband has been talking up Vlado's, as he tends to do with pet projects. At the entrance she observes that the vowel deficient sign announces Vlad's but why start the evening on a critical note? They are made welcome and shown to a table that overlooks water. A lantern box is placed nearby. The candle dances as the last rays of daylight reach over the mountains, a lovely gentle light flickering. Irene also figures that Brendan must have ironed the shirt himself, resisting the urge to point out he missed one side of the collar.

She turns to the menu to see the array of fish on offer.

'What a fantastic selection!

'Yeah, just looking at it here.'

'Did you catch anything yourself today?'

'Not today, no.'

She looks up and sees his head buried in the menu. Man and boy in one. A picture comes to mind of Brendan stomping through the hallway in Portobello, Cathal trailing sullenly behind. A father angry with his son. She recalls her husband gripe at how he had caught a fine trout on the Boyne near Slane, unhooked it and tossed it on the river bank, telling his son to put the fish out of its misery with a stick. The boy said he couldn't do it. Not wanting to hurt the trout the boy suddenly picked up the squirming fish and threw it back in the river.

Irene could not help bursting out in laughter. Brendan stared open-mouthed, hurt by her disloyalty. 'Sorry,' she said, struggling to stifle a giggle. Cathal stood between his parents, facing his father. She placed her hands on his young shoulders in support. Brendan nodded, silently fuming. Already livid at losing his prize catch, he felt she was now encouraging the boy's callowness.

Tossing his wellingtons into the garage he said he would go fishing alone next time. Which he did, two weeks later, brushing away Cathal's tearful protests and ignoring Irene's doorstep pleas – *Don't be such a child Brendan!* – before driving off in a huff. That's years ago now. She can't recall him going out to fish AC, not even once.

'Good evening. I am Anja, your waitress.'

She's pretty and very pleasant and Irene instinctively takes in the gentle curve of her belly. She is so petite she is hardly showing so it's hard to tell when she's due. Irene guesses she is about thirty, thirty-one, jet black hair in a pageboy that only a confident woman would wear. She likes the girl instantly.

Both go for prawn cocktail starters. Brendan chooses lobster for mains and Irene opts for lemon sole.

'Sorry,' says Anja. 'Not prawn, not lobster today. Not lemon sole today also.'

'Oh,' says Brendan, disappointed. 'Swordfish?'

'Not swordfish.'

'What *have* you got?'

'Mullet.'

'Mullet or . . . ?'

'Risotto.'

'That's it?'

'Yes.'

'Two mullet so.'

'You like wine? Mineral water?'

Ever since Brendan did an evening course on wine tasting Irene fears the worst. He opens the wine list but soon as he starts dropping in references to earthiness and sulphates she rejoices at hearing the waitress pull the plug.

'Sorry, I not speaking English very well.'

'Am I going too fast?'

'No. I not know lot in wine. Sorry!'

She offers to find Vlado, the owner, who they are assured is an authority on everything. Irene just wants a drink so she points to the first bottle on the list, savagely denying her husband any opportunity to discuss naughty bouquets with a fellow connoisseur. She chooses white – a Chardonnay from Montenegro – which she declares to be perfect without tasting it. And when she raises it to her lips she finds it chilled and not too sweet. There's no aftertaste, which she often finds with Chardonnay. Realising she has polished off her first glass too quickly she tells herself to slow down. This is lovely and they're both relaxed. She doesn't want to ruin it all by getting pissed.

'Great find, Bren.'

'Don't know what happened the menu.'

'Has atmosphere though.'

'Doesn't it?'

The prawn-less salad is tasty but tiny. The mullet, not such an obvious choice, is charcoal grilled and well presented with salad and fried potatoes. This is the land of simple, not the land of plenty. The breeze off the sea turns slightly cooler. Anja takes a blanket from the back of the chair and drapes it over Irene's shoulders. Brendan doesn't need one. He doesn't feel the cold and is perfectly happy in his half-ironed shirt.

'One man down,' he says, pouring the last drops. 'Will we get another?'

'Aaaah, no.'

His eyes rise in surprise. Anja takes their dishes away.

'Everything good?'

'Top notch,' says Brendan.

'You like dessert? Tea, coffee?'

Against all good sense they agree to share a black forest gateau which they can't even finish. Irene is tempted to reconsider a second bottle but Anja presents an alternative.

'That's it now,' says Brendan. 'Sure we'll take the chicken's neck.'

'Chicken?' pauses Anja, momentarily wrongfooted.

'He means the bill.'

'Of course. You like after-dinner drink? On house.'

'You wouldn't get that at home now,' he smiles, impressed.

'Cognac?'

'Why not?'

'Why not indeed? Two complimentary cognacs and the chicken's neck.'

Sated by dinner and a free drink they feel comfortable enough to sit in silence. A yacht with night lights glides through the bay, pretty as a picture. They watch it pass. A motorboat chugs away to the far side, its small engine echoing a far-off complaint.

'You got a bit of colour.'

'Did I?' he says, examining his arms for evidence.

Anja returns with the bill and two cognacs. She asks where they are from. When Irene says Ireland she surprises them by asking if she means 'south Ireland or north Ireland'. It's not the first time people in the Balkans have made the distinction.

'Meath,' says Brendan. 'Nobber.'

'In the south.'

'Actually, can I pay this in Irish pounds?'

'Sorry. Vlado take only Deutschmarks or US dollar.'

'Hah? Our money's no good here!'

While Brendan sorts through various currencies in his wallet, Irene asks if this is a family business. Anja says Vlado, the owner, had a restaurant in Vukovar but it was destroyed during the war. The city was put under a siege by Serbs but Vlado, himself a Serb married to a Croat, refused to leave.

'For long time fighting but then all change. Vlado fight beside Croatian friends in Vukovar but Serbs stronger. They say five minutes to get out. Ethnic cleaning I think you say. Then five minutes, whoosh!'

'Burned it down?' says Irene, taken aback. 'Jesus, Mary and Joseph.'

'He looks back and this he sees.'

'You're saying this lad is a Serb who joined the Croats to fight the Serbs?' says Brendan, a little lost. 'I thought the Serbs were the bad guys.'

'Many good people in war do bad things.'

She tells them she lived in Sarajevo but originally came from Mostar.

'The Serbs ran you as well?' asks Brendan.

'No. For us it was Croats. But yes, in Sarajevo, Serbs.'

'Right,' nods Brendan, completely lost.

'Please, I allow you have cognac.'

She leaves with a smile. It's just gone half-nine.

'Imagine being burnt out,' says Irene, a little shell-shocked.

'Ah, they'll say anything for a tip.'

Only three tables are occupied. Presumably during the high season this place used to be full. Now it's like the town doesn't have seasons at all. Month-to-month flatlined against a tranquil sea.

Irene pictures the imperious Vlado watch his Vukovar restaurant go up in smoke.

'Just say you've got five minutes to get out. What would you bring?'

Brendan raises his cognac and considers the question. He looks more intelligent when he has a drink in his hand.

'Cash. Passport. And a toothbrush. You can bring the toothpaste.'

He tips Irene's glass in a wordless toast.

'What about your GAA programmes? The whole "priceless" collection.'

'Oh Jesus, yeah, I'd take them too.'

'Hold on, how many is it?'

'Six hundred and four, last count.'

'Hold on Brendan. It's only what you can carry.'

'Oh,' he reconsiders, sipping his cognac. Irene lights a ciggie. 'I suppose if some yahoo is pointing a gun at you there's not much time for packing.'

'Can you imagine running around the house trying to find Mam's ring . . . all our photos, God . . . Cathal's locket would be first on the list but sure, I'd be wearing it.'

He shifts uncomfortably as she fingers the chain. Cathal is never far from his mind but it's not somewhere he wants to go at this moment. Brendan's voice drops, confidential and conspiratorial all at once.

'Here, d'you know something, Irene. This trip. In fairness, I don't think we fitted in with the Holy Joes.'

'Ah, Medjugorje was grand.'

'Could have gone to Knock just as easy.'

'Can't see you sitting in your shorts in Knock.'

'Not with a free cognac in me hand. Here, let me pay this one. Let's see. Forty-three. Plus ten percent. Sure we'll even off and leave it at that.'

'I think the sun must've gone to your head, Mr Gogarty.'

Anja stands by the service trolley. Unused to anything less than instant attention Brendan clicks his fingers. A couple at another table look over.

'Do you have to do that?' Irene squirms.

'Oh now, this one's doing pretty well out of me.'

Anja comes over to gather his cash off the table.

'I get change.'

'You're grand.'

'Excuse?'

'That's yours.'

'Thank you,' she smiles, pausing. 'You know, for us what happen in Sarajevo feel like bad dream. But now we living here so we know for sure it was not bad dreaming.'

'A nightmare?'

'Night-mare. Yes.'

'Shocking altogether,' says Brendan, running low on curiosity.

'*Hvala. Loca noc.*'

'Goodnight,' Irene replies. 'Lovely girl. Notice her bump?'

'What?'

'Bun in the oven.'

'How do you know?'

'I just know,' says Irene, tapping her nose.

She finishes her ciggie. Brendan really wants to pick up where he left off. He reaches across the table, about to take Irene's hand before he has second thoughts and withdraws.

'The point is, coming here to Montenegro has been brilliant. I mean, look at you!'

'I feel great.'

'And don't you look it! That's what I'm saying. I think this place has helped. Even though it's a bit run-down and all. Here's to you. To us.'

He raises his half-empty cognac and they clink glasses, a semi-formal truce.

'And what about you?' she ventures, looking up to face him directly. 'How are you?'

'Never better.'

'You'd say that anyway.'

'You see, what I was thinking was, maybe we should, y'know, spend a bit more time over here. Relax, like.'

'Another holiday?'

'Yeah. Or even longer.'

'Should we not wait till the war is over?'

'Sorry – what war?' he grins with mock incredulity. 'All we've seen is yachts and fishing and kids flying kites.'

'And hotels full of refugees.'

'I'm not saying we move here, lock, stock and barrel. But as a getaway, it's perfect.'

'A getaway?'

Irene's mind is swimming. She goes to light up another cig but rests it on the ashtray. She lifts her glass but does not drink.

'What about Cathal?'

Once she says his name she takes a large mouthful of cognac, draining the glass with a wet cough. Brendan sighs, looking out across the water. The small motorboat has long since disappeared into darkness, leaving the bay virtually silent. Irene picks up her ciggie and flicks the lighter. One fast, urgent drag and one long, slow release.

'The flowers, Brendan. They need changing every couple of weeks. Keep it neat and tidy or you get weeds coming through. They have to be . . . I know you think this is all voodoo but he waits for me. He told me.'

'Stop.'

'You mightn't believe it but we have great chats.'

'Stop, please.'

'Well, I'm not going to let him down.'

'You're not letting him . . .'

She follows the moon's reflection, rippling through water. The mountains across the bay are mere shadows save for a necklace of small houses and, irregularly, the corkscrew headlights of a car twisting and turning uphill.

'Seriously, Irene, we have to get on with our lives.'

'I know.'

'So.'

She wants to scream. She avoids Brendan's stare and tries to control her breathing. She stubs out the cig she didn't really want. She has consciously avoided getting drunk yet still they arrive at this point, swords drawn. Truce over.

'I don't want to talk about it.'

'No,' he says forcefully. 'You're not going to make me feel bad.'

'He's our son.'

'You make it sound like we're doing something wrong. Enjoying ourselves. Even the last few days I see it in you. The weight, lifted. You know I'm right,' he asserts. 'What can we do that we're not doing already?'

– 34 –

They decide to take Lily out of semi-retirement and go for a spin up the coast. It's not that they're all done with Perast but the bay runs all the way to Kotor, a substantially larger town. It has a deep water port where luxury liners used to pull in. Brendan and Irene joke that by the time peace breaks out in Bosnia they will be able to embark on an Adriatic cruise as pensioners.

Brendan imagines something like *Love Boat*. The ship's captain head-to-toe in an immaculately pressed white uniform; a Greek, presumably, but not as big a sap as he looks. The Gogartys would be invited to the captain's table one evening as guests of honour. The suave mariner would be telling them all about his seafaring adventures, piloting the briny deep around Tierra del Fuego on a run through the Panama Canal. As they breeze the channel into Kotor it'll be their turn to regale him with wartime tales of a dodgy Lada and grilled mullets.

Lily starts up on the third attempt and they rumble along the waterfront. Local people sell home-made jam and chutney by the side of the road, the way they sell strawberries in Wexford. The route is generally flat so Lily doesn't have to work too hard.

Irene tries the radio and keeps searching until she finds music. 'Philo!' she exclaims and turns it right up, the tune coming in and out of static. 'I love this song!'

This boy is cracking up,
This boy has broken down.

Irene roars out the window, her hair flying in the wind. She leans back in to clap in perfect time to the music, pointing temptingly at Brendan with a syncopated cry: *Ola!* Then she's playing the dashboard like a piano, laughing along, her head thrown back and they are suddenly twenty years younger, driving through October rain to Salthill.

Brendan is not into music in the same way but it gladdens him deeply to see Irene light up for a few minutes, singing and shouting without a care in the world. He recalls the first time they met. Flying that night so she was, telling him Phil Lynott snogged her at the Lizzy concert after dragging her onstage for a slow dance.

She picks up an imaginary trumpet and plays along until the reception gets fuzzy, starting to fade out of range. She twirls the button frantically to try to tune it back, but they seem to be driving away from the signal. He feels like stopping the car to keep the moment alive but the coast road is tight and there's nowhere safe to pull in. Before the song reaches the next chorus, it's gone.

'Aaah,' she exhales, air let out of a balloon.

She flicks off the radio and slumps back. You can tell she wants to talk and he knows she's going to tell him a story she's told many times before.

'Poor Philo,' she repeats. 'Do you know the clinic he ended up in was in Salisbury? Mother rang to tell me Myles had been asked to collect the body. All they knew was it was some musician from Dublin called Philip Lynott. Can't say I ever heard of him, Mother said. Did you?'

'Small world, hah?'

'Didn't even make it to forty. Thirty-six, Bren. That's all he was.'

Neither of them had ever heard of Kotor but its stone fortifications can be seen long before reaching the city, zigzagging up the mountain like the Great Wall of China. Old Kotor lies behind city walls while the new part of town mushrooms out into forlorn looking Communist-era apartment blocks. It's already obvious which part of town will last longer. They find a parking spot and decide to take a ramble up along the old wall.

It looks manageable but is actually a lot harder when you try it by foot. Under a rising sun it's a fair hike but they make it all the way to the top where they discover a spectacular fort. Even in shorts Brendan is sweating heavily. He keeps thinking of the phrase 'purify my soul' but can't remember where he heard it. Irene has to stop a couple of times to catch her breath.

'Might give you second thoughts about smoking,' says he.

'Dry up,' she replies.

The view from the fort stretches right across the bay. You can see inland too, across plains and peaks in the distance. Whoever built this had the whole shooting gallery in their sights. Plenty of advance warning if restive neighbours had invasion in mind.

'Imagine being a soldier here in ancient times and you get orders to defend the city,' pants Brendan. 'You'd be so bolloxed getting up here in all that armour there's no way you'd manage a proper swordfight.'

'The invaders would probably take you for a conscientious objector.'

'I think I'd just hand over the keys.'

'Well you could forget about your Employee of the Month Award.'

'Fucking sure. Go ahead, lads, ye can have it.'

The air tastes really fresh and pure and you can hardly hear the distant sounds of traffic below. They stay for a while. You'd think it would be a doddle coming back down but putting on the brakes hillside compresses their calf muscles. Still, it feels satisfying to have done the climb together and when they reach street level they stop off for a well-earned Fanta.

It's all there – shops, squares, houses, a water fountain, an ancient old church with candles melted into the stone floor like waxworks. The old city is paved in white limestone. Apart from allowing deliveries at certain times, they don't let traffic through the front gate. It's been modernised as a living town even though, according to a tourist brochure, Kotor goes way, way back.

'168 BC!' laughs Irene, dwelling on the letters in a sad sort of way.

As first-time visitors they ramble slowly wherever the flagstones lead them. They pick up a couple of ice creams, pink and white balls scooped onto a wafer cone. There's no hurry at all today and it's absolutely grand. Irene stalls at a shop window showing apartments and houses for sale in Montenegro. Some are new builds; a couple of them even have a swimming pool.

'Swimming pools will be the next big thing at home,' predicts Brendan. 'It'll be some crack getting planning permission.'

The sign says Adriatika Properties and the office is small enough. A salesman beavers away on the phone while the receptionist files her nails.

'Builders do all the work,' observes Brendan. 'And fellas in suits make a killing. Same the world over.'

'That's nice,' says Irene, picking out a whitewashed cottage.

'Yugos aren't big into bungalows, hah? Not like at home.'

'Terracotta tiles look so Mediterranean.'

'Will we have a gander?'

'I don't mind.'

'Tell you what, Irene, the way you go about this is you act like you've no interest. That you've seen a pile of others way better.'

'We haven't seen anything.'

'Ah, but this boyo doesn't know that. As far as he's concerned, we've scoured continental Europe looking for a bargain.'

She giggles, playing along.

'We're peasants at heart.'

'Sure, aren't we just getting over the Famine?'

'*M'ochón 's m'ochón ó . . .*'

'Will we give it a whirl?'

'Now?'

'Why not? For a bit of crack!'

The opening door catches a bell and in one movement the receptionist drops her nail file into the top drawer. The salesman is talking in his own language and has a deep, gravelly voice older than his years. The Gogartys can tell by the way he looks at them that they are probably the first people through his door today.

'*Dobar dan,*' says the receptionist.

The salesman ends his call and is onto them, fastening his jacket and ready for business.

'Hello! Welcome to Montenegro!'

'How's she cutting.'

'Sasa Blagovic, pleased to meet you.'

'Brendan Gogarty. This is my better half, Irene.'

'Hello.'

'Pleased to meetink you. Come, please, to my office.'

It's an untidy desk. Photos of properties, typed pages, letters. He's only a young fella, maybe late-twenties. The right age and the right game for unadulterated bullshit.

'We were just passing by,' Brendan tells him disinterestedly.

'Looking in the window,' Irene adds.

'Of course. You are English?'

'That's not a great start, Sasa. We're from Ireland.'

'I love Ireland. Where streets have no names. U2!'

'That's right,' shrugs Brendan. 'We have a special relationship with the world.'

'You are on vacation?'

'Just for a few days.'

'We were in Medjugorje,' begins Irene, but Brendan cuts in sharply to move things on.

'Thought we'd have a look at what's on your books. Just for pig iron, as the man says.'

'Please – coffee? Tea? Water?'

'We're grand thanks, we just had ice creams.'

'Adriatic is so beautiful, yes? First time in Montenegro?'

'You could say that.'

'Europe's hidden secret. You are interested to rent or buy? Is very good time to buy. Or rent.'

'If ye weren't in the middle of World War Three you mean.'

'Investment opportunity,' Sasa replies instantly. 'Perhaps you have portfolio in Ireland, yes?'

Brendan notes he's quick enough for a young fella.

'Ah, I have a couple of places but sure they're not worth a curse. You'd be better off buying a mobile home, stick it in Bettystown and hope for the best.'

'How much you like to spend?'

'Ah Sasa, aren't we only looking!'

'Okay but please, what price you like to look at?

'About twenty thousand. Twenty-five max.'

'That's Irish pounds,' says Irene, which Brendan does not consider very helpful.

'Irish pound is same as British pound?'

'Enough as to make no difference,' snaps Brendan. 'Tell you what, Sasa, we're from a place called Nobber in Meath. Ah, you probably don't know it. Anyways, all we see is fields. Every day. So we were thinking of something near the sea. Green to blue. That's what we're looking for. A change.'

– 35 –

Irene is losing interest. The young salesman keeps pushing exclusive mountainside condos that he says will be built over the next year or two. It's all he wants to talk about. They have so many properties on their books she wonders why he doesn't try shifting one that actually exists.

At first it was a bit of a laugh until she knew Brendan was getting into it. Sasa would show them the photograph of a house that obviously needed work and Brendan would be in like Flynn to shoot it down.

'Kip! Next!'

Or a Cetinje apartment, a traditional town that Sasa says is very historical.

'Boring,' says Brendan, faking a yawn. 'Next!'

It's pretty obvious that they can't give anything away in Montenegro right now. She feels a bit sorry for the young salesman. It's like the holidaying Gogartys are toying with him, taking advantage of civil war next door – or Brendan is just being mean. Her husband wouldn't see it that way. He's always banging on that real estate agents would sell their first-born if the price was right. If and when the market turns, he maintains they wouldn't care what hoops they'd put you through to raise their margin.

So Sasa takes the brunt of Brendan's antipathy towards auctioneers, even though he's no more than thirty. The poor fella is so desperate for a sale he probably doesn't realise he's being slaughtered.

She's lost count of how many properties they've gone through. The files are bursting out of three fat Adriatika folders. In a metaphor that definitely gets lost in translation Brendan likes to repeat they didn't come down in the last shower so they won't be buying anything off plans. He adds more than once that he'll leave *all them yokes that's not yet built* to the Russians.

Wondering how long this game is going to last Irene picks up the first folder and starts flicking through. She comes across one they either missed or Sasa skipped past. An old stone house facing water. It's very traditional and seems to be in good condition. A decent garden at the back. Refitted inside with two bedrooms, a big bright kitchen which looks out on the sea.

'Excuse me Sasa. I think you missed this one.'

She thought he might thank her but instead he ignores the interruption. He wants to push something else.

'Beautiful penthouse apartment in Risan? Very good.'

'No, no, forget that. What about this one – is it for sale or is it not?'

'*Da*,' he falters, looking at the property with a discernible lack of enthusiasm. 'The villa.'

– 36 –

They are told the villa is six kilometres away so they follow Sasa's battered Skoda back towards Perast.

'Jesus Irene, that was priceless. Better than Billy Connolly.'

'What?'

'You playing hardball with yerman.'

'To be honest Bren, it was getting a bit . . .'

'When he asked you about viewing the property, you said you could take it or leave it. That was class.'

'I meant it.'

'Brilliant.'

'Sure I didn't know whether I was supposed to be interested or not.'

'Ah no, you got his attention.'

'Wouldn't be used to that.'

'Sounds good though, doesn't it?'

'What?'

'This villa.'

'Don't we have a villa at home?'

'Ah, this is different.'

'Well if you ask me he has a funny way of going about it. First, he tries to flog us places we don't want. And when I ask about this one he tries to drop it and push something else. It's like he didn't want to show us the villa at all.'

'Ah no, no,' says Brendan, rubbing an index finger against his thumb. 'He's a salesman. Look at those condos he's flogging. About three times the price! But wait till you see. They're like puppy bloodhounds – soon as he gets the sniff of a sale, you'll see him light up, bright-eyed, bushy-tailed. Sure they've just one property in the window with a red circle around it. Only the one!'

'I thought we weren't really looking.'

'But sure this is great crack.'

'Suppose.'

'Anyway, priceless.'

Brendan goes to roll down the driver's window only to remember it's stuck. The right side of his face is getting toasted again. He doesn't bother switching on the fan because that would only make it worse. They climb a bit of a hill and then level off before Sasa turns left. Sure enough, there's an Adriatika sign out front with *Za Prodaju* on it, which presumably means For Sale.

'Look at that,' says Irene, sitting up. 'Looks even prettier in real life.'

'D'you know something? I've seen worse.'

The villa sits on about a third of an acre but there's a fair size garden which looks like it might stretch all the way down to the sea. The Lada follows the Skoda into the gravel driveway and Brendan parks up, facing out.

'Don't worry,' says Irene, getting out, 'I'll let you do the talking.'

'Oh I don't know. You tied him up in knots back there.'

Sasa has keys but, oddly, he asks them to wait. Like there's a guard dog about to pounce. He rings a set of chimes. They hear footsteps inside and a man wearing a beanie appears at the door. Brendan immediately clocks him as the fella he saw sitting down at the pier. There can't be too many one-armed men walking around Perast in woolly beanies.

A bandage trails from his right arm. Irene finds her eye drawn to it but when the man notices her staring he reacts gruffly. Sasa speaks with him. The man shrugs, displeased. He stands to one side, his unmoored sleeve flapping in the breeze.

'Come, please!' calls Sasa.

'How's she cutting?' says Brendan, passing through.

The beanie man nods but says nothing.

'Just having a little peek,' smiles Irene, ducking apologetically.

They follow Sasa down the hall. The young auctioneer points out the rooms as they walk through. Small bedroom on the left, bathroom and shower, master bedroom *en suite* on the right – where beanie man must sleep because for some reason he leaves the curtains closed – utility room, storage space. Sasa opens a door to the kitchen which floods with sunlight from a bay window. The Gogartys are well versed in the exigencies of natural light.

'Family live this house for five generations. Now in Canada. Everybody go. Original cottage of Montenegro. Traditional style but now everythink has modern convenience of course – kitchen with new refrigerator, cooker, washink machine.'

Irene notices a soiled bandage unravelled on the kitchen table beside a scissors, gauze and antiseptic. Sasa follows her gaze and whips it away.

'Excuse,' he says, handling the bandage like a primed mousetrap. He drops it gingerly in the bin.

Brendan looks back down the hall and sees the beanie man sit against the Skoda bonnet. Absolutely one hundred percent the same fella, expertly rolling a cigarette one-handed. The missing digits do not appear to impair him unduly.

'In my opinion villa speakink for itself,' continues Sasa, running a tap over his hands. He shakes them dry. 'And come, please.'

He opens the kitchen door and leads the Gogartys out to the garden. A grassy incline slopes down to a deserted beach. There's a patio for barbecue with logs already cut and stacked, all neat and tidy. The cottage axe even rests in an upright position. Brendan and Irene exchange approving glances as Sasa resumes his spiel.

'You want different to Noh-ber? Here in garden, Adriatic. And please, to sit, relax, under cedar tree.'

The tree shapes and dominates the whole garden. A fine mature cedar which Sasa says is over a hundred years old, planted in this very spot by the first people who lived here. They see how it shelters the house from the wind as well as offering shade from the sun, just like now. The price tag on this gem – for God's sake they're only looking for £23,000 – jangles in Brendan's head like a fire sale.

'You like?' says Sasa, smiling at last.

'It's not the worst we've seen, in fairness,' nods Brendan. He turns to Irene like they are a tag team, all but slapping hands as he makes for the rope. 'What d'you think?'

'Does that man live here?' she asks.

'What man?'

'The man who opened the door.'

'He visitink from Sarajevo,' replies Sasa, checking his rinsed fingers for bloodstains.

'What happened to his arm?'

– 37 –

These mornings are like southern California; gloriously predictable. One daily perfection after another. Breakfast on the terrace and a soft breeze blowing across the bay. It's like stepping into a picture except Irene feels warmth seep through her body. Occasionally, the only thing she misses is a half-decent cup of tea.

Brendan wants to get the car window fixed before the return trip to Medjugorje so he goes looking for a mechanic in Perast. He finds a panel beater but says they couldn't agree a price – more like the mechanic wouldn't do it for free, suspects Irene – so Lily will be going back to Marijana in the same sealed condition they got her.

The previous evening they tried a different restaurant in town. The menu was just as limited as Vlado's but the service not nearly as friendly. Maybe they are just slowing down to the pace of things in Perast but after soaking up so much afternoon heat Irene just felt tired and lazy. They were back at the hotel before eleven o'clock and had a glass of wine on the terrace before bed. It sounds very old when she says it but Irene declares how lovely it is to get a good night's sleep.

God, I don't know myself any more!

Neither of them had expected the villa to be occupied but it had been well worth a look, even for curiosity's sake. 'A little beaut,' he called it when they stood in the garden. What wasn't to like? Original stone features, a mature cedar tree in a prize location overlooking the sea.

Yet on the drive back to the hotel she watched him decelerate from a giddy 100 miles per hour to a five mile an hour crawl, from being visibly excited to saying almost nothing. In the spirit of the moment Irene had gone along for the lark. Brendan's u-turn was hardly a rare event – she was used to these vagaries – but having gone to the bother of viewing a place she thought it odd he lost interest the moment they both agreed they liked it.

Hard to know what goes on inside that head of his . . .

Irene thought the villa was lovely but could take it or leave it. Very easy to see its appeal if it was only a short run up the road at home. But they don't live anywhere near here, do they? They live in Nobber.

'I was thinking of walking out the other end of town today,' she says. 'Want to come?'

'No, sure you go ahead,' he replies. 'Them boys down the pier will be waiting for me.'

They catch sight of a tall yacht across the bay letting out its sail. It spools out, orange and yellow, so bright it's almost garish. Once the sail is untied the breeze fills it like a balloon and the yacht picks up speed, heading out to sea at a rate of, well, knots.

'That'd be the business, hah?' says Brendan. 'Just sail up along the coast, stop whenever you like, wherever you felt like. Pick a spot and drop anchor, simple as pulling into a car park.'

'You'd probably tarmac the whole lot if they let you near it.'

'I'm a Captain of Industry,' he refrains. 'If it's development you're looking for, put me in charge.'

'Aye aye, captain.'

'Very funny.'

'Brendan, you don't even like boats. I can still see you going green on the car ferry to Holyhead.'

'Ah, that was different. There was a storm – force whatever – if you remember.'

'And you think they don't have storms here?'

Having picked up speed the yacht soon vanished, the scene emptying like an unfinished canvas awaiting a new subject. They sit, absorbing it all. Over the years they got used to simmering barbed silences, a hundred stored grievances competing for attention. For the first time in ages it doesn't feel like anything is bubbling away under the surface. They have no big plans so there's no real pressure. Their private terrace plays host to an easy *detente*. Brendan tops up her tea and pours himself another coffee. The same thought occurs to both of them at exactly the same moment: You could get used to this.

'What time do you want to eat?'

'Seven, half-seven?'

'What did you think of that place last night?'

'I preferred Vlado's.'

'Yeah, so did I. Though Vlado's probably has the same menu every night – mullet or mullet.'

'Catch of the day – same catch every day!'

'Right, let's go to Vlado's so.'

He finishes his coffee.

'Sounds like a plan.'

Irene's walk takes her up the coast, away from Perast until the path runs out. The road isn't great for pedestrians and on some stretches you need to hug the shoreline. There aren't so many people about. A handful of swimmers, a dog-walker or two, a few kite-flyers. The breeze is quite cool today so you could get burnt without feeling a thing.

She reaches what must be the next town. It's smaller than Perast and there's only a handful of small shops. She treats herself to an ice cream and sits on the wall, not a care in the world. She has to hand it to Brendan, what a brilliant idea it was to come here. Deep down she considers him a good man. It's just they've been through so much and it has taken its toll.

It strikes her as remarkable that she hasn't seen him use the phone for days – has he even recharged it since Medjugorje? Irene is so used to him being half-present, his thoughts far off. Maybe it's sunstroke from driving or he got a bang on the head but it's like he's forgotten all about the marina. She hardly recognises him not being distracted, manically checking for messages or looking for keys. He's as relaxed these days as she has ever seen him AC.

Cathal.

It shakes her. Suddenly she can't finish the cone. Who does she think she is, living it up? Stand-in honeymooners at their once fancy hotel. Did she just imagine she hadn't a care in the world?

Forgive me, darling.

She dumps the ice cream in a bin and reaches for her locket, a heart-shaped Victorian piece resting below her throat. She likes to keep it close. She has memorised the photo it holds of Cathal in a light blue baby grow. Underneath a golden curl she swiped from Jimmy's floor that day. She holds the locket between her fingers and kisses it.

Oh, God forgive me.

She used to have horrible nightmares that Cathal was still alive when they closed the coffin lid over him. That he was knocking from the inside, trying to get out except nobody could hear him over the church organ. Irene got into such a state she wanted the grave dug up days after the funeral, just to make sure. She even rang the undertaker. Brendan told her she needed to get a hold of herself. It plagued her for months and the thought of it still sends a shiver down her spine.

A blonde-haired girl with an unlit cigarette sits on a window sill across the road. It's like a film poster. Bored and glamorous in a quiet seaside town. She's a naturally cool smoker in a way that Irene will never be. The sign above says *Frizer – Viktoria*. It's a hairdressing salon. Half way through she stubs out her ciggie and goes inside.

Irene thinks of the ways Brendan is making a real effort. Whether he recharges his phone or not, at least he is trying. Even ironed a shirt the other night for God's sake! She knows he wants things to be better but Irene still struggles with the fact that when McGeedy walked out of jail, Brendan did nothing. Ran away more like, using the job as a ready-made excuse. She can't let him away with that.

She wonders if she's being too hard on him. She's good at finding his weaknesses because they're not so different to her own. What did *she* do about McGeedy's release? She sat at home, drank a bottle of wine and took up smoking again.

If you're watching me now, darling, you'll know you are never far from my heart. Keeping you near is a comfort but I can tell you it's not easy. You and I know this is how it will be for the rest of my days. Watch your old mam hit forty-one next year. That's more than twice your age, pet. Could you be happy for me if I make an effort too?

Through the salon window she sees the blonde girl refold towels. Irene crosses the road and knocks on the door.

'Excuse me. Do I need an appointment?'

Viktoria looks up, caught by surprise. Picking a magazine off a tubular glass table she glances around, presenting with an exaggerated shrug the gleaming wash basin and empty seats.

'Appointment?'

They both burst into girlish laughter.

– 38 –

He gets back to the hotel at about six and finds Irene doing her eyes at the small mirror. Fresh out of the shower, her hair conically wrapped in a towel.

'Catch anything?'

'Ah, don't worry about that – sure Juventus didn't catch anything either.'

Turning to face him directly, she stands, takes the towel and unwraps the beehive, revealing a new pageboy cut.

'What do you think?'

'Show me . . .'

He looks at her and swallows. She looks stunning even with her make-up only half done.

'You know something Irene,' he swallows. 'I'm a lucky man.'

She smiles into the mirror when he kisses her forehead. She replaces the top of the mascara tube and he goes for a shower. When he's dried off, clean shaven and dressed he finds her on the balcony in her favourite red linen dress. He remembers her mentioning she packed it in case of emergency. How nice to know some emergencies are a delight.

There's been a fair bit of running around but boys oh boys, what a day! It could not have gone better, in fairness. Good weather, a bit of fishing and one hell of a deal. Even Lily did her bit, gammy window and all. He feels energized. You can feel things have finally aligned. This is that sort of day. He can't wait for this evening which will be the cherry on top. They'll do dinner in style – or whatever – at Vlado's and when he gets his chance Irene will get the biggest land since Brendan dropped to one knee . . .

Medjugorje seems like a lifetime ago. With his wife looking like a film star he feels a bit scruffy. He can hardly match her for style if he's wearing the same shirt he had on the other night. A quick sniff of the armpits suggests it's clean enough for one more outing. Otherwise it's a blue Hawaiian ensemble which, truth be told, would secure him automatic entry to a fancy dress.

He remarks on this as they walk through the village. Irene says it doesn't matter but he does feel seriously under-dressed. His wife is turning heads in Perast and he's escorting her in khaki shorts and an unbuttoned corduroy jacket. Not that he minds, not deep down.

Sure, let heads turn! Isn't she with me?!

Vlado's is a bit busier tonight but their table is free. They are glad to see the same waitress on duty. Brendan remembers he tipped her well last time out so they should be treated royally. You could call it an investment.

'Good evening,' says the girl, taking Irene's coat. 'You look very beautiful.'

'Doesn't she just.'

The waitress leaves menus but they know better than to read them.

'On menu tonight is sea base,' she says, sparking up the lantern.

'Sea bass? Now you're talking.'

Brendan looks through the wines but in fairness he already knows what he's going to order.

'That white the other night was nice,' says Irene.

'No, no . . . let's have a bottle of, let's see . . that.'

'Champagne?'

'Yeah, do you have it?'

'Yes, I think.'

'Sure, why not?'

'Very good.'

The waitress turns to go. Brendan feels Irene watching him closely.

'Brendan . . .'

'Oh now.'

She leans across.

'I know you.'

'Indeed you do. I'm a lucky man.'

'What are you up to?

'You've a shocking suspicious mind, d'you know that?'

The waitress returns and presents Louis Roederer by the label.

'Sounds more like perfume to me!' laughs Brendan.

It's ridiculously priced and was probably smuggled into Montenegro but Brendan has a wedge of German marks in his khaki pocket and isn't this a once-off.

'Sir.'

'Good girl yourself. I'll look after that. And if you have a bucket of ice, we're laughing.'

'Of course.'

They are alone again.

'Okay so. Irene . . .'

'Brendan!'

The suspense is killing her, he can tell. Call him heartless but he's enjoying it. He takes a hold of the bottle and starts peeling gold foil from the neck like he knows what he is doing.

'D'you know something? You look a million dollars. Wait till I get this yoke.'

She sighs impatiently.

The cork is wedged so tight it won't budge. It's not like in films where every scene involving champagne goes without a hitch, popping and fizzing on cue. This takes a bit more squeezing and twisting than expected and he can feel his cheeks redden.

'Jesus, why the hell do they have to jam the cork in . . . anyways, I was just thinking how it suits us here. Montenegro. How we both like it, and, you know, maybe if we were able to come over now and again, weekends, whatever. Any time really. So the point of it all is, you know that place we looked at?'

'The villa?'

'It's ours.'

The cork pops loudly but he holds the bottle steady, not spilling a drop.

'I can be fierce smooth sometimes,' he smiles, 007-like.

The cat is out of the bag now and he feels he has to get to the finish. He can see Irene quizzically hanging on every word so there's no time to stop. He talks and pours, pours and talks. The bubbles froth and explode in the glass and dribble over the edge but in a good way, like they're supposed to. If it wasn't such an expensive bottle of plonk he'd swear it was Alka Seltzer.

'Let's just say I took a notion. Took Lily on a bit of a dander when you were out on your walk. Went back over to see yerman the auctioneer. We had a good old fashioned arm wrestle. Knocked a bit off the asking price – ran rings around him, in fairness. Won't put a figure on it now, but, a bargain. Our own villa on the Adriatic.'

'What do you mean you went back? Brendan, you shouldn't have.'

'Oh I know. I'm a terror once I get started.'

He raises his glass, tipping it towards her for the crowning moment. He might even stretch across and give her a kiss. But Irene doesn't even lift her glass. She folds her napkin and looks away. Like, the whole show comes to a complete and utter halt. He hardly notices the waitress bring the bucket.

'Two sea base. And for starter?'

Thrown by the cool reception he lowers his glass and opens the menu again. The young waitress asks if they need a minute or if they are ready to order.

'I'm sure we're ready,' says Brendan.

'No, we're not,' says Irene very evenly.

'Give us a few minutes, hah?'

Don't ask him why this isn't going according to plan but he can see they are already out of kilter.

'I thought you'd be thrilled.'

'You say it's for us but you never asked me.'

'Isn't it a surprise!'

'Some surprise.'

'What do you mean? It was you picked out the villa in the first place! Didn't you love it straight away.'

'We were only looking, that's what you said.'

'Ah that's what you tell them.'

'That's what you told *me*!'

He goes to raise his glass like a Take Two on the telly but the whole thing now feels a bit hollow. All the good gone out of it. He takes a sip before all the bubbles are gone. He doesn't know whether it's too sweet or too bitter and he's far from convinced it 'boasts a broad-shouldered maturity' like it says on the wine list. In actual fact, he'd prefer a pint.

'What about yerman?' says Irene.

'Who?'

'Yerman with the arm.'

'You mean without the arm.'

'The man at the door,' she clarifies, gritting her teeth.

'A sulky whore if ever I saw one. We'll get rid of him, no problem.'

'Where will he go?'

'How should I know? Back where he came from. Listen, we're not here to save the world!'

Irene looks really fabulous, especially in shimmering candlelight, but there's a hard edge in the air. She sits back and starts examining her nails. She does this whenever she wants to shut out the world, like she's having a good *tete-a-tete* with herself. Don't ask Brendan why but all the effort she's gone to with the dress, her new hairdo and delicately applied make-up just seems to make everything worse.

'Where does Cathal fit into this?'

'You're not going to go spoiling it now . . .'

'You didn't even mention him.'

'Didn't we talk about that the other day.'

'What do you mean *that*?'

'You know what I mean.'

She tosses the napkin back on the table and mumbles something about him being so bloody thick. Rising from her chair she asks for her coat. Brendan would really like to know what's got into her but in fairness he's at a loss for words, which doesn't happen too often. He gets to his feet as well but she tells him to stay where he is. To leave her be.

Jesus, it's like being in TJ's of a Friday night except there's hardly a drop taken.

He resolves not to make a show of himself here even though he couldn't care less what the other eaters make of this little drama. The waitress helps Irene into her coat and off she trots like a late entry to the Grand National. He flops back into the chair, silently shaking his head at two barely touched glasses of overpriced champers.

'Everything is okay?' asks the waitress.

'Well that's the $65,000 question, isn't it? You can take these away and get me a beer. Please.'

'You not want?'

'No. I want a beer.'

'And bottle also?'

'Take it all away.'

'Bottle is open.'

'Wouldja relax, I'll pay for the damn thing!'

'And now is one sea base?'

He shakes his head angrily and hands back the menus.

'No.'

'Starter?' she says, hope fading.

The waitress collects both glasses and takes the ice bucket away. Brendan is sure the fish is grand but he's lost his dash and at this point would not say no to getting plastered. He won't though. You might call that a very mature decision, even a broad-shouldered one, but he'd tell you not having the wherewithal to self-destruct is the only fringe benefit of being totally pissed off.

Unbidden, Cross Mountain comes to mind. He thinks of the local men voluntarily taking on that project, offering up sweat and tears to build something in good faith. And what thanks did they get?

Tell you something for nothing, he says to himself, *it'll be a long time before I go the surprise route again.*

He settles for one beer and drags it out until Irene comes back. It's been frustrating. On calmer reflection he wonders if maybe it was too much for her to take in at one go. He's sure she'll come around, common sense returning after a few urgent puffs. Still, it annoys him that the old tropes are tossed out as if nothing had changed. It's not one bit fair her bringing their son into the equation. There'll have to be new rules if she thinks she can throw a sucker punch before the row has even started.

Can she not see he did this for her with the best of intentions? Thought he read her mind correctly. Went and did all the spade work, pulled out all the stops. Something to make her happy. But no! So much for the grand, spontaneous act. If ever he could say he pulled off the deal of the century, this was it. But not so, it would appear, and no time to celebrate. *Obviously.* The deeds still quivering in his hands when they blow up in his face.

– 39 –

Irene doesn't feel like going back to the hotel but you can't walk too far in Perast before street lights run out. She goes as far as the waterfront where a group of men are night fishing off the pier. Dropping a bombshell is Brendan's idea of a surprise.

'Typical,' she mutters, seething.

Drags me into the plot like I'm part of the plan. Says nothing, then goes behind my back so's he can make the big gesture. For you, Irene. No it's not; it's about him. It always is.

She is fully aware that she and Brendan aren't ready to talk about Cathal – God knows if they ever will be – but just because it was mentioned the other night, as in him saying she should 'think about it', he seems to have decided that everything has been sorted. Well it hasn't. After five years does he think a few days in the sun is all it takes for things to fall back together again? Like Humpty Dumpty in reverse! He's so bloody thick at times. Raising a glass of bubbly when he announces this newsflash and expects her to be thrilled skinny.

It's getting a bit chilly so she makes a start towards Hotel St Jovan. The fact is they happened to land here almost by chance. Actually it's all by chance – even down to finding somewhere to stay and, now, falling out over a property deal.

It could only happen to us.

The only constant in tracing back to what led them here is that McGeedy was released. That bastard got out and the Gogartys didn't know how to deal with it. Rather than do the obvious and confront him at the prison gates they end up going on a holy pilgrimage, though she's quite unsure how. And yes, she went along with it.

After all that's happened, Medjugorje was hardly a success. As if! But why couldn't they just settle for this short trip into Montenegro as a consolation prize? Relax for a few days in sunshine with fresh fish, nice wine, a few pages of Jilly. And leave it at that!

So now he wants to make it longer term and turn the villa into a holiday home. What he really means is, provided the war doesn't spill over from Bosnia, the two of them can jump in a plane whenever they want to avoid reality. Travel light, isn't that the beauty of it? Come over with your duty-free for a bit of TLC. They haven't been out of Ireland – even away from Nobber – this long in five years and, if you asked Irene, every extra hour is beginning to feel like betrayal. Her little boy at home. Lying in the ground, abandoned.

When she went to ask about exhuming Cathal she told the parish priest she'd prefer to bring her son's remains to the surface and have him cremated. Then they could bring him along with them wherever they went. Father Coleman rang Brendan who rushed home directly from work.

'You're not the most supportive when I come up with an original idea,' she told him.

The only good thing she can say about Deansgrange is it gives her some place to go – though it's not like she can hang around a cemetery all day. She still grapples with the idea of her child interred deep below the earth. The antique locket around her neck is a comfort. She feels his presence but it's not always enough. They may be sunning themselves here in the Adriatic but you'd want to be a far better salesman than Sasa Blagovic to convince her they haven't walked out on their son.

She shivers. The hotel is only fifty yards away. She sees their room is unlit – presumably Brendan is still over in Vlado's, stewing over fresh fish. He doesn't even like champagne but she figures if he stays put he'll have a whole bottle to get through. He won't let it go to waste. She's not ready to face him but doesn't want to call it a night just yet. When she sees a taxi pull away from the hotel she impulsively flags it down.

Following out the coast road it's easy enough to find the villa. The cottage stands alone facing the sea and she can make out the pole with the *Za Prodaju* sign in the distance. There's a light on inside.

'You want me wait?' asks the driver.

'No,' she replies, sifting through her purse for German coins.

She walks to the front door. The taxi swings around and goes back down the hill. The door chimes shimmer loosely in the breeze when she pulls the cord. There is no answer so she jangles them harder. A shadow fills the glass before the hall light flicks on.

The man with one arm stares at her.

'*Da*?' he says abruptly.

'Hello. I'm sorry to . . . do you speak English?'

'Little.'

'We met the other morning.'

'Yes, I see you.'

He's barefoot. He wears a t-shirt over tracksuit bottoms and a different woollen cap with the letters FK Sarajevo. His right shoulder leads to a stump, dressed, she notices, with a clean bandage. He is almost hostile but him being unfriendly doesn't really bother her. Oddly enough, she feels less put out, even brave, though she's not quite sure why she is here.

'Can I come in please?'

He raises his eyebrows in surprise. She presumes he will refuse. Then he stands back, mock-curtseying like a *maitre d'* for her to enter. Closing the door he points down the hall to the kitchen. She follows the smell of tobacco and a tell-tale wisp from a hand-rolled ciggie on the table. He does not reply when she asks to sit down. She sits down anyway. He remains standing.

'I am Irene. My name is Irene.'

'Damir.'

'Pleased to meet you, Damir. I come from Ireland.'

'*Irska*,' he repeats, nodding impatiently.

'Would you mind sitting down please? It makes me nervous looking up at you.'

Grudgingly, he pulls a chair out and sits.

'My husband Brendan wants to buy this property. It seems his heart is set on it.'

'You need speaking with Sasa. Property his problem.'

'It's you I want to speak to.'

'I?'

'You are from Sarajevo?'

He does not respond. She tries again.

'What happened to your hand?'

'*A šta vas briga?*' he blusters, annoyed.

'Sorry?'

'For why you ask?'

'It was on my mind.'

He faces her directly across the table. He grounds the end of his rollie into an improvised ashtray, the tin lid of a coffee jar.

'I ask question to you. Explain me why war so good for you but for us take everything?'

'I'm sorry, I don't know what you mean.'

'You walk in, take what you like . . .'

'How were we to know you were here?'

'What you care!' he snorts, picking at the bandage and withdrawing into silence. He flicks the coffee lid. 'My wife with baby coming.'

'Where is your wife?'

'She work in restaurant.'

'Vlado's?'

'*Da.*'

'That's your wife?'

'Anja.'

'Yes, Anja. The girl, the waitress. We met her a couple of times. She's lovely.'

His mood lightens a little.

'The baby. Your first?'

'New baby. *Da.* You have childs?'

'Yes. A boy.'

'He come to Perast?'

'Cathal comes everywhere with us.'

He takes a pouch of tobacco from his pocket. The papers are inside and she watches him roll one-handed. She takes a pack from her bag – no Silk Cut in Montenegro but they do sell Marlboro Lights – and he lights hers before flaming his own. He is calmer but his feet shift restlessly. Billowing smoke towards the ceiling he reaches over to push a window ajar. He sits back at the table.

'Anja say will be girl.'

'A child is a gift.'

'Anja says will be girl, but boy, girl, I not care. Good child.'

'We say health is wealth. Nothing to do with money now – the opposite in fact. Good health is a gift.'

'Yes.'

'What will you do next?'

'Next? What means "next" when you have nothing!'

'But Sasa, the auctioneer, said you were visiting.'

'One time we have apartment in Sarajevo. Then bomb come and apartment destructed. Even our cat Mima disappear. This what happen.'

He displays his bandaged stump. Then he removes the woollen hat, startling her. His head is shaven, revealing a jagged, untidy scar. An angry red line zigzags under his ear from the jawline to the back of his skull. She feels like she is intruding and is relieved when he covers up again.

'Souvenir,' he says with an ironic shrug.

'I am very sorry.'

'For why you sorry?' he asks.

Irene grounds her ciggie against the ash tray. Confronted in this way her words feel inadequate, forcing her to safer ground.

'And you made it here. To Perast.'

'Cousin of Anja is Sasa.'

'The auctioneer?'

'He let we stay short time here.'

'But now you have to go.'

'*Da,*' he nods.

He takes one last drag and stubs the butt into the lid. He stands again to close the window, looking past the garden and settling his gaze on the glittering night sea. She notices how branches of the cedar tree move behind him in a graceful dance with the breeze. He remains standing and continues to look out which makes her feel self-conscious and awkward. She can't help picturing the harsh geometry of his stitches. Damir does not turn around when he speaks.

'For why you come?'

– 40 –

Brendan is not trying to make a career of feeling sorry for himself but he's well on the way. Sitting out on the balcony he can see she's really gone and done it this time. Turned the tables on him goodo back in the restaurant and him thinking he was about to put a big smile on her face. Really and truly, they might as well go back to TJ's for old times' sake. The only difference tonight in Vlado's is she was sober and didn't trip over any furniture on the way out. He reminisces about their lively Navan *soirées* back home.

If it involved one glass – or five – too many at Dino's, she might throw a rattler from the pram and storm out. Nothing you couldn't get used to and definitely no need to bring in the riot squad. More often than not she'd stagger up to TJ's three doors away and collapse into one of their big armchairs with a vodka tonic on the go.

Brendan would know where to find his wife so it's not like there was ever any need to go tearing up Kennedy Road after her. He'd take his time. Finish his carbonara and round it off with one of their *crème brulée* specials. Besides, there was always half a carafe to polish off – whenever Irene tipped over the edge you could be sure she'd already ordered way more drink than she could swallow.

He could think of better things to do than watch her crash and burn, but at least back home you knew where she was. Alternatively, Brendan would ring a local hackney to drop by TJ's and pick her up – they know her well – and hope he wouldn't get hit with an £20 puke charge at the end of it. Otherwise, no big panic. Except this is different. They're not at home; they're in Montenegro.

And this crack, get-me-my-coat-please, stalking off high and mighty into the night. You wouldn't get it from a spotty teenager so you wouldn't . . .

He can hear his tummy rumbling which reminds him he forfeited dinner. Maybe he should've ordered the sea bass and ate solo, make Vlado's truly a home from home. All's he could find back in the hotel room was a packet of pretzels, something so salty that he wouldn't class them as food at all. He asks at reception if there was any chance of a toasted cheesy but was told the chef had gone home.

'Chef?!' he laughs, exasperated. 'I mean to say, we're talking cheese on bread under a grill. I'd go down to the kitchen and make it meself if you'd let me.'

It means wartime rations – stale pretzels and champagne. He rescued the Roederer before leaving Vlado's and brought it back with him. No point wasting good plonk at $50 a throw. Next time he makes a killing he pledges to pocket a bottle opener and pick up a six-pack. No more of this do-it-for-show bullshit, shaking it up and wasting fizz like some grand prix eejit.

He expected Irene would be at the hotel when he got back. Sitting out on the balcony, probably. When she wasn't, he guessed she might be down by the pier or having a smoke in the hotel restaurant across the road. But there was no sign of her. He returns to reception where the night porter is playing Patience behind the desk with a very worn deck of cards. It's obviously not the first time he's seen a couple in the honeymoon suite having a barney.

'Look, it doesn't matter about the cheesy. I'm here about my wife.'

The night porter tries hard to stay focused on the game.

'Your wife?' he repeats, scanning the table. Frozen in his upturned hand the next card to be dealt.

'She went for a walk, I know, but that was two and a half, maybe three hours ago.'

The night porter turns to Brendan, popping a sunflower seed.

'What you like me do?' he sighs.

'What do I want you to do? She's a guest at your hotel. Find her!'

Brendan hears a very unmanly shriek in his voice. He should gather himself, starting with deep breaths. One of the refugees arrives and says something in gobbledegook. It sounds like a complaint of some sort but the night porter isn't having any of it. The refugee, a small man about ten years older than Brendan, is pointing at the stairs. They lock horns in angry debate and Brendan is reduced to the role of spectator. It only finishes when the older man walks off, shouting back angrily as he trudges away. The porter spits a shell to the floor and plays his next card, the five of clubs. Brendan waits until he looks up and makes a point of keeping it nice and measured.

'Look, I can see you're busy. It's just this hasn't happened before.'

'She take medications?'

'Not at all! But she has no sense of direction. I can tell you that for a fact.'

'Where she go?'

'If I knew that I wouldn't be standing here, would I? I know it's not your fault but I am worried, you understand? My wife is headstrong, bull-headed. Once she takes a notion, she's a holy terror.'

The night porter's brow furrows. He mouths 'holy terror' like he is trying to memorise it.

'Lookit Horse, go on back to your bloody game.'

Brendan stomps upstairs to get a jumper, gritting his teeth at the uselessness of those who don't give a shit. This does not qualify as a delightful emergency and all he is looking for is a bit of help. Part of him really wishes they were back in TJ's, which is saying something.

He can't even decide where to start looking when he hears a key turn in the door. It surprises him how glad he is to see Irene appear, tossing her coat on the bed. She's got her serious face on but she's steady on her feet which at least means she's still sober. He reminds himself not to wade in all guns blazing. She sees the champagne and goes to the bathroom to get a glass. Louis Roederer in a toothbrush holder. Says it all, hah?

'Had me worried so you had. Running off like that.'

She pours champagne. It's noticeably flatter so there's no big rush of bubbles this time. Sure, what about it? It's not like they're celebrating.

'Didn't mean to worry you.'

'Where did you go?'

She drinks the bubbly without remark. At $50 a throw, he remembers.

'We can't take that house, Brendan.'

'The villa?'

'They lost their home in the war.'

'Who?'

'The pair who live there.'

'Aren't they gone to Canada?'

'Not them. Sasa the auctioneer is her cousin.'

'Whose cousin?'

'You know the waitress. Anja.'

'Up above in Vlado's?'

'That's why he was so half-hearted – remember, the way he didn't bother pushing it.'

'Hold on now, hold on. You mean to say you went over there? On your own?'

Irene takes another sip and puts down the glass. The bubbly repeats on her without making any noise, belching like a lady. Then she speaks slowly, like she's reciting the two-times tables to an *amadán*.

'The couple living in the villa . . .'

'What couple?'

'Anja and Damir. They live there. And Sasa, the auctioneer, is Anja's cousin. He lets them stay there.'

'Squatters?'

'The man we saw at the house . . .'

'Oh, The Happy Fella!'

'That's Damir, Anja's husband. A bomb hit their apartment so that's why he wears a hat. They were under the table at the time. They thought the danger had passed because their cat came in the window. Cats usually know when it's safe, y'know, the same as whenever there are earthquakes.'

'Irene, are you alright?'

'And to top it all, Anja is due in a few weeks.'

Brendan would not be joking if he told you he was really concerned. It's one thing her going AWOL but now that she's no longer a missing person he wonders if the one-armed bandit has been giving her the wacky baccy instead of a rollie. Wouldn't put it past him. Except she's not talking like a mad thing. She's not even hysterical. It's far worse; she's calm and logical, like what she's saying makes sense – which, he can tell you right now, it does not.

'What about it?'

'I'm not setting foot inside that house.'

She refills her glass and drifts out to the balcony. Now that she's rejoined the smoking community she feels obliged to light up at every opportunity. It's a bit windy and she goes through three matches before catching flame. She wraps her free arm around her waist to clamp a slight shiver. Brendan's got his woolly jumper on. Besides, he doesn't feel the cold in the same way so he just sits down at the table and lets her puff away.

'They seen you coming, Irene, d'you know that. Gave you a right sob story. Cripples, refugees, babies, the whole shebang.'

'I talked to him.'

'He ran rings around you more like. Gave you the Peig Sayers treatment – Yugoslavian version. What's this all about, hah? Property deals are *my* business.'

'If this is for us, I have a say, Brendan. As much as you.'

'Well it's me knows a deal when I see one and I'm telling you I made a killing.'

'I don't want to make a killing.'

'Ah, that's just a phrase. Sure didn't you love the place straight away – the garden, the sea, flagstones. Even the oul cedar tree. The point is I did bloody well!'

'I'm not comfortable about it. Do you hear me?'

'This whole thing was supposed to be a surprise,' he pauses, feeling once more a little sorry for himself. 'Is it because I didn't bring you with me?'

'I don't want it.'

'I've signed!'

'Then *un*-sign. Otherwise you'll be coming out here on your own.'

She walks back inside without closing the doors. From the balcony Brendan feels the wind pick up. Some of the boats parked in the bay – *berthed,* as mariners say – bob up and down like wind-up toys in a child's bath. You can hear the odd sail flapping but every so often a gust jangles their metal rings, a shadow of empty vessels in constant rattle.

– 41 –

Brendan figures they have three more days to kill so there's no point rushing back to Medjugorje. They'll have to rely on Lily to get them home and neither of them are thrilled at the prospect of crossing Bosnia a second time.

It's only days since they left behind Rosemary, Packie and the devout sisters. Maybe the prodigal Gogartys will find themselves frozen out as dissenters. The pilgrimage seems like a different story, a different trip, echoing already like a distant memory. Why, when you leave home, does it feel so much happens in a short space of time?

'Looks like we'll have to finish our penance on the beach,' Irene remarks, rubbing sun cream into her legs.

'Pure luxury,' scowls Brendan. 'Grin and bear it.'

She didn't sleep too well. She doesn't think Brendan did either but it was easier all round to feign it and avoid getting into another argument. A sort of unofficial truce across their giant bed. In truth, they knew the other was awake but both preferred to lie there and listen to what sounded like a wild storm hurtle across the bay until it gradually blew itself out.

She cannot clear from her mind the image of Damir's angry red scars. Why did he show them to her? With a head injury like that it must have been touch and go for him in Sarajevo. And if he's in such a state he's hardly out of the woods. For Anja, all the joys of pregnancy clouded by dark, worrying thoughts.

Sunlight floods the room to announce a new day and it's hard to imagine the world can be anything less than perfect. A boiled egg with toast and coffee served on the terrace is a morning routine they got used to very easily. A nice break from regular life. But while Irene knows the imposition of spending 72 more hours in Perast is definitely a first world problem, it does feel like this trip has run its course.

She can tell that Brendan is in a major strop because his master plan has backfired. Irene has told him quite plainly that if he goes through with buying the villa he'll be enjoying the view by himself. She played her part in this charade so count her out from here on in. He'll have to go back to the auctioneer in Kotor and cancel the purchase. Her position is clear – in fact she is rapidly losing interest in whether he sorts this out or not. That said, if he's half as good at undoing a mess as creating one, she reckons it should be all be resolved by tea time.

It was silly of him to go to all that fuss and bother last night. Typical overkill. She's also very annoyed with herself. Yesterday, walking back from the hairdressers, she felt upbeat, even optimistic. Viktoria was lovely and they had a good laugh, even without speaking the same language. Just doing something on the spur of the moment gave her a real lift. Feeling good about herself. She carried that right through to dinner, spending a lot longer on her make-up than usual. Now it all feels puerile and self-indulgent. As for dressing up? Ah stop . . .

It doesn't take much to overdo things these days. This morning feels like a bad hangover. She wants to kick herself for trying too hard. The red *gúna* lies in a crumpled heap on a beside chair. It definitely won't be needed for the rest of the trip. Why did she bring it at all? What was she thinking? Stuffing it back into the suitcase is a glum embarrassment that tastes like defeat.

Not for the first time since leaving Nobber she wonders why even the simplest things trip them up. Is it me, she asks? For a couple of days she thought they were getting on fine, nothing spectacular but comfortable enough. Then he pulls this stunt with the villa and she instantly hates him for it. Maybe on another day it would have come off beautifully, just like he planned, instead of feeling completely and utterly wrong.

'I did it for us,' he groans. Whether that's true or not, it does bother her that he just went off and did it without taking their son into account. It feels so incredibly disloyal.

She leaves him at the hotel and sets off for the beach. Her secret cove is deserted today. She doesn't even get through a few paragraphs before giving up on Jilly. There's nobody around and she's tempted to go skinny-dipping. The only thing stopping her is if someone lands on the beach, she won't be able to come out of the water.

It's a contradiction. She loves having the cove all to herself but today she really does not like being alone. Not that she wanted Brendan to tag along. She'd settle, say, for a couple of swimmers or even a few strangers lounging on the low chairs. Living beings to colour in the emptiness.

The sea is a turquoise bath pooling around her ankles. Usually she wades out a bit and splashes water over her shoulders and chest before taking the plunge. The calm waters now feel deep and uninviting for some reason, an imaginary shark lurking near the shore. She knows it's absolutely stupid but it is how it feels. She's never had this sensation before. Danger, everywhere.

She turns back and towels down. Pulling on a t-shirt she fastens her skirt and climbs through pine trees to the coast road. It wasn't really a fright. Call it a mini-panic attack but she didn't feel comfortable staying here. It's oddly reassuring to see people and traffic around town.

She crosses over to Vlado's. The chef is counting wine stock at the bar. He taps his watch to indicate the restaurant will not open until seven o'clock. Irene sees a figure in the dining room polishing glasses with a dish towel.

'Anja?'

The chef grumbles the way chefs do and turns for the kitchen. Anja approaches, re-wiping the same glass. It's the first time Irene has seen her out of uniform.

'I'm sorry about last night. Storming off and all.'

'You are okay?'

'I met your husband. It was me who visited the villa.'

'Yes, Damir say me.'

'He told me what happened. It's awful. I just wondered what you are going to do?'

'Clean glass Vlado want,' she laughs self-consciously and stops wiping. 'I think we go back Sarajevo. Fighting not as bad like before.'

'But you've a baby coming.'

Their eyes meet. Irene didn't mean to but it feels like she's put Anja on the spot.

'Yes,' she says, tears filling. '*Septembra.*'

The chef reappears, checking dockets at the cash register. Irene stands closer to Anja, screening her from view. She suddenly seems so young, so vulnerable. Irene thinks of her serving them champagne while she carries single-handedly the double burden of pregnancy and a severely debilitated husband. Brendan and Irene have enough problems of their own, but if you're talking about fairness it strikes her that Anja and Damir have drawn a very short straw.

'Vlado not know,' she whispers. 'Say nothing.'

'Of course.'

'Into what world we bring this baby?' she asks, wiping her eyes.

– 42 –

'It's all gone arseways,' he sighs.

Irene's buggered off to her private paradise so Brendan sits alone on the balcony. He recharges the mobile to call the bank in Navan. A machine answers and he's telling it to hurry up before it goes automatically to Richard Clayderman. One forgettable tune will cost him a small fortune. Then he gets through to one of the girls who puts him on hold for Andy, the manager. It's a very tinny line but at least they can talk. He puts a stop on funds being put through.

'Get caught out with a time share?' enquires Andy, like a confessor who has heard this gaffe many times before. 'There's cowboys at that lark every which way.'

'Not at all,' replies Brendan. 'Just saw something, then changed me mind.'

He doesn't even want to think about the expense of the call. He isn't bothered to follow up with Gary or Fiona so he turns the mobile off so as not to get hit with roaming charges. He's sure everything is grand and is too distracted to consider otherwise.

He feels confrontation looming as he takes Lily for a run out to Kotor. Parked up, he makes his way into Adriatika. The receptionist is gone to lunch while Sasa manfully tries to flog some new-build condo in broken English on the phone. Brendan paces the desk in front of him. He can hear the customer back out long before their conversation ends.

Sasa hangs up. 'Belgians,' he shrugs, ruefully. He shakes his head once more before snapping out of it with a loud clap. 'So, Brendan, my friend!'

'We're in trouble, Sasa. Deep doo-doo.'

'What we do?

'The missus.'

'Beautiful lady.'

'That's what you think. She's put the kybosh on the villa. Bananas, pure bananas. And I'll tell you something for nothing. It's all your fault.'

'What I do?'

'Your cousin. That's what.'

'Anja?'

'And her fella.'

'Husband is Damir.'

'Well they've turned my wife's head something wojous. Talk about a sob story! And she's fallen for it – hook, line and sinker. Not that I was there to put a stop to their gallop but the bottom line is the sale is off. Finito. It'd drive you to drink but that's where we are now.'

Sasa straightens in the chair.

'We make agreement, Brendan. I accept. Signink name on paper. You make payment. Deal is deal is done.'

'Now hold on a minute, Horse. Think my wife lost the plot all by herself? No! It's thanks to your cousin Annie's other half. Refugees, cripples, babies, every sob story in the book – even a bloody dead cat dragged into it!'

'Balkan life is full of tragedy.'

'There you go – the soft touch, hah? You never said nothing about this little arrangement of yours. Kept it on the QT.'

'I not know this QT.'

'Lookit, wasn't it supposed to be our holiday home. Now she won't touch it with a barge pole.'

He thinks the penny is finally dropping but you can never be too sure.

'Cancel the sale, Sasa. Because if you don't, I will.'

Enough said. Leaving quickly he hears Sasa grab the phone. Brendan is up and down the wrong street before he can remember where he left the car. It's a pattern when he's at his most agitated. Rustling the keys he tries the next block over. The hinge on the driver's door clearly needs oil. It squeals open, like it's in pain.

I swear to God, this whole thing is way more hassle than it's worth.

The sun is high already and he tries to roll down the window, forgetting that it's banjaxed. He reaches across the front seat to let air in from the passenger side. The stretching movement reminds him of performing in-car gymnastics outside Arbour Hill. He recalls the Range Rover side mirror reflecting the sergeant and two bullocks prowl into view. Talk about timing! A split second before the prison gate pushed open. If they hadn't shown up it could be a very different story altogether.

How far would he have gone?

It's a straight enough run along the coast, then inland for a bit before dropping to sea level for Perast. He ditches the car at the hotel. There's no sign of Irene so he collects the rod and goes down to find Juventus and Tarzan on the pier. They act like he was expected, a hearty welcome for the outsider. There's no sign of the young lad. One of them has landed what looks like a medium-sized bream. It's thrashing around in their red bucket. Brendan isn't great at pretending he's in top form but casting a line over calm water is as good a place to start as any.

The two boys are a tonic. After an hour he feels a little better. They're like a pair of biddies, getting all het up about something, constantly talking, joking, arguing, then sulking or just going quiet. He hasn't a clue what they're on about but it's very entertaining. Juventus catches another bream and he pulls it off the line, taking care with the hook.

'Good!' he exclaims, thumbs up to Brendan and tosses it into the bucket.

Tarzan takes a closer look and nods. Supper in the pot. Brendan wanders over to a shop and comes back with three cans of Sprite.

'There you go.'

They're slow to take the cans, like there's a catch. Tarzan holds the tin sideways, looking askance at Brendan.

'No, no. You better stand that up Horse or it'll go all over the place.'

'*Mnogo vam hvala.*'

'No bother.'

He snaps the aluminium tab and takes a good long slug. They watch him. It occurs to Brendan that they may never have drunk straight out of a tin can. He shows Juventus how to pull the ring back. The older man nearly jumps when it hisses loudly. Tarzan follows more cautiously but the Sprite fizzes all over. Juventus shouts at him to be more careful. The pair of them have Brendan in stitches. Tarzan lifts the can to his mouth and it spills over his chin. He laughs and tries again.

'Try tilting your head back a bit!'

Tarzan takes another mouthful, then rests the can on the ground. He steps back in concentration and belches loudly. Juventus gives him an earful about manners and insulting the visitor from *Irske*. Tarzan bows apologetically and tries to cover up another belch. You'd never think you could beat so much crack out of a tin can.

Brendan is still in kinks when an old Skoda pulls in at the end of the pier. Sasa gets out of the car and makes a beeline towards the trio. He's got the cheque in his outstretched hand and he is not happy.

'Brendan!' he roars. 'Why you do this?'

Brendan devotes his attention to changing the bait but that doesn't stop Sasa shoving the cheque in his face. Juventus and Tarzan watch on, taken aback.

'Why you do this?'

'I'm from Nobber, Sasa. We're no fools.'

'You break word. This not legal after we make agreement.'

'Ah, what about it!'

Juventus asks Sasa what's going on. Brendan presumes that Sasa explains in their own language that this fucker from overseas reneged on a deal. It sounds like the two boys take up the argument on Brendan's behalf but Sasa waves them away. He's come for the *Irske*, not for them. Their voices rise higher and higher and it's hard to know whether they're fighting his corner or they don't like being told off by some whippersnapper. Sasa waves the cheque one last time and tells Brendan this is not finished. He's really annoyed and, making his way back to the Skoda, he nearly trips over a thick rope coiled at the steps.

The two boys are still in lively discussion but Brendan has had his fill of it. Things settle down and he's back with his own thoughts, busily catching nothing. A gust of wind blows one of the empty cans into the water but Juventus retrieves it with his net. Then the little lad arrives with his divine branch and the two boys give him a big welcome.

'*Dober dan,*' the young lad says to the visitor.

'How's she cutting?'

The boy takes a closer inspection of the bucket and approves the catch in that serious way of his. Brendan calls him over and hands him a five-mark coin.

'Go and get yourself a mineral.'

He raises the Sprite can and points to the shop.

'Go on, take it.'

The boy shakes his head. The codgers say something to him but he digs his heels in. He won't take the money. He sits on the pier, swings his legs over the edge and casts a line. Juventus looks over and shrugs.

'Not a bother,' says Brendan, a little puzzled.

Watching the young fella reminds him of the last time he brought Cathal fishing. Brendan pulled a lovely brown trout on the Boyne outside Slane. A full four-to-five pounder. The boy went pale when it landed squirming on the grassy bank.

'Ah, don't be worrying – sure they don't feel a thing,' says Brendan. 'Unhook him there like a good man.'

'Let him go, Daddy, please,' begged the child.

Brendan laughed at the idea but was ticked off all the same.

'Wouldja stop in the name of Jesus! Give him a clout with the stick. Isn't it a mercy killing!'

Cathal covered his eyes.

'Fishes have blood,' he blurted, sobbing.

'D'you know what,' said his father. 'Do you know who cries? Babies cry. Girls cry. And sissies.'

That's when the boy tossed the trout back into the river.

Brendan had planned to go up to Lough Sheelin a couple of weeks later and Cathal wanted to go with him. Brendan thought he'd teach him a lesson and told him there was no room for sissies on a fishing trip. Didn't want the lad having it every which way. He'd have to learn some time. Cathal was all ready with his anorak and blue wellington boots and even though he didn't want to see a fish with a hook stuck in its mouth, he promised he'd be good. If Daddy caught something he'd look away.

Irene pleaded at the last minute not to be so hard and to just let the boy tag along.

'So he wants to go fishing but he doesn't want to catch anything? Irene, would you ever cop on!'

Brendan told the pair of them no meant no.

And so the drive up to Sheelin was uneventful. He turned on the radio, just for a bit of company. He'd rented a boat for the afternoon and rowed out to the Conleen side, wondering if he'd done the right thing. Let the boat drift with the current from the middle of the lake. It wasn't a day he could say he enjoyed. Didn't catch anything either.

'*Hai!*' says the kid in Perast, pointing.

Sure enough, a jerky movement on Brendan's line. At last! He reels it in and knows from the light pull it won't be anything to shout about. Juventus and Tarzan watch him draw it in. A baby bream. He unhooks and throws it back in the water.

'*Premala!*' says Juventus sympathetically.

'Yeah,' says Brendan. '*Premala.*'

– 43 –

Irene can tell that Brendan has really taken the hump but feels she has to put her foot down. He can wallow in it all he likes for she will make no apology. When she gets back to the hotel she notices his phone housed in the charger, green light flashing. Should've guessed. He's back in the saddle and open for business.

The skies have clouded over a bit but it's still nice. Cardigan weather. She sits out on the terrace. There's a couple of small fishing boats in the bay and she can see people ramble along the main street. An interesting way to pass an hour, people-watching, especially when the people you're watching can't see you.

A shelf of books in the foyer downstairs nestles like a cultural artefact. It supports a mixed-bag of paperbacks in different languages, left there by guests who were either fast readers or hopeless cases. Irene has fully given up on Jilly so she'll be adding to the collection.

Brendan arrives back.

'Did you catch anything?'

'No.'

He's still in a huff and acts like he expects Irene to haul him out of it. She doesn't feel she has done anything wrong so she's prepared to put up with this strop for a little longer. After that he can get stuffed. He calls out to announce he's going for a shower.

She is about to ask him why he feels the need to tell her this. Then she hears the bathroom door click shut, locked.

So that's where we are.

Lighting a cigarette she starts thinking of home. She feels a need to do something with herself. Time is drifting by and when they get back to Nobber she knows she can't spend the rest of her life in a dressing-gown.

A thin man walks slowly down the street and sits on a bench facing the sea. He's wearing a woollen hat. She recognises him. The missing arm is not visible from the angle she is sitting. He produces a rollie and when he lights up she marvels how he can perform the entire action with one functioning hand.

She feels like calling down to him or even walking over to say hello but it doesn't seem right, for whatever reason. She's a bad faker. If she goes downstairs to act all surprised crossing the street he would know she had been watching him. She finishes her ciggie and observes him finish his, like they are smoking together.

She finds it peculiar that they met as strangers two days ago and had such a forthright, honest conversation. Now they are strangers once again, keeping their distance. Sort of like the Kilbeggan ladies. You meet them on a plane by chance and next minute you're having an existential chat about the afterlife. She wonders will Kathleen and Julie forgive them for doing a runner – *Like, they can't pray for our souls and then shun us, can they?*

Brendan comes out bare-chested, a man skirted in a bathroom towel.

'It's getting cool. You should put on a shirt.'

He leans on the rail and looks out at sea. Glancing down the street, he sees Damir on the bench.

'Isn't that yerman?'

'Where?'

'On the bench over there. Does he know we're staying here?'

'How would he?'

'Sure I don't know what you told him.'

Brendan goes inside to get dressed. She laughs at a hint of jealousy in his voice. She knows he isn't jealous – not remotely – but it's a funny notion all the same. Damir stands up and stretches before walking back the way he came, presumably to the villa. She wonders when he and Anja will go back to Sarajevo. Or what will they go back to? From what he told her, it sounds like the whole apartment block was blown up. 'Destructed,' as he put it.

'What do you want to do for eats?' says Brendan, buttoning his shirt.

'I don't mind.'

'Not Vlado's so, if it's all the same to you.'

'Fine.'

'There's plenty of other places.'

'Wherever you like.'

'I'm sure the restaurant here is fine.'

'The hotel?'

'Yeah.'

'Alright.'

Picking the hotel restaurant, which they both know isn't great, is him declaring the sulk period isn't over. She can expect no more from her husband than minimal effort. He doesn't give a damn, that's the way it's going to be. They go for a drink beforehand. Brendan isn't particularly talkative and, in truth, neither is Irene. Familiar conversation can be a painfully tiresome business.

There's a portable black and white TV behind the bar. The screen is snowy and the barman fiddles with rabbit's ears to get a better reception. He bangs the counter and shakes his head repeatedly. He says over and over that some market in Sarajevo has been bombed. The news shows UN soldiers walking around vegetable stalls with a measuring tape.

The images are grainy and unclear. Through the dust-covered lens of a frightened cameraman they can just about make out people lying on the ground, covered in blood. You can hear the underfoot crunch of broken glass wherever the camera roams. Dead bodies being loaded into the back of cars like sacks of potatoes. One helmeted man is lying on top of his moped in the middle of the road, like a narcoleptic who has chosen the oddest place to sleep.

The barman says it's the second time this market has been hit but it could be a trick to get the Americans involved. The Gogartys don't know what he's on about but it doesn't look like a trick. It's absolutely horrific.

'Clinton get NATO to bomb Serbs,' he adds, engrossed in what he sees. 'Finish it, for sure.'

Neither Irene or Brendan really understand where Clinton or NATO fit into the picture, but it's a blessing that they have someone else to talk to instead of gawking at each other in awkward silence.

'*Katastrofa*,' says the barman gravely. These images are now coming in live and the Gogartys, almost despite themselves, tune in.

It may not be a colour TV but the city looks quite green at night. Despite all his re-jigging the reception does not improve and it's hard to make out what's going on. Bombs exploding in the dark. A roar of jets and what sounds like automatic gunfire. Some of the refugees come downstairs and watch the small screen in silence. Some are tearful. One woman, clearly shocked, whispers to herself in prayer.

'Get us another two drinks there, chief, when you get a chance,' says Brendan, momentarily indifferent to the sight of mass murder.

Dinner is passable but neither of them enjoy it. All the staff in the restaurant are talking about NATO and how the siege in Sarajevo will end after more than three years. Out on the street locals and refugees are arguing, presumably about the same thing. For all the talk of war being so far away it now feels very near.

When they return to the foyer Brendan says he's going to bed. There's no talk of a nightcap, which is probably a sensible move. They drift upstairs. Irene sits out on the balcony for one last smoke. The temperature has dropped so she slips a jacket over her shoulders. She hears familiar tinny notes play inside, Brendan checking his mobile for messages. It feels like quite a while since he last played that tune. Just before midnight he makes a call himself.

'Yeah, it's me. Grand, grand . . . listen, the phone is working again so you can get me if there's an emergency. Anyways, I'll be back in three days. Bye.'

Listen to him, counting down already.

Irene feels like they are getting right back to where they started. Things were looking up for a while but now she really wishes they were home in Nobber. Even if she'd left the bloody charger in the bushes they'd probably end up in the same old cycle. Her, fully withdrawn from reality on the balcony; him, reaching for his mobile as a lifeline.

The bedside light clicks off, bed springs creaking. A small fishing boat chugs through the night. She tries to follow it and sees a man on board shine a torch briefly before steering towards an island on the other side of the bay. He must know these waters like the back of his hand.

Black and white images from the snowy TV come to mind. Damir's scars and bandaged stump. Anja's bump. She lights another cigarette and hears the mattress object when Brendan shifts position. She follows the trail of lights up the coast road trying to pick out where the villa might be.

He is still awake when she steps inside and switches on the bedside light.

'Brendan, we need to talk.'

– 44 –

Talk about humble pie. Following a big heart-to-heart in Adriatika Properties they are tailing the old Skoda back to the villa. Sasa probably imagines his chest-thumping display down at the pier did the trick. If he only knew! That whole act was water off a duck's arse for Brendan. No, no, that wasn't it at all. And no prizes for guessing that the master plan the Gogartys are about to unveil is one hundred and ten percent Irene's.

What really frazzles Brendan is that he had the whole thing sorted in the first place! Not just a bargain – a proper steal! And now, thanks to his wife, he has to unravel everything and pay extra. Never mind the fact that, again thanks to his wife, he has to go back and grovel. Why? Because last night, she had a little think for herself while smoking her brains out on the balcony. In between all her puffing and huffing, she came up with a solution.

Figured it all out and came in to enlighten him. Went through it point-by-point. Brendan, blinking in harsh lamplight, sat up to fold an elbow across his eyes. Once she started laying out what she had in mind he began rearranging the pillows.

'You know this pair will get a toehold here and we'll never get rid of them,' he countered. 'And how are we going to keep an eye on things from Nobber?'

She suggested asking Sasa to be the local agent. Brendan said he had no intention of tacking on management fees to what should be the simple acquisition of a private property. All these extras coming out of his pocket, of course. Throw in the fact that Sasa is Anja's cousin – conflict of interest between landlord and tenant – you could say they were asking for trouble by keeping it all in the family.

'Well, they're not really tenants,' replied Irene, 'because they won't be paying rent.'

All of which leaves Brendan feeling like a proper clown. Whatever about coming up with your own harebrained scheme, when you have to follow someone else's – and have absolutely no say in the matter – you are goosed, plain and simple. He never thought he'd say it but he's beginning to feel nostalgic about commuting in drizzle along the N52 where he could run his business without outside interference

So it's out the coast road from Perast. The *Za Prodaju* sign is still standing and so it should be because, strictly speaking, yesterday, Brendan walked away from it all. One of the thousand and one ways a property deal breaks down. Many the slip between cup and lip – sale withdrawn, you could say. He's not the first investor to have second thoughts but as he broods over it he wonders if he is the first entrepreneur in the free world who now takes instruction from his missus.

He has both hands on the steering wheel. Nine-fifteen. Usually he drives with a single thumb but he's too immersed in how they've arrived at this turn of events. Don't make him laugh because he's not in the mood for laughing. They've had to do a 360 – or is it a 180? – because Irene saw scary pictures from Bosnia on a gammy black and white portable. Bodies all over the place, fair enough, but nothing they haven't seen in the bad old days up North. It's not like either of them have a clue what is going on over here. Really, what has mortar bombs landing in Sarajevo got to do with the Gogartys signing off on a holiday home in Perast?

Sasa parks up. He's acting all official and waits for them at the door this time. He yanks the chimes and Damir comes out, unshaven, like he's just out of bed. He's in a t-shirt and tracksuit bottoms, as usual, and the beanie and bandage also remain in place, like a uniform. He's barefoot, of course. He takes a second look at his unexpected visitors and there is no big *dobrodosli*.

'I don't think anything would surprise this boyo,' mutters Brendan.

'Hello again,' smiles Irene.

Damir is not a big fan of small chat. If he and Irene were to find they had anything in common that could be it. Maybe he knows the score already. Advance notice of this latest development, a Balkan squinting window. The way things seem to operate around here that would not surprise Brendan one bit.

'Damir, this is my husband Brendan. The man who bought the house.'

'Yeah, that's me, "the man who bought the house".'

'*Zele da pricaju sa tobom,*' adds Sasa, translating into gobbledegook.

'Can we keep this in English please?' interjects Brendan. Two nights of broken sleep and a mutiny by his wife have left him tired and emotional. 'If that's not too much bother.'

Sasa leads the way down the hall into the kitchen. The waitress from Vlado's comes in from the garden. However effective the grapevine may be in Montenegro, you can tell with 100 per cent certainty she did not expect the Gogartys to come calling. She hugs Sasa and kisses Irene on both cheeks, continental style. Brendan settles for a handshake seeing as they hardly know each other. No need to go entirely native, is there?

'Please, come,' says Anja, leading them outside.

There's a very slight breeze and you can tell it's going to be a scorcher, in Irish terms at least. A wooden bench is set under the tree in the middle of the garden. It's positioned to catch shade in full view of the sea. Simple but clever. Imagine that same tree standing there a hundred years ago, thinks Brendan. And people under it talking shite back then, just like we are now.

'Anja, this lady is Irene and gentleman is Brendan.'

'Yes, we meet before,' Irene cuts in.

Brendan is tempted to correct her grammar, mildly irritated that she is deliberately using the wrong tense to get the message across. In no time they'll all be speaking fluent gobbledegook.

'You like coffee? Water?' asks Anja.

'No thank you.'

Brendan shakes his head glumly. The way he sees it, Irene has worked it all out so he lets her do the talking. He sits, twiddling his thumbs. Damir stands off to the side like he's not really interested either. Instead of taking a seat he kneels to listen in, constantly fidgeting with the bandage the way a kid would annoy a scab. Now that they are all present and correct

Sasa pipes up like a UN peacekeeper to bring this impromptu gathering to order.

'Good afternoon every bodies. Brendan make agreement to buy villa. Now he want change agreement. Is not normal like normal business but Adriatika is professional service for investment property so this we do.'

The confusion of verbs absorbs Brendan's full attention. He does not actually take in what Sasa is saying. Instead, he makes a mental note of this syntactical delinquency, committed with such abandon it should turn the villa garden into a crime scene.

'Well, to be honest this has all happened very fast,' begins Irene, directing everything to Anja. 'We were in Kotor during the week and saw pictures in Sasa's window. We went in, sort of on spec. We had been talking about a getaway.'

'For why want you get away?' interrupts Damir, the spell of the Adriatic temporarily broken.

'I suppose it was more Brendan's idea. Just, you know, a place to get away from things.'

Brendan feels a finger of blame suspend from the cloudless sky.

'Things?' persists Damir.

'Well, yes,' continues Irene.

'We get away also but not want,' shrugs Damir, reverting to silence.

Brendan sighs theatrically, for effect.

'That may be the case but for us it was a good idea, a great idea,' Irene continues, paying no heed to her husband's sideshow. 'And it turned out, the villa was exactly what we had in mind. But we didn't know anything about your situation here. And I know you feel we just barged right in and – '

'Please excuse,' objects Sasa, raising his hand. 'I takink you here because villa is for sale.'

'Correct!' says Brendan, slapping hands off his thighs with relish.

'I do my job. I present you new Adriatika properties – condominium in Kotor, Cetinje, Risan. But Irene want to see villa.'

'Now you have it,' nods Brendan, warming to this.

Sasa picks up the slack.

'And at the end of commercial discussions Adriatika sellink property to Brendan Gogarty, citizen of Noh-ber, Ireland. We sign legal document. Everythink, like you say, correct. I explain Brendan whatever is new agreement is not possible go back.'

'There is always a way out,' interjects the purchaser.

'Don't worry, Sasa, the sale will go through,' assures Irene with a glance in her husband's direction. 'Brendan and I have agreed to that. We also agree that Anja and Damir can stay on here for up to six months after the baby is born.'

Sasa translates this. Damir is interested once again. From the look on Anja's face you wouldn't know if she has taken it in at all. She looks shocked, even dismayed.

'After that, you'll have to sort out a place of your own.'

'If that's not too inconvenient,' adds Brendan. 'Why don't you tell them we're an international charity while you're at it.'

Irene sees that Anja still can't quite grasp this. The young woman places her hands on her slightly swollen belly and earnestly asks Sasa to repeat the translation once more. At the end of which Anja looks like she is going to start crying.

'Ah here,' shifts Brendan, allergic to tears.

'She say she not know what to say,' shrugs Sasa.

'Oh now,' grunts Brendan.

Damir gets to his feet, like he too wants to check the small print. He's taller standing but his English is patchy, to say the least.

241

'Until baby is born here we live?'

'If you want to,' nods Irene. 'Yes.'

'Where is catch located?'

'There is no catch,' replies Irene. 'It's what we want to do.'

She turns to Brendan, awaiting one hundred and ten per cent confirmation.

'You're the boss,' he says, happy to be unhelpful.

'We not have money to pay,' Damir reminds them. 'I not working.'

'It's not about money,' says Irene. 'Thanks to Brendan.'

'At home we call it sponging,' says Brendan, eager to rain on this sunny parade.

Anja is beside herself, talking about *februar*. Brendan presumes correctly she means February. 'Thank you, thank you,' she says, all excited, looking for strangers to hug and kiss.

'She does not believe this,' explains Sasa.

'Oh now,' rejoins Brendan. 'We'll say nothing.'

The Gogartys have already launched the short version of the grand plan but Brendan suspects Irene, its originator, is blind to all loopholes. Dropping out of second year Arts twenty years ago is not ideal preparation for the hard scrabble of real estate. He doesn't feel he has much choice but to go along with it. You could easily be convinced he had just swallowed a lemon.

'*Hvala*,' says Damir, offering his good hand. 'Thank you.'

'Oh, don't thank me – that's your fairy godmother over there.'

'You are welcome,' says the fairy godmother, wishing the fairy godfather could be a little more gracious.

'It is,' Anja struggles. 'You are, you are . . .'

'Two big, thick eejits from Nobber!'

Brendan looks pleadingly to Irene as though seeking permission to withdraw from proceedings. He wants to leave. If entrepreneurial life has seen him through a few scrapes and the odd mis-directed punt, he reckons this has got to be the worst transaction ever. He may be legal owner of the villa but now he just wants to get away. Price-wise there's nothing wrong with the purchase – and a lot right, he consoles himself – but it's just not the same if a deal can leave you with such a bad taste. Ask any speculator worth his salt. He finds the whole thing so farcical that he'll leave it to the UN to tidy up the carnage.

'Okay, everybody happy?' asks Sasa, like a ringmaster. '*Dobro*. Please, Brendan, we requirink new cheque. One that does not jump.'

'You mean bounce.'

'Do what it say on tin,' elaborates Sasa, nodding.

'Tellinya,' swears Brendan under his breath. 'You couldn't make this up.'

He takes out his cheque book and feels a shadow loom over him when he goes to sign. Call him superstitious, but he doesn't like people standing over him when he's writing cheques.

'Do you mind?' he says.

The Gogartys have already discovered that cash is king in Montenegro. Travellers' cheques are for the tourist museum and personal cheques are viewed with distrust. The young auctioneer made a big show of accepting payment first time round. 'Take it or leave it,' Brendan told him, explaining that he doesn't usually go on holidays with twenty grand-plus in his arse pocket. The only option was for Brendan to sort out a credit transfer when they got home. And that's not a runner – ever see a real estate agent settle on a promise?

Sasa steps aside, waiting. He's apprehensive. Brendan fills it out slowly, adding a full stop after his signature. Brendan will probably have to ring Kells again to clear this. Otherwise Andy might confuse this cheque with yesterday's call and put a stop on everything as a precaution. Then again, considers Brendan, if he doesn't call Andy and no cheques are honoured, he could say the bank messed it up; the Gogartys would be long gone by the time Sasa would find out. Couldn't you call it an honest mistake?

'Won't you ring Andy?' says Irene, one step ahead. 'Just so there's no mix-up.'

Brendan detaches the cheque along a perforated line and hands it over. He even borrows one of Irene's tricks, waving it in front of Sasa and telling him once again to take it or leave it.

Sasa takes it.

'Now. Are we finished with all this hullaballoo?'

Handling it carefully Sasa examines the signature. He's not entirely convinced but Brendan couldn't be bothered putting his mind to rest.

'Anglo-Irish Banking Corporation?' queries Sasa.

'Safe as houses.'

With a bit of a *grá* for the dramatic, Sasa takes the first cheque from his inside pocket, rips it in two, tears it again and hands over a tidy pile of strips. Then he hands Brendan an envelope with a set of keys.

'For second time, you are owner of villa. Congratulation, again. No funny business this time.'

Irene tells Brendan that even though he's made a killing he does have a big heart. He suggests she's just being nice because she got her way. He's tempted throw another strop – the deal is nearly done this time so it'd just be for show – except Anja invites them to stay for refreshments now that they are all best buds. More like a lemonade party for a soon-to-be absentee landlord and his rent-free tenants.

'That would be lovely,' says Irene, getting comfortable.

'I'll leave ye to it,' nods Brendan, rising.

'Where are you off to?'

'Somewhere people aren't looking for something.'

Sasa shakes hands with the new proprietors before getting wrapped in his cousin's embrace. Anja is in hugging overdrive. With a bun in the oven Sasa reminds her she should be resting. He's heading straight for the bank to make a lodgement before the cheque burns a hole in his pocket.

Irene is happy to stay on. Which is grand because Brendan would just as soon leave her there. He feels he's been boxed into a corner and has a right pain in the arse with her meddling. At this point the only thing he'll concede is the villa is a beauty and they might even get to enjoy it some time, provided their new squatters up-sticks when they're supposed to.

Damir stands in front of him.

'I take you where fish is better.'

'What's that?'

'I know where is fish.'

'Ah here – you want to come with me?'

'Is no problem.'

Brendan feels outnumbered.

'Be the hokey there's no stopping this fella, hah? Signs me up to put a roof over his head; probably wants me to catch his dinner while I'm at it.'

He sees Irene cover her mouth to pretend she's stifling a cough. 'You always say Bren, you can't beat a bit of local knowledge.'

Damir stands at the table like a lost puppy.

'Where's your rod, man? To fish!'

'I not fish,' says he. 'Just for looking.'

'Oh sweet Jesus, the crack will be only mighty.'

Anja walks to Damir and leans her head against his chest. She's still buzzing. Only after he was given the heads up about her bun-in-the-oven does Brendan see the outline of Anja's bump more clearly. He now watches her beaming. He admits it's a wonder to see a pregnant woman smile at the world. She even comes towards him with open arms and a warm hug in her sails. He heads her off at the pass.

'Good luck, now.'

'Brendan!' calls out Irene, wiping her eyes.

'Hah?'

'Enjoy yourself.'

– 45 –

Irene only knows Anja a few days but she feels so glad their paths have crossed. The young Bosnian woman is just one of those people you warm to straight away. Of course, there was no way of knowing that their first night at Vlado's would prove to be such a significant encounter, something so unexpected and worthwhile. Don't we live our entire lives like that? How a chance moment might reconfigure everything that follows.

Brendan would laugh if he heard this sort of talk. At home all Irene's friends have virtually deserted her. She will readily admit their gradual withdrawal was more her fault than theirs, that she set about dropping them rather than they gave up on her. After Cathal she just didn't want to be around anyone. It was easier that way.

She basks in the Adriatic sun. This hiatus has got her thinking. How, over the years she contrived to burn off the most caring, the most loyal. Some were incredibly forgiving – stubbornly, maddeningly so – but she methodically worked her way through every last one of them. Which eventually left her with silent empty days to mope around the nameless mansion while Brendan ghosted in and out like a delivery boy. Now and again she'd have a go at him for using the job as a getaway, but if she was brutally honest she could not blame him.

So Damir is going to take him fishing this afternoon – they might as well be going to a GAA match in Navan. Talk about *The Odd Couple*! She just hopes Brendan won't blurt out anything too crass or stupid. And if he was going to insult the Bosnian he'd do it Nobber-style, so indirect and obtuse that Damir wouldn't even know he was having the mickey taken out of him.

It's too hot for tea. Anja goes inside to get refreshments. Irene notices the garden well planted and full of colour. It drops down a few steps to the beach and she loves the way the cedar tree brings it all together. Sitting here is immersive, almost hypnotic with the turquoise Adriatic sparkling and shimmering. There's a lovely sense of peace in the garden and now that everything has been sorted out with the villa she feels pleased. It's the first occasion in a very long time she has felt positive about anything.

Didn't think I had it in me anymore. Maybe the goodness in her draws it out.

Anja brings a jug of water with peppermint leaves and lemon slices floating on top. She smiles as she pours two glasses, giving thanks for the umpteenth time until Irene's upturned palms cut her off mid-sentence.

'Okay,' nods her host, finally understanding. 'I not speak English good.'

'Your English is a bit better than my Yugoslavian.'

They watch a fishing boat chug slowly out to sea.

'You must be very excited about your baby.'

'Six – five weeks maybe,' replies Anja, sounding less apprehensive than before.

'You won't notice the time passing.'

'Damir say he want son but I know he not care. Boy, girl, he worry same anyway.'

'That's what men do.'

'Oh!' she cries, startled. 'Baby moving! She move!'

She takes Irene's hand and places it on her belly, moving it gently to follow the source of life. A minute tremor, a low hum of electricity.

'Yes! I can feel it.'

'Now is stopped,' says Anja, still searching before she finally lets go. Her voice drops to a whisper. 'Sleeping.'

Irene sips from the glass and tastes a minty lemon tang.

'Cathal was like that. Kicking all the time. Brendan would say, boy or girl, that's a footballer. Went out and bought a Meath jersey, so cute with its little sleeves. He used to bring Cathal to all the matches, carry him around on his shoulders.'

'You have photo?'

Irene unfastens her necklace to remove the locket. The antique casing is bronze with enamelled bluebells shaped like a heart. The button is concealed at the side. She opens the locket partially, shielding it from the wind. Anja leans over to see the baby photo.

'For why piece of hair?'

'His first haircut.'

Anja appears taken aback. Irene wonders if she should not have shown it. It opens a mystery, leaves too much to explain. She snaps the locket shut, kisses it and reattaches the necklace.

'Please Irene, for why you go Medjugorje?' Anja asks quietly.

'Ah things were a bit, y'know,' Irene begins, stepping into the treacle that usually leads to silence. She resolves not to allow herself get stuck this time, to push herself through troubled thoughts and find the right words. 'It was Brendan's idea from something he heard on the radio. People like us went there and found it peaceful. Which, it is.'

'You look for peace in Bosnia?'

'We're not religious now but it just seemed like something worth trying. I don't know what you can expect from lighting a few candles. Suppose it didn't do any harm – sure, didn't we end up here!'

'Something happen your boy?'

'Now is not the time, love.'

To her relief Anja lets it go and returns with a bright, breezy optimism.

'We come to Montenegro with nothing; now we have everything,' she pauses, breaking into laughter. 'Everything!'

It makes Irene laugh too. She is happy for her new friend. Then in a sudden change of mood Anja appears less buoyant, reaching for the tree, running her hands along its bark.

'Damir here sit many times, all quiet. Maybe he change a little. But still he is Damir. My Damir. And when I find I am with baby, it is, you know, something too good.'

'Too good to be true.'

'Yes, too good to be true. Except it *is* true.'

'You shouldn't worry yourself.'

'How you know?' Anja says sharply, checking herself. 'Sorry. We live nice life in Sarajevo. Then . . . it go bad like hell. Danger to look out window.'

'The world can turn like that.'

'Yes. This we see happening.'

'We've seen it ourselves, God knows. Protect your child, Anja. Boy or girl, doesn't matter. Children need to be kept safe because if you don't protect your child, you'll never forgive yourself.'

– 46 –

For someone who won't be casting a line for some time Damir has a good eye for the right spot. A bend on the river, about two miles inland. Willow trees on both sides with branches stooping and dipping into water. Sunlight frames the glade so it's warm where they stand without being exposed. And all so quiet. Brendan takes it in, baits a hook and casts the line.

Damir sits on the bank, looking on. Which seems to be all he wants to do. When he removed the hat Brendan got a bit of a start. Irene did mention something about the man having brain surgery but hadn't prepared Brendan for a skinhead sitting in front of him with heavy-duty scars. His eyes appeared to sink deeper into his skull, which made him look younger and older at the same time. Been through the wars this fella, thinks Brendan. Damir settles in shade, forever fiddling at the bandage below his elbow. He tosses small pebbles into the water.

'Glad you came, hah?'

'Cigarette?' offers Damir.

'I don't smoke.'

He has one rolled but foosters around with matches. Brendan goes over and lights up for him.

'Irene took the coffin nails up again recently. For Lent.'

'*Hvala.*'

'In films they always have the fella lighting up a smoke for the girl. It means they're going to end up riding. Don't get me wrong now, Horse – that's not the case here.'

'Excuse?'

'Ah, don't worry about it.'

Brendan goes back to his spot and casts again. He can see small huts downriver, more like sheds patched up with timber and corrugated iron. Somewhere for fishermen to sit out of the sun or shelter from rain. A couple of rods angle anonymously into the water. Birdsong speckles the air.

'Grand spot alright. Fair play,' says Brendan. 'You like fishing yourself? I say, do you like this?'

'River fishing good in Bosnia.'

'We have rivers in Ireland. Good for trout, salmon, perch. Takes your mind off things so it does.'

Sometimes Brendan can't tell if Damir is listening. Like he's distracted or maybe retrieving fragments from the chaos of his mangled head. He leans to his side and cradles the stump.

'That get sore? Your arm.'

'Head is badder. Inside head. Noise, all day.'

'That's rough, hah? I worked with a fella once who had tinnitus. Years on the roads using a drill and never wore ear plugs. I'd say yours is a bit worse. Tell us, what was your game before all your bother?'

'Excuse?'

'Your job. Your work.'

'*Ja*? *Sajdzija*. I make time. Make this,' he says, brandishing his watch.

'You fix watches! You must have a shocking steady hand.'

'But now I not do.'

Damir withdraws into his own thoughts, taking a drag from his cigarette. A lad with a lot on his mind. Reaching into his jacket he pulls out a small bottle. It has no label. He unscrews the lid and passes it over.

'What's that – *poitín*?

'*Rakía.*'

Brendan puts the bottle to his nose. The liquid has no colour and smells strongly of plums but you can tell it's pure rocket fuel.

'*Sláinte.*'

'*Ziveli*. Man in Perast make this but we make better in Sarajevo.'

Brendan is cautious with his first swig.

'Whew . . . that's hard tack, hah?'

He hands it back, his throat on fire. It does not go down easy. Damir takes a bigger slug, no bother to him. It's not exactly nectar but there's a definite afterglow.

'*Poitín* we call it. A few of them and you'd be bulletproof, hah?'

'What you do job?'

'Boats. Hire them, rent them, sell them.'

'Boats?'

'On the river. Tourists mostly. It's all about seeing potential. Taking opportunities. Was a bit slow for a while, in fairness, but it's beginning to take off. Ireland's on the up.'

'Bosnia is not on up. Sarajevo one time very nice city. Very beautiful, good life. First war start in centre – Archduke Ferdinand?' he prompts, handing over the bottle as they go into Round Two.

'You're talking about yerman from World War One?'

'He shooted by Serb in Sarajevo. Big history.'

The second mouthful is easier.

'Will ye go back?'

Damir talks about the end of the siege like he is talking to himself. Friends and neighbours getting shot when they went out for firewood. Neighbours praying at a funeral blown to pieces by a mortar. Now it's changed. Serb artillery in the hills running from NATO air strikes. He's glad it finally happened but questions angrily why it took so long.

'City not same now. What place for living? For I, no job. Not making time. What I do when baby come?' He drinks, rubs his neck, lost in thought. A man without a plan.

'D'you know you should write a song about yourself. Country and western. Bit of a dirge about all your woes.'

'You have childs?'

'Just the one.'

'Boy?'

'Yeah. Cathal.'

'Co-hal.'

Brendan rests the rod and picks up a stick. He spells out the letters on the riverbank. It's strange seeing it displayed there, a shallow carving in dry mud.

'Co-hal. Is good name. What age your boy?'

'Ah, we lost him.'

'What means lost?'

'He was killed. That's what.'

'I so sorry,' says Damir quickly, getting to his feet. 'What I can say?'

'Ah, you're grand. Sure five years later meself and Irene haven't really figured that out.'

'Five years?'

'Ah, it went to court and all . . .'

'*Hej grize*!' shouts Damir, splashing into the river. '*Hej! Otkachi je sa udice*!'

'Jesus I do, right enough! Something's after biting!'

Brendan raises the rod and feels the drag. Damir tells him to let the line out. He's focused on the catch and paces the bank like a demented basketball coach. He's more excited than Brendan. The line spools out fast as the fish pulls upriver, zigzagging underwater out of sight. It'll be a real test for this rod, made in China or not.

'He's a big bastard, so he is!'

'*I izvuci je, polako* . . . take slowly.'

'Come to Papa! D'you know, I'd call this quare teamwork, hah? A watchmaker from Sarajevo and a boatman from Nobber.'

'*Polako* Brendan, *polako* . . . '

'Yeah, yeah. *Polako* . . .'

He's coming back downriver and Brendan moves to reel him in. Spooling quickly, winding as fast as he can. The line jerks suddenly and lightens and they see a silver splash. The angler is on automatic so he keeps reeling but feels the nylon dance free, suddenly weightless. The hook dangles before them, loose and empty.

'Fuck it, hah!'

Damir second glances but he's already laughing and can't stop. Brendan holds his spot, checking his pockets for fresh bait.

'Alright, alright . . .'

He wouldn't say it's *that* funny. He watches Damir collapse hysterically on the bank, wiping tears from his eyes with his good hand. You'd want to be made of stone for it not to set you off.

'Aaaaahhhhh. *Dobro*,' he says, recovering slowly.

Brendan allows himself a smile – he is on holidays, after all. It's just he hates when things get away.

– 47 –

An easy hour passes by. Irene wonders if she said too much about Cathal and is relieved that Anja didn't press it any further. They talk for a while and relax in the idleness of the day. This visit has really settled her. She's thinking of wandering back to the hotel when they hear chimes at the front door. It's Dzana, who does part-time waitressing at Vlado's.

She's younger than Anja, a confident early twenties, slim and tall like a lot of Montenegrin girls.

Her American is perfect. It turns out she lived in Baltimore with her father for a couple of years and then came home. She knows about the pregnancy so Dzana and Anja are more like co-conspirators down at the restaurant.

Anja goes inside to get another glass.

'So when do you guys go back to Ireland?'

'In two days. One more night here, then we'll drive back to Bosnia.'

'Cool.'

'Anja just told me you'll let them stay here until after the baby is born. That's awesome.'

'Yeah, it worked out well.'

Anja returns and pours for Dzana.

'Did you like America?'

'Yes and no. I was fifteen and my parents split up, so I guess it was a hard time. My mom lives here in Risan so I came back. Dad is still in Baltimore.'

Anja goes to refill Irene's glass but the colour suddenly drains from her face. Off-balance she stumbles forward and reaches for the table in an attempt to break her fall. She hits the ground softly, fainting like slow motion, water splashing from the jug still in her grip. Irene rushes over and reaches under Anja's shoulders, cradling her head. Saliva bubbles from the corner of her mouth.

Dzana rushes over to take her hand and they try to sit her up. The fall stuns Anja, visibly frightened at the risk of impact. They can't believe how everything has changed so suddenly, so drastically.

'There's a hospital in Kotor but maybe we should go to the main maternity hospital,' Dzana says urgently, panic creeping into her voice. 'Except that's in Podgorica.'

Irene has no idea where Podgorica is or where they should go.

'Why don't we call an ambulance?'

'Could be an hour before an ambulance gets here – I have a car.'

'Let's go wherever is nearest!'

Anja cries for her baby, touching her stomach with her fingertips as though checking for cracks. They help her to her feet. She's light but Dzana is much taller than Irene so it's awkward walking Anja through the house. Dzana's Mazda is parked right outside so they slide Anja into the back seat. It's a sporty-looking car but the interior is strewn with sweet wrappers and empty cans of diet Coke. You'd never think such a stylish girl could be so untidy.

Irene sweeps everything to the floor and runs around the other side to squeeze in. She can't fasten the seatbelt so she hangs onto the head rest for balance when Dzana takes off. Anja lies across the seat, propped against her lap.

Anja has absolutely no energy. She sobs quietly and moans, blaming herself for falling. Irene wishes she brought some water to cool her forehead and moisten her lips. They stop at a red light in town which delays everything. All these lights should be green. As soon as it turns, the car lurches forward and they fly along the coastline. Thankfully, Dzana is a good driver and not afraid of speed.

The young pregnant woman is drifting, whispering to herself, praying, raving. She wears pink tracksuit bottoms and the sight of a bleed between her legs shocks Irene. She tries to distract Anja because she's afraid any sight of the widening stain would create panic. Dzana spots it in the rear-view mirror. She lets out a gasp and grips the steering wheel knuckle-white, looking to overtake an articulated truck.

'You'll be fine, Anja,' insists Irene.

Dzana hears a siren and wonders if an ambulance has somehow made its way from Kotor. But no, it's a police car bluelighting right behind them. Dzana brakes hard at a bus stop and pulls in, breathing fast and shallow. Irene punches the head rest waiting for a policeman to appear. It seems everything has ground to an unnecessary halt but she is wedged between Anja and the door and can't get out. She sees the policeman in the driver's seat taking notes.

'How do you say hurry up?'

'You don't want to annoy him.'

'What is it?'

'Jebo te poquri vise.'

She rolls down the window and lets out a roar.

'Jebo te poquri vise!'

The blue light on the roof is still flashing but there is nothing urgent about this. The policeman gets out in his own good time, adjusting his hat.

'Will you fucking *jebo te poquri vise!'*

He reacts like he's been pinched and swaggers to the driver's side. Dzana tells him they have to get to the hospital. The policeman bends to look into the back seat and sees Anja stretched out, groaning. He swallows and nods.

'Prati me.'

They watch him waddle hurriedly to his car. The siren wails into life. He pulls ahead to let Dzana tuck in behind and it's breakneck speed, hazard lights blinking all the way to Kotor. Dzana follows him right into the emergency bay where ambulances usually park. She runs in and gets help. Irene repeats again and again that everything will be fine, like she is reciting clichéd lines from a tired matinee.

Two orderlies come running to lift Anja onto a gurney and race inside. Irene watches her being taken away. Such a gentle young soul, now flat and lifeless. A hospital porter appears to ask Dzana to move her car. Irene leans against a low wall and asks him for a cigarette. The porter stops, surprised at the request.

'*Engleski?*'

'No.'

'*Americanak?*'

He loses interest and pats down the pocket of his blue coat. He takes a Drina from the pack and lights it for her. Dzana returns and they hug each other in shock. Only then does Irene notice her hands shaking.

– 48 –

The fish aren't biting. Even though Brendan's total haul in Montenegro is, without putting too fine a point on it, abysmal, a wise old angler on the Moy outside Ballina once told him the art of fishing isn't always about the catch. Besides, it's been an agreeable few hours.

Brendan watches Damir doze uneasily on the grass. He awakens when it's appreciably cooler, a light mist blowing up from the mouth of the river. Damir shivers, shaking out his legs to get the circulation going. Hotel St Jovan is twenty minutes away on winding roads. They will leave what's left of the *rakía* to another day.

'Looks like fog coming in below. Suppose we should make tracks before they start worrying. Anyways, I'm getting a bit peckish.'

He reels in one last time and starts tidying up. Damir appears extremely quiet, even withdrawn, but the silence suits them fine. Brendan is already getting used to it. Damir sits up and fixes his cap, gently touching his head like he's making sure it's still there. He closes his eyes.

'Fog in August if you don't mind. Would you get that often – of course you're a Sarajever. Or Sarajevan, which is it?'

258

He's not listening.

'Are you alright?

'Noise in head,' he says. 'I need lie down in house.'

'You probably shouldn't have drunk that stuff.'

'Do not say Anja.'

'Oh I'll say nothing, don't you worry. Do you have tablets or something?'

'In house.'

'We'll get you home big fella, no panic.'

'I so sorry.'

'Ah don't be thick.'

He's not so steady on his feet as they make their way back to the Lada. It's hardly the drink but reaching the car he seems particularly fragile. He gets into the passenger seat like every movement is a mini-earthquake. Brendan pulls the passenger door shut, hearing the metal clang too late.

'Sorry about that, Horse.'

He needs Damir to direct them back to the main crossroads. Brendan even feels a little nervous carrying such a delicate parcel. He'd prefer to drop Damir off at the villa in jig time because as long as he fills the passenger seat the burden of responsibility falls to the driver.

There's no chat and no crack in the car. Brendan tries to take it handy. He's not making excuses, but he feels he should remind Damir that this oul banger is nearly sellotaped together. If a gear slips, put it down to a gammy clutch; if they clatter over the odd bump, worn shocks.

Just don't start thinking it's my fault.

Damir closes his eyes again like a barnyard owl and shields his gaze from the window. It's obviously not for show. When he places his hand close to his temple it's more like he's absorbing waves and does not want to make physical contact with his head. He's well and truly banjaxed. Even his ex-watchmaker fingers can't seem to settle. He rests his palm against his jaw, unsure and trembling. Brendan interrupts to ask which turn to take at the junction and soon enough they're back in Perast.

'Door to door,' says Brendan as they pull into the driveway, Lily's sticky handbrake an exclamation mark.

He switches off the engine. He expects Damir to be chomping at the bit for his tablets but, instead, the stricken man just sits there dejectedly, facing straight ahead. Shattered and frozen all in one, he doesn't even unfasten his seat belt.

'C'mon so. Are you right?'

'No, I not right.'

'Ah, I don't mean it like that.'

'Look me, Brendan. This is I.'

'Ah, would you relax.'

'And when baby come, what good is I?'

'You'll be as much use as I was. That's the honest truth of it.'

It's time to get this fella off his hands. Brendan does not wait for Damir to shake himself so he flicks open both seatbelts and leads the way only to find the villa front door locked. He peeks through the window but it's lifeless inside. He calls out for Irene, then Anja, but you know an empty house when you see one.

Damir trails him to the door.

'Why is it locked?'

'Anja have key.'

'Well she's not here. There's nobody here.'

Brendan remembers the manila envelope Sasa gave him. He takes it from an inside pocket and pulls out the Adriatika Properties keyring.

'Well I do own the fucking place,' he shrugs.

Springing the front door like a first-time buyer he stands back to let the patient through. Hands to his head, Damir trundles forward and ducks straight into the bedroom, half-heartedly dragging curtains after him. Brendan follows through and takes a look in the kitchen. No sign of life. Outside, he sees fog drifting in, thicker than earlier. Two glasses and a jug lie on the grass beside a slice of lemon. Another glass rests further away.

There's a loud groan from the bedroom. He finds Damir burrowed under the duvet, his outline sketchy in the gloom. If he's this bad Brendan can't see why he doesn't take his tablets. He asks where they are kept. Damir mumbles that Anja puts them in the kitchen so Brendan starts rooting through drawers. He finds another bottle of *rakía* in the cupboard, then spots pills in the press above the sink. He hasn't a clue if they are the right ones but sees D. Tomic written on the label.

'Is this them?'

Damir reaches for the tablets and swallows a couple. He sits up to swish a mouthful of water.

'No note or nothing,' muses Brendan, wondering if Irene might've walked Anja down to Hotel St Jovan. But why leave a jug and glasses on the ground outside?

Damir retreats under the pillow. He looks terrified, suddenly blabbering in his own language, rocking and jabbering like it's the end of the world.

'Give over with the gobbledegook, hah?' snaps Brendan, irritated at such a loss of control. What use is being helpless?

But there's no stopping him. Brendan can't tell if it's migraine or tinnitus, but whatever it is you'd only wish it on your worst enemy. Tears fill the stricken man's eyes as he rambles on disconsolately about Anja and the baby.

'I don't know what you're saying man. What do you expect me to do? What can I do?'

If the one-armed refugee was helpless a few minutes ago it's Brendan who feels quite useless now. And he wouldn't mind telling you he doesn't like it one bit. He'd actually like to help the lad, in fairness. But sure, how? He remembers his barstool companion in Kells pointing out that you can't help someone who doesn't want to be helped.

'Why don't you shut the fuck up and go to sleep!'

He knows that's not the most constructive thing he could come up with, but standing there speechless does not help the situation either. The migraine is not listening and Brendan hasn't a clue what Sarajevo's war wounded is rabbiting on about. He leaves Damir to his nightmarish visions, closing the door after him.

Let the tablets do their work.

His whimpering comes through the walls. Brendan can even hear it percolating into the kitchen. He wishes Damir would stop. He swings the cupboard door, grabbing the unopened *rakía – don't worry, I'll replace it –* and brings it out to the garden. He is bothered by the incongruity of glassware discarded on the grass. It lies rudely out of place, like a calm scene disturbed. He picks up the lemon slice, brushes off a blade of grass and bites it. Grimacing from its bitterness he unscrews the bottle cap and knocks back a mouthful of *rakía*. It's hours since the last drop and this tastes every bit as harsh. He has to force himself to swallow. It carries a right kick and leaves him sucking for air.

Wisps of ghostly fog billow up the garden from the sea. He stops to listen closely, glad that finally he can't hear anything from inside the villa. There's no question that lad is in the horrors but it's no excuse for unmanly sobbing.

Pull yourself together, Horse. I can't help you.

The mist triggers the long, slow blast of a foghorn somewhere up the coast. Brendan shivers involuntarily and takes another greedy swig. It's rough tack by any standards but blotting out everything right now feels like a good option. He feels a vague resentment towards the lighthouse operator, perched up there like he's saving the world. Sure, all he has to do is press a button in between making tea and dunking a digestive. This saving sailors business is probably done by computers at this stage.

He tilts the bottle to his mouth and lets the *rakía* pour down his throat. It's a little more bearable when he can't taste it but the surge rushes him, goes up his nose and explodes into a sneeze. He wipes his face with a sleeve.

The foghorn blasts again.

He thinks of when he and Irene turn on each other at home in Nobber. Once ignited, their fights usually burn through to full combustion. Cutting remarks and deep scrapes followed by a sharp-elbowed race to a *coup de grace*. If their mansion was a bullring Irene would be the more skilled matador, coolly proficient at gliding the sword through bewildered quarry. Except in the Gogartys' case it's not about killing for mercy. It's about sticking the knife and turning it one more time.

'You are the boy's father,' she reminds him when the gloves are well and truly off. 'Why couldn't you protect him?'

He never has an answer for that. Irene knows it too so it's a weapon she likes to keep in reserve for special occasions. Even though she's stuck it to him more than once it lands every time with the same damning efficiency. He is literally struck dumb, unable to muster a reply, unable to separate regret from guilt from anger from shame. It usually brings these full and frank exchanges to a finish without any need to declare winner or loser. The victor, if there is such a thing, is whoever has enough energy left to storm off.

The weary aftermath of these domestic barneys can run for days or weeks, during which he reflects long and hard on the unfixable nature of a deeply harboured grievance. He tries to come up with an answer so he'll be ready next time because, one thing is certain, there will be a next time. But a smart riposte, or honest reply, invariably eludes him. Driving home of an evening, or sprawled sleeplessly across soft Egyptian cotton, the rhetorical taunt haunts him. Guide and protect, isn't that what a father is supposed to do?

Well life goes on – for some at least. As for the bastard who brought all this on them? Didn't they say he is now the prison's star gardener? Must have green fingers! The thought of it just gives him the sick. Flowers and plants need care. Kind fingers to bring delicate things to life. Not in this case. *Brutish* hands. How could he even have got picked as a gardener! And while you're at it, take that gaggle of prison psychologists and probation people back to the scene of the crime. Want to find clues? Red specks under green fingernails, if you looked closely enough.

Of course he knows what they'll say. That McGeedy has turned the corner. He has been rehabilitated. They'll put him on public display as a shining example of how the prison system works – sure, isn't that why he's out way ahead of time! It's a joke. One big fucking joke.

What did I do? What could I have done?

The foghorn sounds.

Their beautiful son, twelve years old. Not even a teenager. Cut. Down.

Brendan tosses away the bottle and grabs the long axe from the woodpile. The first blow glances off the trunk, scraping bark, grazing the tree's skin. In the fog he doesn't see each strike hit the mark cleanly but he swings the blade overhead, building up momentum until it drives a wedge through sap and chippings. Sweat runs free as oil over his arms and upper body, making the axe handle very slippery. No matter. He won't be stopped this time.

Each high lift is followed by a hefty *thunk.* He keeps going, faster and faster, cutting a deep gouge until he sees the tree tilt like a drunken sailor, falling in on itself. When he finally stops, it bends and splinters with a loud crack that sounds like gunfire and crashes slowly to the ground, burying bushes and flowers along with the wooden seat and a couple of garden chairs.

He breathes heavily, turns around to find Damir staring open-mouthed from the kitchen. Light from the hallway reduces him to a shadow. He's not wearing his hat so under low wattage lighting Brendan sees the sutures of his shaven head defined with perfect clarity.

He drops the axe. Enough.

'That's that,' he says, sliding to his knees.

Damir emerges slowly, stepping into the garden. He joins the plaintive boatman and sits on the ground beside him.

'Maybe I not give you *rakía* again.'

The cedar tree comes to rest with a series of sighs, heavy branches settling inch by inch under their own weight.

'We miss him so much,' says Brendan, wiping away a sheen of perspiration with his sleeve. 'Every fucking day, in fairness.'

For a while nothing is said. A foghorn splits the silence.

'In winter in Sarajevo we burn chairs, bed, table. Even some wood of floor.'

'You think I give a shit about your floorboards?'

'And books. Anja work in library, so we burn many books. Anja say me one day, Damir, when war end I think we not want chairs.'

'What are you on about?'

'When things not normal we try make normal.'

'You can do that all you like,' snaps Brendan. 'But sometimes, nothing works.'

The cedar tree finally reaches its level. The garden is still.

'Anyways, what about that head of yours?'

Damir sits up. He shrugs, then smiles.

'I still here.'

– 49 –

There was no time to leave a note. Irene half-smiles at a thought that for the second time in a week her husband might be worried about her. She was going to go straight to Hotel St Jovan but guessed Brendan would stay on at the villa with Damir. Several attempts to call from a hospital payphone rang out – she vaguely recalls seeing his mobile left in the charger back at their hotel room.

She and Dzana are both exhausted after spending six hours at A&E. It's a nervous drive home because of fog. At the end of all this Dzana is either going to get a speeding ticket or be asked out by Latko, the policeman.

'Kinda cute but not my type,' she shrugs, a girl clearly used to male attention.

They don't get back to the villa until after nine. Irene is relieved to see Lily parked outside. At least Brendan is here. She pulls the chimes and Damir hurries to the door. He's not wearing the beanie and the criss-cross of angry red marks makes it look like he's stitched his own skull together. He panics when he sees Irene and Dzana show up without Anja.

Dzana explains calmly in Bosnian that everything is okay. That Anja's sugar levels dropped suddenly and she had a light bleed so the hospital kept her in. Irene doesn't understand the words but she can sense Dzana play down how serious it could have been.

When Damir asks about the baby, Dzana says they might have to induce next week. That decision will be made tomorrow. They did a scan and she says the *decak* is absolutely fine. Irene figures *decak* must mean little boy because Damir covers his mouth with his good hand like he's in shock. Seized by emotion the discovery stuns him. Not only is everything okay but he will have a son.

'Anja say girl but doctor say boy!' he tells her.

He practically begs Dzana to bring him over to the hospital. Otherwise he intends to walk. She is beyond tired but Damir can't be denied. She agrees to take him.

'Where's Brendan?' Irene asks.

'In kitchen,' says Damir, running inside to get a coat.

'Are you okay driving in the fog?'

'I'll be careful,' says Dzana. 'Hey I didn't mean to let slip about it being a boy.'

'Well you can see what it means to him. After everything today, it really doesn't matter.'

'What a day, huh?' smiles Dzana.

They embrace warmly like two near-strangers brought together by circumstance. They now have a cherished memory to share. Dzana walks to her car. If they ever meet again this will be an experience to remember, a cross between nostalgia and fright.

Irene hears Damir talking with Brendan in the kitchen before he reappears, hurriedly pulling his jacket over the stump. He slips the beanie over his head and makes for the car. Dzana starts the engine.

'Goodbye!' he shouts, theatrically kissing his good hand and waving from the passenger seat. Dzana swings out of the driveway, tail lights swallowed up in mist.

'Brendan?'

She closes the front door and walks down the hall. Brendan is sitting at the table, preoccupied. It astounds – shocks – Irene to find him like this, his face flushed bright red, hair wild and matted with sweat.

'What – you're covered in . . . look at you, Brendan. What's going on?'

She touches his shirt. It's damp right through, the perspiration cooling into dark stains. He regards her in a strange way, like he's petrified. She has never seen him look like this before.

'Is everything alright, Irene? Honestly.'

'You tell me!

'The baby . . .'

'We had to take Anja to the hospital in Kotor. They're talking about inducing. It was a scare, that's all. Brendan, what is going on?'

'Damir was sure the baby wouldn't make it. Had me convinced so he did.'

'What's wrong with you? The baby will be fine. The baby *is* fine!'

A heavy shadow fills the window where she sat this afternoon. She steps out to the garden like she's being hauled slowly by rope. Through the fog she sees the silhouette of the cedar tree on its side. An axe lies on the ground, an upended bottle nearby. She struggles to take it all in.

'Oh my God, what have you done?'

She looks around and sees Brendan shift uneasily in the doorway. It's so obvious he did this but, in a way, he looks broken too. She doesn't know if it was some sort of madness or drunken rage. Or if it's just beginning to dawn on him what he has done.

'Why, Brendan? How could you destroy something so beautiful?'

'If Cathal cried out for me, Irene, I didn't hear him. I swear to God.'

His words are saturated with guilt and pain, a sound so gut-wrenching that she hardly recognises her husband's voice. She is floored and it takes real effort to find her own.

'It wasn't your fault.'

'If he called out, Daddy! Except it'd be more like Daaaaaaaaaddyyy!

'Don't do this to yourself.'

'How could I protect him?' he cries, an ache erupting from deep within. 'Nobody heard him, Irene,' he adds. 'But I hear him now.'

His body shakes like a rolling wave. Small tremors leading to convulsions. She has never seen Brendan cry. Not through the trial or even at the graveside. He is literally shaking here, from head to foot. If those tears banked frozen for the past five years they are now melting in torrents.

When they first heard Cathal was gone they refused to believe it. Then they saw him laid out on a chilly mortuary slab. You'd think he was sleeping except for a dislocated shoulder and a dark bruise around his left temple. Irene wanted to kiss away any marks and breathe him back to life. She could not say how much time passed before they were asked to make way for the coroner. Their own child in front of them, laid to rest in cold quarters under a plastic white sheet.

It was an image they could never un-see. From there on they could either carry grief like a burden or let it bury them whole. Not knowing what to do with it, they discovered that it was occasionally useful for slashing each other. Irene sees from the shards now before her that they have cut themselves deeply.

She realises and regrets in the same instant the extent to which she has deliberately reopened these wounds. She recalls making her trustiest accusation from time to time, choosing a particular set of words in moments when she wanted to really hurt Brendan. Now, serenaded by a foghorn, he returns it to her as a festering sore. When she reaches out for him he squirms free, his shirt damp and loose. They stand apart in the garden, a static twosome clothed in mist.

– 50 –

The projector is whirring away and he can't shut it down. Closing his eyes makes no difference. Just when he thinks the screen has finally gone blank, other images gatecrash the party. All are unconnected but one leads directly to the next. The projector illuminates dust motes before being fed once more by the carousel. Sleep isn't going to come easy tonight, if at all.

I mustn't be in great shape, inside like. Not if I take it out on a harmless oul tree . . .

He is bone weary but doesn't feel sleepy. He observes that the ceiling in the honeymoon suite could do with a fresh coat, notwithstanding the fact Hotel St Jovan needs a lot more TLC than a lick of paint. Looks like a hairline leak in the far left corner. You don't need to be a boatman to know water will always find its level. He'll tell reception in the morning when they check out. It's not the worst he's seen, in fairness, but these small wrinkles can get exaggerated if you stare at them long enough.

An image jumps in before being pushed away by others. He sees Irene feeding Cathal in the kitchen in Irishtown. The fountain pen drying up when he is about to sign for the marina. Was that a sign? Straight to Las Vegas. Brendan and his school pal John Phillips counting chips at a roulette table. His mother and father respectably dressed for Sunday Mass. Where now? Feeding the swans in Portobello. Time, for some reason, jitterbugged, working backwards. Irene with house keys. Opening the front door to *Avalon*. Their own place. Irene turns to him; the way she is smiling you can tell she is beyond happy.

Now he's lifting Cathal over the turnstiles at Páirc Tailteann. A proud father carrying the young fella to his first GAA match. The boy sits on his father's shoulders, both of them roaring on the Royals. You'd think he'd be a bit scared, crammed in among so many people and the noise and the shouting and cursing what-have-you. Not at all! Now and again Brendan has to tell some young buck to soften the language but Cathal is in his element every bit as much as his dad.

Fast forward to Croke Park, 1981. Meath have lost to Wexford in the Leinster quarter-final and Brendan is fit to be tied. The championship gone again for another year, by one bloody point. They are walking back to the car in Drumcondra and Brendan doesn't feel like chatting. In this black mood he's unaware how quickly he walks and the boy is half-running on shorter legs to keep up. When the father feels his son's soft small hand take his it catches him by surprise.

'Daddy,' the boy tells his father. 'Don't be sad.'

Brendan's eyes blur thinking about it. He wouldn't describe himself as a regular crier. Like, he'd never get picked for reality TV. Okay, he might've shed a few tears at his mam's funeral but they were strictly private – even Irene missed that. He could've blinked them away if he had to but not these ones. He can feel the pillow rinsed out under his neck. In the name of Jesus he doesn't know what's wrong with him.

What keeps returning is the day at Lough Sheelin. It's not that he was entirely wrong to leave the boy at home – tough love, isn't that what you call it? – but what he would give to re-run it very differently. Just give the lad the nod and watch him scamper into the car with all his little fisherman stuff. Would have redeemed Brendan for an eternity instead of putting him on the hook for something he can do nothing about.

Like if their boy was with them here in Montenegro Brendan would have bought two fishing rods to take down to the pier below. *Me, Cathal, Juventus, Tarzan and their little fella tossing lines into the Adriatic and d'you know I couldn't care less if I caught nothing all day.*

Ah, what is he saying? Sure the boy would be seventeen, going on eighteen. This whole set-up would bore a teenager. He'd hardly have come out to Yugoslavia with two old fogies. And if he did, wouldn't he be off doing his own thing – discovering girls, discos, gargle. Probably looking for a bit of action – a loud race in a fast boat or wherever they do the water skiing outside Perast. More likely he wouldn't be here at all. Excitedly on the phone back home telling his pals he had a free house in Nobber for twelve whole days.

But listen, am I tripping meself up here? There should never have been any need to leave Portobello. Nobber wouldn't even be part of the equation. No fancy holiday required and no free house either. We'd never have been charging up a holy mountain in Bosnia or getting sunburnt in Montenegro if we hadn't lost him in the first place.

He closes his eyes, an itchy trickle down both sides of his face.

Some specimen, so I am.

He rubs his eyes and more tears come. It's windscreen wipers he needs, not eyelids. He holds his breath and tries to let it out slowly. There isn't a peep in the room. He can see Irene's outline on the balcony, feeding smoke to the night sky. The internal projector is motoring away of its own accord, playing this horribly seamless exhibition that whirrs through segments of his life. Displaying all the things Cathal and his Dad did – and cruelly adding for spite everything they would've done if the future hadn't been written off.

Teaching him to drive the same way Brendan's oul fella taught him; taking him to TJ's for his first pint, or the first one his father might know about; doing chauffeur for his school debs; going to his college graduation or maybe he'd have joined the marina to learn on the job. Or he might've gone travelling for a year or two beyond in Australia or the Far East to 'find himself'.

In the name of Jaysus I can't do that – and I stay at home . . .

As for spilling his guts to Damir? I'm not usually like that, Brendan tells himself. Getting all blubbery. It's just not him.

He probably hadn't a clue what I was on about. Just as well . . .

Normally he could explain whatever he's done but not this time. Hard to make sense of what you don't understand. Maybe the whole build-up – five years! – bursting after the Arbour Hill fiasco like a big dam. If that sounds like an excuse he's not trying to go soft on himself.

It's just that lying here in the gentle swish of the Adriatic he realises he has no control over what comes to mind. Some of it would surprise you but he knows it all comes from the same deep, empty well.

Cathal isn't with us any more. Well, he's with us and he's not with us, if you know what I mean.

Brendan is genuinely glad for Damir and Anja. The pair of them have lost so much but the way things have worked out at least they have something to look forward to. Truth be told, the only one he feels sorry for is himself.

He hears Irene come in from the balcony, nicotine stale on her breath. She climbs in without a word. This bed is huge and there's an open prairie from his side to hers. He doesn't want to keep her awake with all his sniffling but it's hard to stay quiet in the dark. He keeps his eyes shut and submits to the silence. He senses her lifting the duvet and sliding closer. He turns the pillow upside-down so at least the part under his neck is dry. She lies on her side, rests an elbow under her head, watching him. He doesn't want to turn to her.

'Sssssssssshhhhhhhh,' she whispers.

He is conscious of her softness and her warmth. He ignores the taste of burnt tobacco. She runs her finger gently along his cheek, tracing to source until tears go dry. His eyes flicker open and he looks her way. They lie like that for a long unbroken moment, facing each other. From images racing unbounded all over the place his mind empties out. The projector unplugged.

He suddenly feels weary but Irene inches across the cotton divide. Her lips touch his, breath catching as he sniffles. They kiss slowly. They've hardly kissed for years, not like this. Her hand reaches under the duvet and rouses him to life. She leans back and peels off her t-shirt, throwing it to the floor. Locking together they kiss hungrily now, as though her tongue seeks out the salt on his skin. She lifts her leg across, his hands pushing up against her breasts, feeling her nipples harden. She straddles him and with a free hand guides him inside her. She is drier than she'd like but she's ready for him.

They haven't done this since losing Cathal. Yes, they had sex over the years, a few emergency rides, but this is something totally different. He looks up and sees her rise and fall to her own secret rhythm, tightening her loins around him and drawing him into her with a contracted squeeze. He goes to speak because he knows he won't be able to hold on much longer, not when she grips him like this. She places her finger against his lips and continues to rise and fall and rise. His mind floods with strange sounds and colours and he feels himself erupt inside her, jolting forwards. Tears flow again and Irene clamps him with her thighs until he is entirely spent. She leans over, her hair draped across his face, her breasts pressed against his chest. She regains her breath and rolls away. They spoon each other, avoiding a small damp patch in the sheet underneath.

Irene drifts off to sleep and he is happy to let her go. After a while the duvet feels warm and stuffy so he rolls onto his back without pulling away. It's like he wants to stretch free without losing the contact. He feels her skin glowing against his body. They stopped sleeping together at home years ago so this is all very new and very remembered. Only minutes ago her fingers and mouth, her touch, her smell brought him to life. Something feels right. The sound of her sleeping softly eases him into a heavy, pleasant drowsiness, the pair of them following different paths into turbulent, troubled dreams.

– 51 –

Lily takes them to the hospital in Kotor after breakfast. It doesn't look like an Irish hospital. It feels emptier, less hectic. Anja appears pale in her blue gown but Irene is glad to see her look so much better than yesterday. She sits up slowly when they enter the ward. Says she got so used to hospitals in Sarajevo after Damir was injured, the oddest thing is to find that now she is the patient.

Back then it was Anja who slept by his bed, keeping watch while her comatose husband drifted restlessly. She tells them she got used to 'living in chair'. Twice the surgical team was going to operate but were afraid what might happen if they couldn't safely remove the offending shrapnel. When Damir regained consciousness he had lost the power of speech. Words and syntax returned very slowly, day-by-day, familiar sounds sometimes coming to him unaccompanied by meaning.

Surgery was aborted on the third attempt, the doctors in Sarajevo opting to leave things as they were. He was likely to suffer side-effects they explained but this was probably better than the alternative. And once that decision was made they put his file into a large envelope and said he could go home. Anja told them they had nowhere to go. The hospital said that was unfortunate but it was not their problem. They needed the bed. Thousands of seriously injured people around the city requiring immediate medical attention.

Then this morning in Kotor she awoke to find Damir watching from a chair beside her.

'We change place,' she says, without her usual lightness.

Half an hour earlier Sasa took Damir back to the villa, the father-to-be so overwhelmed by it all that he insisted on taking the scan with him. Irene says little. She can't help thinking how close Anja came to losing the baby. And if that was something the young woman went through, who knows where it might have led.

A colourless drip feeds her arm. Brendan shifts his feet as he glances around. He doesn't like hospitals and gets weak at the sight of blood. It's just the way he is. There are five other beds in the ward and even though it's nearly midday, most of the patients are asleep. One woman in her forties shuffles up and down the corridor in her dressing-gown; another rocks gently in a chair at the window.

'For twenty-three days in Sarajevo Damir sleeping. Lucky for living, doctors say me,' she continues, wanting to talk. 'Today, he so happy.'

The Gogartys feel they should distract Anja rather than let her upset herself. But instead of resting, as she is told, Anja reaches for Irene's hand.

'Before he get better in Sarajevo I think terrible things. I think, please let God take baby if he give to me back Damir. But this not happen. He give me Damir and he not take baby. Yesterday I think maybe God change mind.'

Irene doesn't know why Anja wants to tell her this but the Gogartys have nothing to add about God. Five years ago they gave up figuring out how anything is decided, who is saved and who is taken away. Or why. Irene places her hand on Anja's drumlin belly and searches for a kick. There's a glimmer of movement which thrills and frightens both of them. It's a sensation Irene remembers well eighteen years ago.

'You need to rest.'

'Right so,' says Brendan, grateful for escape. 'Is there anything we can get you?'

'Need baby to come,' Anja replies.

Holding Irene's hand she locks fingers.

'*Hvala*,' she says.

'No, thank *you*.'

The Gogartys leave the ward and don't look back. Irene knows she will worry about Anja's pregnancy until this child is delivered. There can't be any more scares like yesterday, such a random overlap of moments, big and small, each one affecting the next. Irene wonders what would have happened if Anja had fallen on concrete, not grass. If her friend hadn't called in at that time? If Dzana wasn't a fast driver. Or if the policeman didn't clear the road ahead . . .

They drive back to Hotel St Jovan in silence. Brendan chews his lip like he always does when pensive, but Irene doesn't feel the oppressive stillness that usually hovers over them. He shifts gear as they swing uphill. She wonders what is running through his mind when he wordlessly reaches over to touch her wrist, pressing it ever so lightly before changing gear once again.

The receptionist gives them a cool welcome when they return, glancing reproachfully at the clock as though to remind them checkout was two hours ago. Up in the honeymoon suite Irene feels a little nostalgic. She retrieves her red dress, shakes it out and re-folds it into the suitcase.

With everything packed away, she takes one last view from the balcony. The same sunny panorama criss-crossed with ever-changing details. It has been home for the past six nights but their time in Perast feels a lot longer. A nest of butts, lipstick-kissed, sits in an ashtray alongside an unfinished bottle of red and two stained glasses. She wouldn't mind staying another night or two but it really is time to move on.

'The honeymoon is over,' remarks Brendan.

He settles up at reception while Irene waits outside. God help them if they try to add anything extra to the bill, she thinks. She finishes off a ciggie she'd kept from last night, observed in silence by an elderly refugee couple sitting in the shade. She waves but they do not respond. She wonders will they ever get home.

Brendan appears with the fishing rod but it won't fit into the car. Only by rolling down a back window and feeding the rod through to the well of the passenger seat is he able to lever it in.

'They won't let you on the plane with that,' says Irene.

At least they are ready to go. The sun is already hot.

'Should've got this fixed,' he complains, banging the driver's window.

He reverses onto the coast road and continues slowly along the waterfront before pulling in sharply at the pier.

'Just a sec.'

He eases the rod out the back window. Irene watches him stroll over to where two pensioners are fishing – one in a striped football jersey, the other heavier, topless and very tanned in shorts. The three of them shake hands, all smiles and laughs.

It's getting too hot in the car so she unbuckles and gets out. Brendan points in her direction and they wave. She waves back. He's hardly going fishing, is he?

A young boy joins the trio at the pier to show Brendan a red bucket. He's only about nine or ten, wears a t-shirt and shorts but no shoes. The boy seems delighted with himself and Irene laughs when the pair of them exchange high-fives.

Brendan starts baiting a hook with worms they pick from a jar. The young boy retakes his seat on an upturned crate. Brendan stands beside him and swings a line into the water. Irene watches them, four unlikely lads facing the sea in quiet concentration.

Just as she wonders how long this will take she sees Brendan kneel and hand the fishing rod to the boy. The older men make a big scene and the boy wraps his small arms around Brendan's waist. Irene watches her husband ruffle the boy's hair and return slowly to the car.

'Who are they?'

'Me fishing pals. Juventus and Tarzan.'

'And the boy you gave the rod to?'

He smiles and restarts the engine. They have one more stop to make. They leave Perast and chug loudly up the coast to the villa. Ascending the hill he sees Sasa plastering a red sticker across the *Za Prodaju* sign. The cheque must have gone through. As the Lada pulls in Sasa finishes off the job, jumping off the wall like a circus showman.

'How's she cutting, Sasa?'

'Is cuttink good.'

'You lads are the same the world over, d'you know that?' says Brendan.

'Marketink opportunity.'

'You're not leaving that sign up forever, Sasa. I'll give you a week.'

'*Nema problema. Dober dan*, Irene.'

After everything that happened last night Brendan is a bit embarrassed that his handiwork is still on display. Can't undo this one, sadly. He is relieved that Irene has been so forgiving or he wouldn't be able to face it. Damir appears at the front door with a rucksack. His hand is blotched inky black, like he's been painting.

'The hard man himself!'

'*Zdravo*! Brendan, Irene. You like a coffee?'

'No, no,' says Irene. 'We won't delay.'

'You see baby?' he asks, carefully producing the scan from his pocket. He holds it up for Irene. She can make out the shape but all Brendan sees is a blob. Damir traces the x-ray outline of the body and head like he's figuring out a puzzle.

'You see? Face. Little hands like this? I teach him how fix time. Sasa say he is beautiful baby.'

'All babies same,' shrugs Sasa. 'But yes, he is good baby.'

'Sasa say he look like me.'

'Yeah, the same happy face,' suggests Brendan.

'We saw Anja this morning at the hospital,' says Irene. 'You had just left.'

'Yes and now I wait there until baby come. Doctors say maybe one week. Or they take baby out.'

'They're going to induce?'

'Anja stay for one week, eight days whatever she need. Then come here. *Ne zaboravi sok od brusnice*, Sasa.'

'Cranberry juice,' explains Sasa. '*Nema problema*.'

'That's good,' says Irene. 'The baby is going to be early so they'll want to keep a close eye. And Anja is going to need a lot of rest afterwards.'

'Were you painting, Horse?'

'Yes, get ready for Anja. Sasa get other things also. What is in English – red, blue, yellow, green.'

'Balloons?' interprets Irene.

'We not put air in until Anja comink home,' says Sasa.

'That'll be lovely, Damir.'

'Like family, we have party for baby when Anja here. Maybe you come, please. Special guests.'

'Do you know, we'd love to,' says Irene. 'But Brendan will be back at work and I'll be sorting out a few things at home. Just make sure you take loads of photos.'

Damir throws his rucksack into the Skoda.

'Brendan,' begins Sasa, 'I see you make interestink changes to garden.'

Brendan's not sure if he's looking for an explanation or just stirring shite. There's an awkward silence.

'Yeah, it's a bit different alright.'

'What about getting a new tree?' suggests Irene.

'Oh,' replies Sasa, scratching his head. 'You want same?'

'Yeah, the exact same, more or less,' says Brendan. 'A nice cedar.'

'Where I get new tree hundred years old?'

'It's not that complicated, Sasa. Just have a look around and see what you can find. You'll have to get a digger to take those roots out. Then plant a new one.'

'Is your property,' shrugs the auctioneer, going to his car.

'Don't go overboard on the bill now.'

'I make sure he do good job,' whispers Damir, itching to get away.

'Sure you boys go on ahead. I'll lock up.'

Damir wipes his hand on a rag but the paint has dried in.

'Mind yourself, hah?'

'Give Anja our love.'

'And the little fella.'

'*Da.*'

He pulls the beanie from his pocket and eases it over his head.

'Since war start in Sarajevo, I think nothing good. Only bad things,' he pauses, flexing his good hand, trying to figure it all out. His stump follows the same direction. Muscle memory. A smile breaks across his face. 'And now, only good things.'

Sasa starts up the Skoda. Damir slaps his thigh and grabs both of them in a one-limbed bear hug. He squeezes hard before releasing.

'Only good!'

'Good man yourself.'

He gets into the car and rolls down the window, a big grin on him.

'Brendan, Irene, please!' says he. 'Tea, coffee, what you like. As we say in Balkans, my house is your house.'

'Cheeky bugger,' laughs Brendan, shaking his head.

Damir shouts a bit of gobbledegook out the window and blows them kisses. And they're away.

The front door is open. Irene ripples the chimes in passing and goes down the hall while Brendan checks the rooms. Nothing to be done, really. Going into the kitchen he can't ignore the fallen cedar stretched out the back like a museum exhibit. Man's inhumanity to trees. He feels stupid and embarrassed but what's done is done.

Irene walks slowly around the garden. Even in daylight it looks and feels oddly asymmetrical. A scene out of balance. Despite the carnage there are signs of activity which are strangely cheerful. A step ladder points to a ribbon of bunting and coloured bulbs. A paint brush resting on an open tin stiffens in the heat of the day. Beside it, a canvas banner flaps against a pole like a homecoming for county champions. All that's missing is a bonfire.

The banner has snapped away from the far pole and it shakes loosely in the breeze. Irene lifts the axe and returns it to the woodpile. She picks up the *rakia* bottle and glasses scattered around. She is glad her husband is going to sort this out. The villa needs a tree. She tries to imagine the cedar tree replaced in kind, bringing the garden back to some sort of order. To put it back the way it was.

A yellow sail catches her eye, a fancy yacht heading out of the bay at a fair clip. The crew won't need to stop until they run out of grub or wine, just drop anchor somewhere along the coast and stock up again.

Brendan wanders into the main bedroom. Damir left the curtains closed so he swings them open and pushes the window ajar for air.

'Brendan! Come here!'

She's not panicking but her voice is sharp and urgent, like when she recognises someone on the telly. He walks through the kitchen and finds Irene holding one end of the banner in the garden. She steps backwards, stretching it tight from the pole. Damir's homemade capitals spell out as she goes. When Brendan walks outside she unfurls the last piece of canvas. Irene stares at it, then looks at him. She's crying and laughing at the same time.

Brendan walks closer to make sure he's not imagining this. Irene stretches it further.

'A dark horse, hah?' he says. 'Never said a thing.'

He grabs the end with her and they pull the banner taut, attaching the loose end to the second pole. Once secured it holds tight. They both step back, Irene wiping her eyes, only laughing now. Big capital letters painted in black over their heads.

DOBRODOSLI KUCI ANJA I CAHAL!

'Isn't that something, hah?'

'Isn't it just.'

'A dark bloody horse.'

A breeze gathers behind the banner, filling the canvas like a sail and making the letters look even bigger. They stand for a minute or so, which is no longer than it takes for the yellow yacht to disappear from view.

'You alright?'

'Never better. Yourself?'

She smiles with a beautiful sadness. Reaching for her necklace she unclasps the locket and kisses it, then passes it to Brendan. He closes his eyes, holds it like secret treasure, puts it to his lips and returns it with a little prayer. Irene glances at him, as though seeking the slightest encouragement. Brendan nods gently. She holds the locket carefully and touches the release button to spring it open. Wisps of golden hair catch in the breeze, billowing and fluttering into the air above. Their eyes turn to the neatly framed black and white photograph inset. A little blond face smiles back, a dimpled bundle starting out on life.

photo by Matt Naughton

About the Author

Frank Shouldice is a Producer/Director with RTÉ Investigates. He is author of *Grandpa the Sniper*, which Diarmaid Ferriter called 'rich, evocative . . . vivid and absorbing'. He won the Prix Europa (2015) for his investigative radio documentary *The Case That Never Was,* and is writer/director of documentary feature films *Once We Were Punks* (2025) and *The Man Who Wanted To Fly* (2018). He lives in Dublin.

Acknowledgements

This novel did not happen overnight. What started out as *A Villa in Montenegro* – actually a stage play – evolved over years as a hesitant first foray into fiction. Strangely enough, the play is yet to follow . . .

It can be difficult to assess the worth or quality of one's own work. My sincere thanks to esteemed authors Martina Devlin and Andrew Hughes for their keen observations on an earlier draft, and to Sam Millar, Paul Howard, Ethel Ronan and Michael Harding who also took time out from hectic schedules to cast a cold eye. Reading a debut novel is a big favour to ask and their generosity is very much appreciated. Thanks also to Kevin Lavin, Nora Kirrane and John Givens for welcome appraisals.

Seeing this novel finally go to print takes me back to primary school where my teacher Vincent Conway fostered a creative spark. Dedicated educators can make such a difference. Approaching literary agents many years later I recall warm enthusiasm shown by some – particularly Jonathan Williams – making up for a general sense of *ennui* conveyed by others.

My thanks to the endlessly inventive Steve McDevitt for conjuring up a provocative cover design and to Peter O'Connell for guiding us through the choppy waters of marketing.

Publisher and editor David Givens at The Liffey Press has shown great belief in this novel from first draft. Safe to say that without his stewardship and support *Beneath the Cedar Tree* would not have come to life.

Hope you enjoy it.

Frank Shouldice
Dublin, July 2025